GHOSTS OF OCELOTS

THE BLIND IMPOSTOR AND OTHER STORIES FROM GUATEMALA

by

Jonathan Reynolds

ISBN - 978-0-9887328-2-7
EPUB - 978-0-9887328-3-4

Published by AMPERSAND BOOKS
St. Petersburg FL
www.ampersand-books.com

Cover design by Matthew Revert
Drawings of Maya glyphs by Matthew G Looper
(from The New Catalog of Maya Hieroglyphs -
the Classic Period, by Martha J. Macri and
Matthew G. Looper, University of Oklahoma Press)

*"Fulano and Mengano" previously appeared in slightly altered form
in*
Ampersand Review 5

*For Jasper —
(and Bucky)*

GHOSTS OF OCELOTS

The Blind Impostor and Other Stories from Guatemala

FOREWORD

For those eager for adventure the country described here is an exotic place, and adventure is a relatively short flight away, in normal time and space. Reasons for the "otherness" of the Republic are not limited to the myriad ruins of the greatest civilization of the ancient New World, found almost everywhere within the borders of the modern nation. The exotic blooms also in the fevered consciousnesses of the largely illiterate poor, who earn, on average, two dollars a day. How do they survive? Are there brilliant ingenuities? Is the Republic a playground of miracles?

Differences between the city and the *campo* – the countryside, the hinterlands – are not simply those between urban to rural. Most apparent to the visitor is the difference between modern slum and feudal peasant life. Out of a population of some fourteen million, only a tiny group of a few thousand owns or controls seventy percent of the land and wealth. Not surprisingly, the murder rate is the sixth highest in the world.

In the *campo*, "civilization" is like a light bulb left on somewhere and someone forgot to turn it off. Its benefits are dreamed up, don't exist, or the light bulb is so impractical few know how to flick the switch.

As historical fact, memory, integral to consciousness, struggles to avoid repression or erasure. Is it naive to believe there are prices to pay for this? When someone has been kidnapped and killed – "disappeared" – do the malefactors hear ghostly violin elegies? More likely, after centuries of exploitation and violent repression, the powerful permit tame trinkets of a reified culture for the tourist seeking the exotic. *Recuerdos* (mementos) make this preference seem merely new, even gentle, preoccupations of Power. Mention of justice for massive crimes against humanity, or for acknowledgment of the social contract, is rewarded, as often as not, with "disappearance."

There is true and false memory, although, at street-level, the distinction may be very hard to see. For the ordinary citizen the difference between existence and non-existence equally is blurred.

My twenty-year sojourn in the Republic began in 1990 as a young student and has yielded up for me my own sense of the exotic. What seems palpably the devil's smoke lingers in wisps, tapers and tailings in the air around the thousands of raw-skinned five-year olds begging in the streets of the capital city. A malaise ("suffering" seems too obvious a word, "pain" too tepid, *dolor* too Castilian, delicate) overwhelms, asphyxiates buds of consciousness – ironic, because flowers bloom everywhere. A better term is needed for what feels psychically on fire, pulverizing. But however one might search for that better term, the sensation it would name is so unremarkable, and there is so little available to alleviate it, that perhaps no fitting word exists. How vivid is the life! observes the tourist from the safety of a sightseeing van, his feelings of whatever emotional color immediately, transparently, ridiculous.

The usual physical categories of gravity, motion, inertia, and so forth – the laws and dimensions of space and time – seem different from those of the *gringo*'s universe. Subsistence determines all action, which, efficiently, is only automatically and at all times action necessary to survive.

Life is lived at the bottom of the bottom; mistakenly, the tendency is to believe primeval impulses flourish there, innocent and unchecked. On the other hand, the fundamental economic unit is the maize plot which, because of centuries of land theft for the great *finca* , is relegated to the highest, hardest-to-reach patches on the uppermost sides of volcanic mountain ranges; seen from far below these make a tiny, pretty quilt.

Discerned from the bottom of the bottom, looking up, is what is known only through a pirated, second-hand stream of commercialized, cartoonish, imported imagination – advertisements on pink-tinted, slipping television screens of American objects for sale. Because these media are at eye level, the citizen artificially, briefly, believes he could be equal to the rest of the world. On billboards his consciousness rides a confused, frothy surf above the streets. Giants with white teeth and wearing sunglasses toast each other with Pepsis, Cokes, Fanta, rum. In the sunken places below the signs, where garbage accumulates and spills down *barranca* bankments, trash fires emit the gray-black smoke of burning plastic bags. Despair and panic freely radiate, expanding to other corners of the land – or as far away as the *campesino* can take himself on a "chicken bus."

If the Republic *is* a place of malaise – of suffering, pain, or *dolor* – it is curious that it is populated by nobodies or non-persons who, *ipso facto*, because of their inconsequentiality, one must conclude do not feel. If the outsider thinks about these nobodies or non-persons at all, in their own norms we find their exhaustion is nowhere, as if Nowhere is a place: a negative of a negative not yielding a positive – except, at times, in the Indian markets, for example, a little smile, a strange peace.

If you happen, for some reason, to spend time in the *campo*, one irony among many is that the individuals met there are so sharply defined you might wonder how it was possible that you never knew them before or that they had not always been a part of your life. One thinks of the fish, called *mojarra*, who lives in shallow, quickly disappearing muddy ponds and comes up to the surface, now and then, hanging there, fixed eye staring, to swallow a bubble of air.

Some of these sharply distinct people appear in the stories here. One who does not is a woman of seventy, a cook for an archaeological research project whose screen presence, as I refer to it (she, like others in her little village, is unaware of the existence of the popular culture of the West), resembles the magnetic persona of Anna Magnani, the great actor of Italian neorealism. No more than five feet tall but bulking large in every other way, Doña Maria Zapeta de Noriega seems rooted in a deeper surety of life, though her world goes as far only as the horizon of the next town, her universe extending no farther than the close high mountains around her.

Perhaps the seeming resilience is because of what appears as the *campo*'s "unspoiled nature." This may be, also, because of the continuous difficulties of survival – ever-starting, ever-finishing, at the bottom. Without dividends otherwise, these difficulties lend the citizen a greater sharpness *and* a sense of the universal – helped by folk deities like the ambiguously evil, rum-drinking, cigarillo-smoking Maximón, or the ambiguously good skeletal god, San Pasqualito, who bend the walls of the possible in the interiors of *xamanes'* incense-filled temple-huts.

This more-than-real quality, a people's "genius," exists despite a frail hold on life for reasons of the most final kind of violence. From slaughter, slavery and disease, the coming of the *conquistadores* killed ninety percent of the indigenous within a hundred years. The genocide of thirty years ago erased whole villages, many that had never even appeared on maps.

One night with Doña Maria I sat outside the project kitchen – refurbished for use in the ground floor of a several-story high, wood frame "hotel" that the former owners of the great German plantation built for visitors. It was a customarily dark, quiet evening in the *campo*, burning with stars. Somewhere mariachi music was playing. A feral dog barked now and then. She and I looked across a tame courtyard to the old headquarters of the once-giant cashcrop-for-export combine. In answer to a question, risky no matter how tactfully put – with brows raised and an almost comically solemn nodding of her head, comical because how else can one relate such drama? – she told me, yes, it was true, and leaned forward to share a secret that not only she but every adult in the village remembered as if the things had happened just last night: that in the basement of the great stone building a few meters away, regularly, for years, people were tortured and killed, and their corpses disposed of in a burial pit somewhere secret and unmentionable.

Ay Dios! she sighed...

Another hidden truth, like bone within flesh: many in the Capital work in the sex clubs of Zone Nine or in hidden brothels scattered throughout the finer residential neighborhoods of other *zonas*. Their prettiness, their bare skin, seem consigned to transience – hugely, overcompensatingly, dreamed up, yet contingent, finally unknown, unknowable. Along with confessions of the secrets of mortality, Zen illuminations offer themselves. One cool early morning in the Capital – before *tiendas'* broken sidewalks were wet from mops, before trucks revved up and horns began to break the quiet – I woke up, lonely, in a room in an inexpensive hotel in Zone Ten. I experienced a vision I came to call "the burning surface." I saw, consumed on the blade-edge of the purely ephemeral, the futility, the resistlessness, of all desire in the forms of young women glimpsed, again and again, profiled orange in the tawdry sunlit streets. They walked resolutely in the billowing diesel fumes, they skipped across the trash-laden streets. They lingered, or hurried along, threats to their existence so routine. Were they aware of a special drama?

The Republic is one consolidated dream, the resonances shut in. Its constituent dreamers wait inside rain-slashed huts. When the rains stop, among iguanas and howler monkeys, in the black night, not far from the little town square where a broken ancient stela has been crudely replastered, they swing in the cocoons of hammocks. The stars are so enormous you can read by their light. But these dreamers never realize much of themselves, swinging in bare-earth floor rooms, on porches. Yet the face of the now seen and then forgotten little child, playing in the great city's gutters, is greater in every detail to the same degree her life soon wastes away and so quickly is lost.

There is relief then when, at night, you hear the laughter and banter of families piled in from the dark in their little rooms. Arrived safely home, they have escaped the threats for one more day. The night is a haven, though they know that, somewhere else, someone is taken. As is frequently the case among the *pandillas* or gangs, everything can be punctuated by a bullet to the head.

In the same way that life histrionically is cheap, like many other places the Republic boasts dramatic natural wonders. Perfectly conical volcanoes mount the sky. Rivers flash, drum, roar unseen and unheard except by those immersed in their own isolations, out of the cognizance of the world. Cattle-and-ranch Wild West red lands abut the coast. Gazing over huge horizons of hundreds of kilometers of sugar cane are the house servants of the *dueños* of the monocrop *finca* . The sweet green monotony merges more and more with the saline air of the Pacific, which makes itself known, eventually, in lagoons of river drainage where manatees sleep, drugged in their isolation, beyond the black sands of the delta. A single light bulb hangs from a pole, outside a cantina, *ranchera* or salsa faintly playing on a radio.

What impresses is how life has routines despite most intense, most enervating pressures. Very frequently the visitor finds the little stores like oversized phone booths: *tiendas* selling *gaseosas*, bottled water, *chicharrones*, firecrackers, cigarettes, cell phone cards, *cerveza, aguardiente, rón*, pans of homemade candies, other sundries. And despite the lack of a national entity – a ghost only of an identity, enforced by visor-capped federal police, by a largely invisible but ubiquitous military – evidence exists of public works: roads and sewer drains, ministries of agriculture and tourism, bottled water trucks, battered propane tanks, in the city electricity bills.

The tourists go on diversions into the "wild." If lucky, they find themselves not hopelessly lost, because a river, say, the Chixoy, *does* appear, wisely, on their map – though its shallow gray waters, scuttling under the brilliant, tranquil sun over sulfurous, chalky cobbles, are somehow alarming. A little later, around the elbow bend of a tiny, high, dirt road, one looks down a hundredand-fifty meters to the rusting skeleton of a chicken bus that tried to fly – its name, as likely as any other, a crude joke for those who died, EL CONDOR.

Later still, the tourists touch a fine filament hanging down
in the utter darkness of the night sky...

The filament brushes their faces. They think this gives the mystery away: all is good, safe, recovered. One of them tries to follow the filament up with her eyes. It disappears among the stars in the warm ghost-darkness. The stars are so enormous they pulse to their own frequencies.

They are charmed by the "wild." Worldlier they are, though, and the terrors seem far away: despite squanderings, life, though misinformed, transformed, cannot die. That mud-covered, beat-up pickup truck is *theirs*, and not some *campesino*'s. From somewhere, they smell – inevitably – tortillas baking on hearthstones.

As compulsively as I have tried to record both the intensity and the brevity of life, the citizenry manages. The people make do in fine old colonial homes, serving generations of *Castellanos*. They make do in little hamlets around the *Lago de Atitlán,* the great lake slapping inside an enormous caldera. They make do in the scantest maize plots in the furthermost passes of the mountains.

They make do, walking many kilometers – the icon of the countryside the sombreroed pedestrian on foot because he lacks bus fare and has just himself for transport. They make do in the brutal *Oriente,* given over otherwise completely to narcotics trafficking and routines of great violence. They make do where the morning shadows of other secrets hide in smaller cities in the highlands' *tierra fria.* They make do in the *tierra caliente,* in great conifer groves with hidden rubber plantations and processing plants producing a foul smell you think must emanate from Hell. They make do where crude-carved wood shelves and other useless furniture set out on the tiny road to sell, bespeak, in the night, a peculiarly elaborate, surreal, and profound solitude.

These things are there to be picked up by the quickened senses. And you can read about them, in summary fashion. On a wall in beautiful old Antigua, protected behind barbed wire, a historical plaque with family crest informs the visitor only that in that place once stood the house of Bernal Diaz del Castillo. There, retired from his service to Hernán Cortés, in his *Historia verdadera de la conquista de la Nueva España,* the venerable soldier wrote of war and the fabled, improbable victory over the *Mexica.*

Consider the itinerary, seemingly so short, that walked up to present times: in Western history, Bernal Díaz' witness is not really so very long ago. But all that the modern tourist is provided as proof of the *Conquistador* is this unremarkable inscription, containing the slenderest of facts – so sparse it's as if the greatest event thus far in human history, the meeting of Old and New Worlds, never happened.

PICO DE ORO

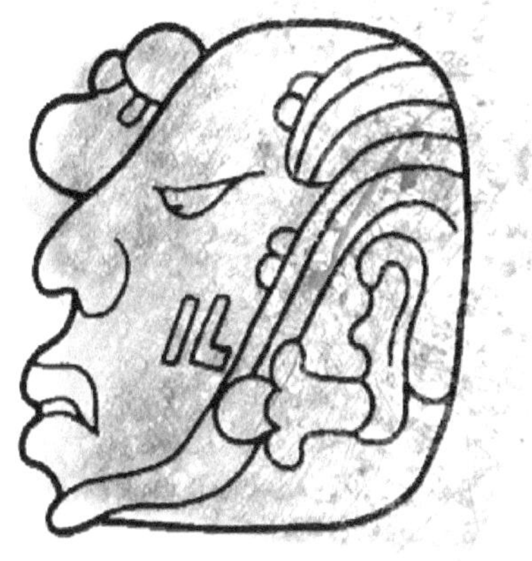

In the capital city of the Land of Many Trees, the Land of the Replacement Parts, a few might be aware that they live in a new age of progress, of freedom and fabulous technological inventions, and of a plethora of goods and services to buy. In other great cities around the world vast wealth has accumulated that makes such progress possible. Hand-in-hand with commercial development seemingly of entire subcontinents, ingenious financiers have catapulted physical assets into microsecond-to-microsecond "virtual" gains. No matter how unconnected the equation to life's material constituents, the gains bring astronomical reward, reapings continually recalculated in digits running on computer screens and the billboards of the bourse. There is a new world, and the arrival of its wonders is trumpeted to everyone everywhere with access to the popular media – though the news of these wonders penetrates only so far into the other world.

In the hinterlands of the Republic one realizes that this text of the new world, an enormous blanket of sense or context, reaches only so far. Within hours, on battered roads that peter out and end, outside the Capital, there are places that are "wild" because in these places no one can read the text of this new world, and not just because in these places no one is literate. There is almost no common reference to the rest of the world; "almost" because, despite the remove, there are yet some things recognizable if, for example, the *gringo* might stumble into these places.

In the mountains, on the slopes crouching below the cones of ruminant volcanoes, below their occasional wisps of smoke, the fabric is stretched and wears thin, or it tears, or it just does not reach. Accordingly, there are *campesinos* in the Republic's hinterlands who have never heard of the great cities of the world. They have not even heard of the Spanish Conquest, the greatest extinction of people in history, although these modern-day woodcutters and water carriers know to distinguish themselves from others not like themselves, and might speak about this at night, by the three-cobbled hearth, the children drowsy and secure within it with the smell of corn gruel and the compacted dirt floor. The children are secure in it even when, in what to them is the center of the world, the winds are slinging around the limbs of the trees and whipping the vines as the rain slashes down outside the doorless pillbox and wood-slat walls and then, when the rain stops the sodden earth is steaming and the birds start up again as if singing in the morning of the universe – although that universe is strewn with garbage – secure in the bigger cycles of rainy season to dry that, if they possessed clocks, they might say are as regular and predictable as clockwork. They know this even when giant fireflies alone illuminate the blackest night, revealing dim knees and fingers of brothers and sisters. At such a time there is nothing else. This *is* the world. To venture into this world – again, if one is lucky enough to realize it – there, an abiding text of its own exists, otherwise illegible to the visitor who, adventuring, might think he has plotted and arranged to arrive there although what really has occurred to bring him there is, in the greater scheme of things, complete accident.

Most people know only one little song, thought the man named Pico – liking the metaphorical aptness for the limitations of others. He felt the urge to hum. If not for being under the canopy of the unpruned coffee trees Pico would be stung with starlight radiance. Under the branches of the coffee plants and the shade trees was like a perch on the ledge of shadow. Pico was thinking, as he often did, how very profound, how extremely complicated, was survival. For days, weeks, months, how long? – as long as he could remember! – he felt he was on the verge of being overwhelmed by this realization. But he had come up with a plan, the contemplation of which was satisfying for his opinion of himself.

Alone, letting dispassion penetrate the haze of overreaction earlier in the day to this or that and the useless talk that accompanied the this or the that, he stood now in the close darkness of his gone-to-seed coffee plot which grew in untended tangles – and which reminded him, despite his self-congratulations, of what he was more accustomed to: endless difficulties, failure after failure. But his ability to think, to penetrate the haze of the quotidian, had provided him with a great and prudent solution for future exigencies, the confirmation of which he could hear like a tiny buzz in the silent darkness, new life to which his hands had given birth: a dozen two-centimeter high saplings which he had just planted and which, in twenty years' time, would become mature trees he could cut down to sell for firewood. The long-term security of the investment made him realize that his sagacity was at least as great as that of the other men in the town and gave him confidence that he could, after all, make shrewd decisions.

He knew, of course, that the saplings represented a long-term investment. But time did not change much. There would be so little change, or no substantial change, at all, in the world in the twenty years it would take for the saplings to grow tall and thick, that the value of the investment was absolutely secure. One of the other men, who had not only a coffee plot but grew all sorts of other trees – he clearly had a gift Pico lacked – who possessed an air of sagacity and patience, was excited, entirely too plainly, by his idea to start growing cacao again. When prodded the man protested that he had heard the *gringos* in *los estados* were paying great amounts of money for cacao. No one believed him. Beyond the rashness of the assertions, Pico felt the man would have been better off keeping his plans quiet because, if the idea did work out, someone else might steal it and then poison the man's trees. Pico wondered again if there might be some basis for the man's hopes… but no – it had to be just another woman's tale. He, on the other hand, was hard-headed, realistic.

His patch was on the top of the plateaus rising successively higher north of the town past the hedgerows of trash, garbage deposited in strata visible in the road cuts and ivied in by the footpaths up. A hundred meters west, in a hole in the steep bank overlooking the deep ravine cut by the narrow rushing river, was La Ventana, the *xaman*'s cave, around which lay the reaches of the *bosque*, the forest, so wild only some in the town ventured there to hunt. Being near the cave that led to the underworld reminded Pico he was near the Center of Everything. If he was an apostate from religion at that moment, since he was thinking about money, or long-term security, at any rate, it all fit together, he reminded himself, however, since the underworld was full of money.

He turned to the east – where every day the sun was born. Then he held himself completely still, relaxed – anyone passing in the dark on the dirt road east of his plot, the road that marked the end of the plot, would not see him among the vine-tangled stilts and little branches of his ruined coffee trees. If there were passersby they would be from the scant villages higher up, villages so small they had no markets, and who, in a few hours, would be hiking the several kilometers down in dead silence, bundles of sticks or baskets of vegetables balanced on their heads to sell in the town market. These people would come in the pre-dawn dimness, in an dead gray that penetrated the spirit but which anticipated the renewal of the world, everything minted new and brilliantly bright, even the garbage everywhere.

But now the sun was still making its way through the underworld and was some hours away before it would emerge triumphant from the jaws of the east. Also invisible now were the impassive volcanoes to the north and east and west. The ocean was down below the town, a half-day's bus ride away, reached on smaller and smaller roads dwindling ultimately to grassy paths and mangrove swamps and black sand beaches. The town was perched between the volcanoes and the ocean which was another reason Pico knew he lived in the Center. The cave, the volcanoes' cones, the titanic rains, the rushing streams, the black fertile earth, also confirmed this.

Pico shut his eyes, thinking ahead to daylight when the busyness of the market and the little section of cobblestoned street would be humdrum – the normal everyday activities that were the opposite of the night and its dreamworld frights and clarities. In a few hours the sun would rise, casting its powdery glow over the horizon, revealing in the slanting mint-cream rays the town nestled in green and the early morning mist mingled with the smoke of cooking and trash fires rising around the slatboard-walled shacks and their corrugated metal roofs.

For some reason, into the calm mindfulness of distance from all of that, the picture of Don Avellino intruded. Avellino blustered around with sly self-importance, always looking to grab the attention of somebody important, because he still thought *he* was important, all because he had been the first president of the cooperative. Sometimes, Avellino wore the garb of a K'iche'. He was ranting some days previously to one of the latest crop of do-gooder *gringos*, holding the man with hand and eye full of a humorously caricatured righteous anger. Lately Avellino had been going on and on, on an indignant tear, because some person, a Kakchikel! had dared to speak up at an assembly.

The *gringo*, who was smiling in amused but embarrassed interest, listened as Avellino, his big grizzled head shaking no, no, no! this was not correct! The Kakchikel were the traitorous enemies of the K'iche', having cooperated with Pedro de Alvarado in the killing of the K'iche'. The *gringo* who, apparently, was some kind of student or expert or something, had pointed out, "But that was five hundred years ago!", to which the old man, aware of being comically full-of-himself and not aggrieved outrage, agreed, nodding his head vigorously as if the length of time that had passed, centuries, rather than undermining the grievance, only affirmed the righteousness of his indignation. Old fool, thought Pico. On the other hand...his good opinion of *himself*, so hard-won with his tree scheme, was wavering: Pico the titterer. He quickly put this aside, but then doubt in the wisdom of the scheme poked up. Then again at night everything could seem wrong, or at least so different – full of potentialities the routine of the day did not permit – "it was impossible to judge if they realistic or not."

As he stood now in the silent darkness he felt that the earth, the soil itself, and what grew from it, was vast, if reluctant, company: needing to be coaxed to cooperate. That the coffee plot had gone to seed represented this stubborn, evasively seductive reluctance. He did not understand, for example, why the plants had grown old and stopped producing enough beans. This resistance – the failure of his plants to produce – redounded to his shame. Other people in the town knew his plot was now a tangled wreck. As if revealing past follies and failures the silence creamed somehow, present all around such that it seemed to dim the darkness – as if there was a light in the darkness immediately around him in the *cafetal* revealing: Pico the Fool... But he was quite alone, and he felt a determination returning: he was not just Pico. As distillates of confirmation of this, jewels sparking like eyes on their backs, the glowing caterpillars now and then he could make out and which he knew hung twisting from their threads; one of them meant business: the barest touch of its white fur could send a man into forty-eight hours of terrible pain and malaria-like sickness. The *uxnayera*, a little, brown, poisonous snake, must be around somewhere, too, hanging where it liked – at shoulder level in the branches of the coffee. Absently, he prayed to the snake not to bite him.

As he was thinking these things he could hear the hum of the little saplings stretching their tiny roots, tentatively exploring out and down into the soft black earth. A mosquito buzzed by his ear and he slapped at it. He felt a wet smear on his finger: his blood on which the creature had just engorged itself. Mosquitoes came from the underworld and this one must have zoomed out of the cave; he suspected that when it first came out of the gloom it was a gigantic fanged beast but, to disguise itself in the middle world, then shrunk itself down. Strange, but true. But he refused to be overwhelmed. He refused to be superstitious, even though he could picture easily the elongated fanged faces of the mammoth and bloodthirsty underworld mosquitoes. One of the other men, Rogelio Tuy, believed that the ancients lived in the mounds scattered throughout the town and that if you dug deep enough into the mounds you would find them there, alive and ready to share their secrets and their wealth; the proof of this, said Rogelio, was in the frequent discovery by virtually everyone in the town, in their maize patches and their house gardens, of sherds of pottery and, every now and then, of a whole pot, beautifully colored creamy-orange, or incised with strange and delicate patterns. Pico had no quarrel about anything with Rogelio, who was strong and worked harder than almost anybody, but he doubted Rogelio was right about this.

Blood; Rogelio... Earlier that day there had been an altercation. Pico had not been present to witness it but heard about it from another man. For some reason the ever-belligerent town bully, Álvaro Pacheco, had attacked Felix Monrroy with a machete. Rogelio was the only one ever to beat up Pacheco, who threatened a lot of other people and always seemed ready for a fight. Pacheco's victim this time was Felix, Felix-with-the-bad-skin who was always loudly, false-patiently, somberly, indignantly, explaining the wrongs he suffered, but always in a way that set Pico on edge because it seemed Felix might at any moment do something really crazy, causing a lot of blood to be spilled – much more blood than one of the mammoth mosquitoes could suck out of Pico or, for that matter, certainly than what had come from Felix's injuries, which weren't that bad. Álvaro hadn't used the sharp edge of the machete. He'd just whacked Felix several times with the broad side of the blade, though some of these whacks were right on Felix's head and Pacheco also had slapped Felix hard in the face, leaving angry red welts, as if boiling water had been spilled on him, making his complexion even worse. At this thought, Pico felt like tittering. Felix hadn't fought back, which was sensible, because Pacheco would have beaten him up much more thoroughly. The witness, the man telling Pico about it all, described Felix standing, stunned, bent down under the sudden fast blows, and then running away, holding his hands on his head. While recounting this to Pico the man had laughed, a tickled falsetto. But the assault was serious – the ignominy made it dangerous, and not only for the next few days after which with other people the whole thing would just blow over, because Felix held grudges. Felix was a coward but he had a limit to what even he could endure which, as with all cowards, was more than what anyone else would tolerate.

Pacheco had a wood business. It was against the law to log without permission but no government inspector came to the town so Pacheco rightly was not worried about being caught. In fact, as Pico well knew, it was as if the town did not exist to the government in the Capital and the only possible connections elsewhere as reminders that the town belonged to the Republic were the names of other larger towns scrolled by crank sticks for display in the panels above the windshields of the chicken buses. In these larger towns even if one could not find a bus with the town's name on it the bus driver's *asistente* would affirm that the bus passed through the town and, when luring passengers on board, would include it in his rapid-fire, tough-kindly, con-artist shouting of destinations.

Pico reminded himself he had to keep quiet about his tiny saplings because Álvaro might think him a future competitor. He felt like laughing because he was engaged in a clever deception by secretly planting the hardwood saplings – *volador* trees, perfect disguise for future firewood since they also were shade trees for the coffee. Pico again felt how smart he was because he had a fallback plan for Pacheco. If Pacheco found out about his firewood tree crop Pico could just promise to sell him the wood and, in the meantime, somebody might kill him. But for now he reminded himself to avoid Pacheco.

He hadn't taken sides in the Felix-Pacheco dispute, but had just stood around when, later, showing up after running away, Felix described the attack, nodding with the others when Felix's voice, strained hoarse and breaking but reinforced with anger, described in detail the offense upon his person. Felix's oratorical powers were particularly sharp, which had led him to success in the recent elections in the cooperative when the new president chose him as Secretary. For a small, boylike man Felix's anger had an extra size and solidity and this, too, was what made the situation dangerous. Anything could happen in the next few days if Felix decided to make a big issue of the assault, demanding action, leading to another confrontation, with others pulled into the fight. Felix might, for example, continue describing, loudly and with well-chosen but highly inflammatory words, how unjust and unwarranted had been Pacheco's attack on him; Álvaro might hear of this and come looking for Felix; this or that committee for this or that side of the dispute might be created; and then, as had happened before, vigilante committees would select guilty parties and warn them or kill them. For now, Pico agreed with the others that it was wait-and-see. Even though Felix was the Secretary of the farm cooperative's current leadership – held an official position in the town, as such – nobody wanted to fight with Pacheco. But, again, Felix, too was scary – especially when that big, obscenely embarrassed, agonized, false grin spread over his face, and which signaled that no matter how cunning and treacherous he could be beneath his indignations, he had sensitivities. When pushed beyond toleration and with nowhere left to maneuver, Felix could become a giant, dangerous firecracker, with ramifications for everyone. The town's two mayors, the town precinct leaders, the *cofradía*, the secret managers of the nine sacred springs – who knows, all of them might be pulled into the mess.

The whole thing had happened that afternoon. A group of men were standing beside a corn field, under some avocado trees, talking about it. Aware he made a comical figure – skinny, cowlicked, reticent, smiling, barefoot, tittering, vague about everything, in pants that rode high above his ankles – Pico went up to them in his solemn, silent way, anticipating the usual fake-innocent grins, rough jokes and snuffling laughs about his nickname, "Pico de Oro," a nickname he had been given because, after a stroke that had laid him up for a month, he went on to father several more children.

Unlike Felix, Pico agreeably played the fool – why not?

but, inside, he was really a serious person. At the jibes Pico just smiled, not taking anything to heart the way Felix always seemed to. Felix was much *too* serious. Pico knew that when he was next around Felix he would have to listen to the same list of grievances, described painstakingly and overly clearly in a loud, sober, aggravated voice, as if he was orating in church or something, talking over everybody else's heads. Pico knew to assume a serious face as he would pretend to listen sympathetically to Felix, pretend to take his side. Like most of the men he was capable of automatically changing the expression on his face from smiling laughter or cackling fool to seriousness or indignation. A fourth option was complete impassivity, as if needing more understanding, followed by dumb unacknowledgment. He certainly never let the *gringos* lately in the village – those do-gooders interested in old pots – know his real name! Hah! He kept everything inside. Even how ugly his woman was. Though this wasn't much to admit since all the other men felt the same about their women.

His mind wandered away from the fight and back to his own sagacity. He thought now, again, about the great rains that came and that would come, the beginning of all that would saturate the world and feed the tiny saplings that would grow, in twenty years, to be ready to be cut down for firewood – a secure investment for the long term. And how if the hurricane winds did not come too far inland, into the piedmont, below the slopes of the volcanoes, the firewood would bring him a fine return. This *was* a great idea – his stay for preservation, his trick up the sleeve, his bulwark against future exigency. He was *Agosto* – not Pico – and he lived inside himself. His life was good; the night was sweet.

With this self-congratulation, he felt he had been up in his patch long enough. He had left the woman three hours earlier to climb up to his coffee plot and plant the saplings. As he made his way out of the thatch of gone-to-seed coffee to walk down to the ghostly calm of the main street, cobbles sunk or protruding here and there, he set to thinking again. There were others he had to watch out for, and he was tired of this, tired of being tense all the time. Every now and then he admitted to himself – guarding against the admission because it made him vulnerable even to admit it – how he had to keep his guard up, and this made him really tired. And he could not afford to be tired. He had to keep dancing. Like the boxer he had once seen on Doña Blanca's little black and white television.

He had watched the little screen through the metal grate and door Blanca always kept locked and behind which was a small terrace with plastic tables and chairs set up as a little *cantina* lit up by a single naked light bulb. Blanca didn't let Pico, or any of the other men inside, because they did not have the money to buy anything. But she did cheerfully sing out jibes in answer to the men who wanted to watch the fight, and she didn't object when four or five men had collected in front of her grate to look at the television she had set up on the terrace, even angling it a little so they could see better. Of course that had been a one-of-a-kind circumstance and there was no guarantee Blanca would be so obliging in the future. The boxer, apparently a Guatemalan, was fighting a Mexican and, until he got knocked out later in the fight, was always hopping up and down on his toes and snaking in a punch now and then, flicking back the Mexican's face.

Doña Blanca was another one of the ones he had to guard himself against, though. Hah! This was what was also so funny:

watching with other men the boxing match on her television, having to worry about Doña Blanca because she was powerful, wealthy, and dismissive, her big bulk much bigger, probably by two or three times, than Pico, himself. Who would win if Álvaro were to fight Blanca?! He would ask this later of the other men, for a laugh.

Watching for a few minutes on Doña Blanca's television was by no means the first time he had seen television. When he went into the big, crazed, bottom-up bedlam of the nearby city there were windows in appliance stores with images, gray, sometimes pinkish, rolling and skipping, jittery...funny. He didn't think much about where the people and the things were or came from that appeared on the television. But he was pretty sure that what he saw could not be real. What was real was the Center in which he lived – woke up into before the glow of morning to the sound of his wife heating water on the hearthstones and slapping and rolling out tortillas.

Now, as he descended down the road, on the outer boundaries of the town center were the dim yellow lights of buildings. He passed the few *cuerdas* of someone's cow pasture which separated the dirt road from the cemetery and its blue-painted homemade memorials and markers, the bigger ones miniature replicas of the old, semi-abandoned Catholic church.

He came to the dirt road, cut deep with almost impassable ruts, and stood for a moment, remembering when the politician had made a speech there about building a real road, then, after being elected (this one paid a hundred *quetzales* a vote), getting an appropriation for the money, and pocketing it – but still claiming to the newspapers he had built the road, because, with some obscure logic of his own, the money had been appropriated for it.

As he approached the intersection of the road and the potholed cobblestones of the main street, he saw the light cast by a moss-green bulb from a concrete-and-metal shed on the road from the town to Santo Tomás, the next town up – the last one out on the single road west, the road which then ended, with wilderness only ahead – and then, in barely illuminated darkness, the ruins of the old German plantation headquarters. Inside the massive walls were many chambers. Even the bathrooms had been enormous.

In the basement a decade ago – during the Bad Times there had been torture and killings. Pico knew for a fact that several men had had their penises chopped off by machetes and that others were hacked to death, or shot in the head. But nobody talked about that – even now, so many years later. Why would you discuss these things? Some of the killers were still around. And not all of those who had died were truly gone, anyway. They had come back as the caterpillars that turned into moths or butterflies, or maybe some as fireflies – he was unsure which since only a *xaman* knew.

He passed the concrete-and-cinderblock construction site of the new church Pastor Estéban was building, which was going to be the biggest *evangélica* church, by far, according to Estéban, in the town. There already were some thirty other *evangélica* churches each with a would-be preacher, as grim-faced and righteous as possible to gain adherents and tithes. Estéban lately was walking around with a bodyguard who had a big gun stuck in his belt. The explicit meaning, no matter how the bodyguard smiled to set one at ease, was that survival was complicated... What if, he thought to himself, there was a fight between Estéban and Don Oscar, the powerful black magic *xaman* who had *two* bodyguards, wielding shotguns? Oscar's men would win, obviously. But who knew? Good luck, bad luck, he thought: it's all the same in the end – there was little one could do about it. Except be smart, be prudent...so, his saplings.

He avoided the center of the town – where the road passed the market in its cavernous room, now shuttered with a pull-down grate, where the town drunks had loitered but now sprawled, unconscious, under the corrugated roof covering a raised walkway and out of the glare of the sodium light. He avoided, as well, the crossroads and the evil things that happened there.

The road in front of the market passed metal-roofed dwellings with more permanent cinderblock walls, and included the meeting room for the *cofradía*. He also avoided the road here. If he stepped into the road he would be in the middle of something bigger, worldly in its own way like all roads are, where the buses stopped and started. He would be in the middle of the wider world or at least where one could connect to that wider world where the buses went and where people like him did not belong.

Now he headed for the break in the hedge that bordered the cobbled street to take a shortcut past the old plantation headquarters, mystery of mysteries of the long-gone *alemanes*, the white bosses who had constructed the great buildings. He entered and then left the shadow of the bolus of a great tree, the ancient ceiba that reached far over the straight poles of *volador*. Crossing these boundaries he felt exposed again, but also somehow godlike – maybe the only one awake to the myriad mysteries of the town at this late hour. Even the town drunks were asleep, even *La Cihuanava*, the young woman – seventeen years old – who was the Evil Temptress, with a reputation for loose morals.

He walked past the *papas fritas* vendor, asleep in his chair by his little blackened cart, cap pulled down over his face. He passed down the other street that wandered south on great broken, slanted, concrete slabs – "improvements" from years ago into easements of sewage; leaped over the deep sewage ditch onto the concrete abutment some *gringos* had built years ago for the town; walked down an alleyway so narrow his shoulders almost touched the buildings' sides, out into a field of starting corn; crossed a bare patch in front of a little shack with walls of big, flat rough-cut boards – his house – and went in the door. He stood in the dark on the earthen floor, listening to the woman's raspy breathing, sleeping out her exhaustion. He was aware then of pairs of eyes on him, silent children, awakened by his entry. He motioned at them to go back to sleep. Then he eased himself in beside the woman, turning his back to her warmth and away from her sour breath, and, congratulating himself again on his saplings as navigation around all of the disputes and purposeless wrangling between people – Monrroy and Pacheco, Doña Blanca and the other wealthier families receiving *remesas* from relatives in *los estados* and putting themselves above other people, little groups forming sooner or later in the town fighting other little groups.

As he waited for sleep, with no remarkable reflection about it, his imagination began traveling down a broad white way leading triumphantly to the utterly primeval, where the World Tree, laden with mirrors and blue-green jade, rose high, glittering in the smoke of burning, bloody bark paper. And he thought how, in the afternoon, as always, would come a great loud sigh of wind, followed shortly by the dense patter of down-pouring rain here, at the center of the world, where his saplings were now growing. Life will always make use of life – no more, no less. But, he thought, he would live to a great old age, when his saplings were great *voladores* casting shadow on his coffee plants. He, Agosto, was a secret king.

Fulano and Mengano

All of this happened under a different sky and stars and before the new epoch of the hard hand of justice in the Land of the Many Trees, the Land of Replacement Parts, of the social cleansing – when people turned to vigilantes and hired assassins to kill the tattooed gang members who were considered the cause of a great plague of violence in the cities. Whether this new phase has been for the better or the worse, who can say?

At seven thousand feet in the great barrel of the valley basin the city overflowed down *barrancas* and up mountain slopes. Beyond was the *campo* with its smaller towns with shack hovels and evangelical churches, its howler monkeys and trackless wilds – still, now and then, coveted by mining companies but neglected and, hence, unknown because these parts were simply outside the pale of history, still occupied by Indians wearing vividly colored traditional clothing, who disappeared up little beaten paths to places no one visited or could imagine.

Present as a dormant forethought everywhere except in the city's two rich zones, this remnant image of the wild was mindful in the laser-quick traffic that ran all day through the devolving *avenidas*, and even in the vast reaches of the city's poorest and most primitive and haphazard *barrios*, where the social norms were upside-down, obeying their own counterlogic because this was where the *maras* ruled, and where, like a giant zipper down the side of a dark whore, a *marufa*, the lights on the *avenidas* were dim, intermittent. In these places where one did not go, the great engine of life throbbed of such dangerous deterioration it seemed like the haunts and rumors of the four hundred little drunken ones, the *Tzitzimime*, about to descend to wreak their havoc from the black night sky, the stellar blackness which, otherwise, was above appeals for intercession in the real lives of humans. Yet, bursting out somehow, like the tiger flowers leavening the air, the firespike that drew the hummingbirds, were oases of civility. Within the high yellow walls of the Flanagan estate, the rump of a very old and once much larger *finca* in Zone Thirteen, were twenty-five acres carefully tended for repose, an island of a past time. Just outside the walls, dogged children begged at car windows or, with barebones props – red button nose, facial paint – garishly mocked up as smiling clowns, deadly serious beneath the fixed farcical grin, juggled balls or walked on their hands in the midst of tubercular, hypercaffeinated traffic.

Within the wall, at the great estate house, four friends sat under a giant parasol at a table by the back entrance to the kitchen. Two professional men, Horacio and Mauricio Flanagan, owned the estate, an inheritance; their guests were Alberto Fulano, a retired small businessman, and Guillermo Mengano, a dentist. All were on their way to being *jubilados*. Strewn with scarlet and purple bougainvillea bracts, set into the coarse, broad-bladed grass cropped close by the gardener's machete, beside them was a square, four-legged, ash-colored basalt monument. Joining in the reunion, cunningly carved skulls in each corner grinned at whatever joke, in general, shared, of whatever happened in life. The monument had been identified as an ancient throne by a hugely enthusiastic *gringo* archaeologist studying the great ancient city beneath the modern one – more than two thousand years old, the young man had said, captivated by the iconography – sacrifice by decapitation, he added, helpfully, pointing out the cavity on one side of the block serving for the runoff of blood.

"It must have been like a crab scuttling after too few bits of crackers," said Mauricio Flanagan, inviting the others to laugh with yet another analogy about the difficulty of Fulano mounting a bicycle business in the city. Under the fronds of a cigarbox tree and a bird-of-paradise's kingfisher-like flowers, Fulano, as usual, looked fixedly ahead, a gleam in his eye, however, indicating appreciation of the comment. Guillermo Mengano lifted his upper lip in a silent shrugging laugh, revealing his yellow teeth. The tired joke, which the Flanagan brothers still managed to enjoy after many years – repressing smiles out of consideration for their friends – was that, of course, in Latin countries, "Señor Fulano and Señor Mengano" meant "Mr. So-and-So and Mr. Whoever."

It was not until after years of running the shop, not until a few years after Fulano had the cement business, that he seemed finally to acknowledge the unlikely odds for success for him and his clients, young shop clerks in cheap permanent-press pants, who bought a bicycle lock as if this would prevent the inevitable theft. He finally seemed to accept that the shop had not been such a good idea. Horacio added, "It would have challenged Hazlitt: if you think you can win, you can. Faith is necessary to victory."

With a doctorate in metaphysical philosophy from the University of Buenos Aires, received before realism forced him in another direction and he became a urologist, Horacio was apt to wax learned at times. For the sake, in his own mind, of sharing what delighted him, although knowing he would not be understood and the effort was wasted, from time to time he would drop admired names, Hazlitt, or Lamb, or his favorite, Swift, as if to help elucidate a particularly difficult topic. When he did this the other three would listen respectfully – Mengano nodding to indicate that he, of course, understood the reference. When he was done, a long pause would ensue after which the conversation would strike up again, returning to the more prosaic context as if Horacio had said nothing. Horacio took no offense at this and, as the discussion continued, would break in now and then with a companionable "Precisely!" as if the impediment to understanding and agreement had been dislodged since his comment.

Seesawing on the favor scale with the increase in crime and violence, the topic that day was the usual one – the social divide in the country.

"The whole problem in the Americas is one that goes back to the Moors," Horacio was saying. He liked to provoke the others with sweeping assertions; today he wanted to share a thought to see how it would be received. Mauricio looked at his brother.

"Explain yourself."

"Well," said Horacio, distributing little plates of appetizers. "We all know that what has happened over the centuries, with us and the Indians, has not worked. And it has not worked in a particularly terrible way," he added, eyebrows raised as he looked at the others. "This topic we hate to speak of in good society, the terrible gap between the rich and the poor – this, of course, due to historical actions, the Conquest, colonialism – the *encomenderos* whipping the peasants not to God but to the fields of the *finca* with the help – the great help! – of the friars...and then those governments a hundred and more years ago that pretended to serve progress and democracy but merely opened the doors to the neo-Colonialists, the Dutch, the Belgians and, mostly, the well-disciplined Germans – who had the greatest success here, to make great amounts of money – "

" – and intermarry and produce *us*," said Mauricio, a little impatiently.

" – the Moors," Horacio continued, raising his hairy-knuckled finger, "with their authoritarian traditions, so firmly underpinned by Islam, distrusted any notion of the individual, and the social order came from Allah. Whatever benevolence they displayed during the height of the Muslim expansion – and they *were* enlightened with regard to the arts, philosophy, the natural sciences and so forth – was due to the pride they felt in their god-given role as conquerors. But the problem was that we, the Castilians here in the New World, mostly Catholic, ancestrally influenced by another overly pious civilization, the Moors, have held on so rigidly both to offended pride and an ancient, demoralized half-European, half-Moorish status quo that permits nothing but obedience from those considered beneath us. In the end it threatens to suffocate us!"

Except for the occasional reference to the Indians as children needing enlightenment but who must be dealt with firmly, discussions of race were untouched, or islanded, if mentioned at all, by smiling non-reaction. Accordingly, Horacio's comments were greeted without comment, but, again, because of his two advanced degrees, no one ventured to dispute him. This was so even though this particular topic could be aired only among old and trusted friends. Alberto Fulano, because of his darker skin, never denied that more Indian blood flowed in his veins than in those of the others; he had now a somewhat still fiercer expression.

"Explain what you mean about the Moors," he said gruffly. Horacio turned to him.

"What I mean is that we – that is, Latin Americans – are the inheritors of a mixture, unique in Europe, of two proud, aristocratic traditions, both of which were trampled – unable even to write our own history, to define ourselves, because of defeat.

North African Islamism reached, at the greatest extremes of its expansion, to Spain, but then fell to Christian Europe. The baser elements of this twice-defeated culture, those who came to the Americas, have never recovered from these insulting events.

"First, they were conquered by the Moors, who changed them in many ways, and then the Moors were driven out, leaving them defeated again, this time by the Christians. The attitude and behavior of the *conquistadores* and the Church's men here were dictated by this double fall. Hence, our particularly brutal ways with the unfortunates around us. And we have been unable to change it – change ourselves – that is, in how we treat the *campesinos* – "

This was said as Moises, the resident help, reached between them to collect the dirty crockery.

" – our brothers and sisters! Just look at what the Jews are doing fighting the Palestinians, on the other side of the world – " "The next thing you're going to say is, this is where the violence comes from?" asked Mauricio, a bit heatedly, but segueing neatly into the other common topic. Mauricio was an economist and a complete materialist.

"Oh, the gangs. Well... " said Horacio, rubbing his ruddy, sagging face, "this I can tell you: the *maras*, the *pandilleros*, even if their violence has much to do with drugs these days, it is also due to something much older and longer-lasting. This, as we all know but so rarely admit, is the brutality that has existed in this country for five hundred years now." He paused, then added, "I have to admit that if I were a young man living in the bad parts of the city I would probably join the gangs. In order to survive."

This was a shocking thing to say not only because it came from the learned elder of the group but because the threat of violence in the city required the threatened class to band together, to decry the threat and the perpetrators of the violence as inhabitants of another country, almost another universe. Mauricio was accustomed to his brother's European-style politics, and he shared them, to some extent, even if he made exasperated objections when others were around. Guillermo Mengano was more conservative and always murmured accolades of the military but he, himself, had hidden a university professor suspected of being a Communist in his great country house on Lake Atitlán; this was when the national university had been attacked by the army and the police and hundreds of people, supposedly radicals, were murdered – "like chickens with their heads cut off," had been Mauricio's sickened comment at the time. Alberto, who had been a Communist, a fact known to the other three – and which was no hindrance whatsoever to their affection for him – opened his mouth and picked at a piece of food in his teeth; the impassivity was customary but, to Horacio's assertions, the reflective expression on his craggy face, his friends knew, meant something was forthcoming.

Horacio continued, as if summing up a daily lesson,

"We sit on top of a seething mass of misery. We're on top of the volcanoes." He gestured behind him towards the immense, perfect cones of Agua and Pacaya. From the streets outside the old yellow *finca* walls, hollow of hope, came the shallow crackling sounds of backfiring vehicles, reminders by the gunshot noises of the prickly dangerous whims of the body politic.

"My friend, you're wrong," Fulano said now. "We would not be like them. And, by saying this, you forget the many poor people who do not choose to sell drugs, and steal, and kill. You take away one of our freedoms – to choose."

With this rebuff, at that moment Horacio could see, in his mind's eye, Che Guevara and Miguel Angel Asturias sitting together, sharing a coffee in El Portalito, the old cantina located just inside the great market in Zone One where, legend had it, the two had sat in the early 1950s discussing Marxism and revolution and literature. He felt quite weary thinking of all that had happened in the country since then. Mauricio knew where the conversation was going. He, himself, had fretted about the problem almost as much as Horacio.

Horacio's son was Federico, a humble but charismatic young man who studied both political science and graphic design at the university. Federico was living then in a boxlike apartment immediately above El Portalito. Fede's two roommates were Palestinians – a curious touching by the rest of the world of the otherwise sealed Republic. Fede said he and they almost never shared a conversation, though the Palestinians were nice enough. It was sufficient for Fede that they were not *gringos*; Fede was still in a somewhat nationalist-revolutionary mode, principally because of his Salvadoran maternal grandfather, a leading Communist who had managed to survive the civil war in that country. Fede was leftist – sometimes he could seem a bit the angry young man. For all his somewhat blurry allegiance to the impoverished and uneducated, he was an *artista*, and was capable of commenting in good society how the rich loved only dead artists because when alive genius was so messy – all that depressing in-your-face suffering. For Fede, as with many talented young men, life did not yet consist of so many compromises that you still thought you possessed one identity.

Periodically the Palestinians would leave for weeks at a time – their business was "import-export," said Fede, with a big appreciative smile, because it was all too evident, from the enormous bundled crates of goods they stored in a dusty adjacent apartment, that they were merchants of pirated clothing and CDs. When they left on their mysterious trips they would leave great amounts of food in the refrigerator, telling him to help himself. Fede did not much like the food – somehow, Middle Eastern fare had been obtained – hummus, baklava and the like – but, since he was usually hungry, he managed to eat a good deal of it when they were away.

Mauricio, Fede's doting uncle, joked about the possibility the Palestinians were terrorists. Guillermo Mengano took this seriously, being the most conservative of the four, though he made clear that he thought that, given the sophistication of the intelligence agencies – trained, ironically, by the Israelis – if a plot was being hatched it would be nipped in the bud well before any bombs went off. Mauricio was joking because, as anyone with any sense would agree, Guatemala was the least likely place for international terror: it was *pura mierda* to think that anyone outside the borders, except for the drug lords, cared what happened to the country. And what was there left to destroy, since the *politicos*, the big family businesses, the great *finque os*, had looted everything already? The saying was that subsistence in Guatemala was like a crate of pirated goods that fell off the truck, and the truck-owner didn't know that the crate was the life support for all the little *Chapines*.

In retrospect that was when the first whiff of trouble rose in the air. Unbelievably – since who can believe in their own death? – it would try to smother one of them. Death in the Republic, no matter how it manages to come, surprises.

The Flanagans had known the two other men from boyhood. Fulano was a wiry small man with a brushy salt-and-pepper mustache and coarse hair more silver than black, combed past his ears so that it curled on his sun-wrinkled neck. The assumption was that he possessed no sense of humor at all, and when the "Fulano and Mengano" jokes flew around, inevitably his face darkened and it seemed that cartoon steam would start puffing from his nostrils and forehead; he stared straight ahead with a set demeanor, the stolidity of which suggested he was on the brink of an explosion of anger. In truth, he was not a violent man; when he was much younger he had boxed a little at a rundown gym in the city, but, despite some talent and success in the ring – he was not fast but he was tricky because of an erratic stance – he had hung up the gloves after nearly killing someone with a stunning right cross to the jaw.

Mengano, his closest friend along with the Flanagans, was a tall, pale, sere man, who spoke very rapidly and conveyed the impression, when his bright vague eyes were upon you, that you were the most intelligent confidant he could have, that it was natural that he would have only brilliant acquaintances, and that the only discourse possible was that of the greatest sensibility and acuity, there being no other communication worth uttering. Even the most trivial of comments was received with the presumption that it could be nothing if not superbly apt.

In defiance of the Fulano-Mengano joke and although, in general, Fulano and Mengano resisted the urge to associate precisely because of that, the two men did manage to meet a few times a week in cafés or to share a plate of street food on a bench in the crazed, bottom-up city, usually choosing a shaded spot under a giant magnolia tree near the parrot vendors on 20th Street in Zone Ten.

This was despite the fact that when the parrots were fed *jocotes* or bits of tortillas the racket sometimes was so deafening that conversation was impossible. One might have asked what the ruckus was about – did they miss the jungle? Hate the city, as impossibly degraded as it was?

Like many in the city if they survived to old age the four had kept in touch through the ups and downs of life. Two of them had lost their wives to cancer, two to fatal house entries by burglars. The main reason for long acquaintance in Guatemala was that if one survived *la lucha* that was *la vida*, well then! Survival itself capped a life, and those who managed to endure to old age shared that surpassing fact, obliterating almost everything else.

Yet there was something special about the Fulano-Mengano bond. When they were together it was as if the joke of their names did not exist – it was never alluded to, indeed, never, when addressing one another, did their last names cross their lips. When the two sat by themselves in the smoky streets eating tacos or *papas fritas*, rearing back in their senior years to glance at the bedraggled pigeons, they were content apparently to take in what life had to offer at the moment and, no matter what it was, as symbolic in some way of experience and wisdom – a difficult affirmation, given the infinitely jaundiced perspectives of a Third World capital metropolis.

Señor Fulano, then, the little firecracker with a long fuse, and Señor Mengano, with a self-effacement peculiar because of his height – an ebullient and anxiously affirming ghost – complemented one another in mysterious ways despite the joke: defying the expectation that the only way to permit themselves to associate was to agree tacitly that the friendship was of a higher and more rarified nature. But then who could know the convoluted connections between them going back so many years? They were like Philemon and Baucis, Horacio observed to Mauricio, if one of the two had been the wife – and who could know the shared moments and glimpses of life, through the decades of the death squads and the Disappeared, the pinching of finances oscillating with the slight augmentations of fortune, the hurricanes and earthquakes devastating life periodically within the physics of the city, so strangely fallen at seven thousand feet?

The fact was that, indeed, their friendship had come about because the complete absurdity of their last names, singly, and the even greater absurdity when they paired up, had pushed them together as children by the jeers; they were the comic duo. But as the years went by the joke had the effect of placing them in a special niche in an absurd world, like a double negative that returned them to surpassing sanity and seriousness. It was possible that if they had not lived in such an ocean of life's trouble they would not have been so close. But this was their milieu, they had no other, and their friendship seemed, at times, incongruously permanent.

As a result, bending down to feed a pigeon scuttling amid the trash and shredded plastic bags near a twisting, rough-barked *jobo* tree, they represented to themselves, and quite likely to others who might merely have glanced at them, a charmed oasis of communion, if not a colossal mistake of gentleness. They seemed not merely a rich blend of what the country had to offer in the way of an hermetic history and identity but a testament to the improbability of life and reason within the confines of the bandit-fast city in which regard for humanity could seem so remote or accidental.

Fulano, despite his slow, somewhat plodding pace in life, had been the more adventurous. After his short stint as a boxer, he had opened a bicycle shop in a neighborhood that was a mixture of the transient and the traditionally poor-mercantile, in this case, about thirty or so wooden furniture makers. The sense of optimism, the sense of having been delivered to renewal – even somehow sporadically evident in the one female entrepreneur, a black-garbed widow with an exhausted air, who ran a school supply shop in their midst – seemed materialized by the sick-sweet smell of varnish and the hammering and sawing sounds of indefatigable production. Fulano apparently had been convinced by all this that his enterprise could succeed, despite the fact that the perils of city life did not permit bicycle transport.

When it was sunny, as it was every morning, the light was so white, harsh and blank it seemed as if the force of nature, by its bleaching of the plaster walls of the buildings, painted, repainted, repainted again employing the most lurid palette, could break through the mess, the sprawl, the depredations of struggle that seemed inevitably to mean one step forward, two steps back. It was as if one could make an appeal to the light for something bigger, older, and longer-lasting than the grind of life, although, of course, this was an illusion, one of the many necessary illusions one needed to guard deep within oneself in order psychically to endure or, somehow, to gain a small advantage in life. In this way, the improbability of his shop seemed like those fragile cement block frames of houses cropping up in strange places, halted during construction for lack of money or will to complete them, a big tree growing inside the roofless walls testament to nature's luxuriant rapacity, indifferent to any effort to establish some order to things.

A few days after the reunion in the Flanagans' garden, Horacio received a phone call from Fede. Horacio's first thought, a happy one, was that Fede had a working cell phone again. After the customary exchange – Horacio asking how things were going, hearing the somewhat halting reply, "Great!" (despite an undercurrent of fiery impetuosity, his son was an extremely polite young man) – Fede told him that he had a problem, and he didn't know quite what to do. It was rare that Fede sought paternal advice, given the usual resentments of son towards father which had made Fede insist on getting his own apartment.

Horacio asked what the problem was.

"Well," Fede began, stammering a little, "it's a little difficult to tell you. But, here goes. Uh, you know my roommates? Well, last night they came back from a trip and, well, they seem to have brought a lot of drugs with them!"

"No!" said Horacio.

"Well, yes. Not no! And... And they also seem to have brought back a bunch of guns."

Horacio felt a familiar start of alarm and fear, the ugly negativity instantly reversing everything else, like a razor doing emergency surgery in the open-air theater of the streets.

"Federico Alejandro!" "Yes?"

"Federico, you need to leave that apartment. What has your uncle been saying? I think now he's right. These people are bad." With Fede one needed sometimes simply to emphasize the obvious.

"You're right, you're right..." his son said softly, in a low, thick voice, as always ready quickly to mollify.

Then, after a long pause, and as background street noise suddenly mounted, Fede said,

"Papa! I have to go. I don't have much time on my phone, anyway. I'll call you later. Promise. Don't worry!"

A moment after ringing off, holding his phone so tightly it became painful, his comment some days ago about the Moors returned to him: how pretentious, how irrelevant to the real world! He felt his life was like those old, useless, cast-iron trellises attached to a crumbling building one could see even in the more extreme of the run-down parts of the city – ridiculous remnants of a second- or third-hand "Castilian" gentility – his "intellectual" propositions a ridiculous pose. Through the window of his office in the old great-house the sun was calm, the air buoyant as always. But, waiting for the afternoon clouds that would quickly fill the sky through the eucalyptus and bring the clockwork heavy afternoon rain, every bit of the flowering garden lining the driveway, every bit of the office with its books of literature seemed suddenly fatally at risk, as if a giant fist was about to punch through the walls, knocking everything to pieces, reducing everything to the gray-white dust ubiquitous in the metropolis. And Fede's problem was yet further evidence of the real operation of life and death here, fear and random violence underlying every moment even of cordial social ritual. The only calm Horacio was able to muster came from knowing his son's slightly malicious pleasure in creating drama, stirring things up a bit.

When Fede next called, Horacio asked to meet him for dinner. Horacio had not yet told Mauricio or anyone else about the problem so it was just the two of them, father and son. They met in a Chinese restaurant in Zone Ten, not far off the Avenida Reforma, the great boulevard that separated the two rich zones. One could still hear cars whishing past from the remnant wetness of the afternoon rains. Like all restaurants for those with enough money, the entrance was cloistered behind hedges, with a narrow driveway opening and a shotgun-wielding guard patrolling the cobblestoned courtyard.

He had driven to meet his son thinking, as he had many times before, how, for the easily lost, a drive through the city at night was a surreal odyssey amid racing, pollution-coughing vehicles lacking taillights. The danger, somehow intoxicating, the sights somehow epic, one strove to avoid, in the jammed underworld street life of the more extreme *zonas*, passing through vast neighborhoods of battered warehouses and streets littered with endless filmy plastic bags, splatters of melted dough, corn, fruit, and other jetsam from great common markets, grates and lockdown everywhere.

Sitting down Horacio looked at his son, his face asking, *What? what?* unable at first to talk amid the quick, sullen bustle of the restaurant. He saw, with mingled relief and alarm, that Fede had brought some belongings in a big duffel bag – relief that his son seemed to understand the seriousness of the situation, alarm that it all had arisen in the first place. The darkness outside was held at bay only by the scarce reflections of pinks, reds, and oranges from other establishments, restaurants with large open patios, discotheques for the cosseted children of the tiny overclass, ready for the evening business. The poorly lit walls of the restaurant seemed spidery-webbed, the waiters' joviality transparently false. Of course there was no question of telling the police. Payoffs were the grease that kept things moving and, as everybody knew, the police were more criminal than the criminals; many of the street robberies were carried out by the cops, who knew the schedules of businesses and the other rhythms of the city since they had time on their hands – paid their pittances not to prevent crime but to watch and take note of opportunities for themselves.

Fede was in a calmer mood and tried to lower the tension. "Look, don't worry. I'm staying with a friend tonight. Tomorrow I'll go back and get the rest of my stuff...and while I'm there, you know, I can kind of see what's going on. Probably what'll happen is they'll be killed by some other narcos, or by the gangs. So, when they're dead I'll just move back into the apartment. I'll have the place to myself again!"

Horacio looked with dismay at his son heaping more rice and noodles onto his plate, spearing gibbets of meat as if nothing was wrong. Horacio had no appetite. All he felt he could do was nod – things were going too fast. Nothing was different: nothing was good. As always, there was the perilous reality of the great zones of poverty into which ninety-nine percent of the citizenry was banished and then abandoned.

Horacio dropped Fede off in front of his friend's building and watched as his son knocked and then disappeared inside. Then he drove back to the house and called Mauricio. Mauricio, who defended Fede to his brother whenever Horacio had a complaint, said, "I told you so!"

"You haven't told me anything other than that his roommates were terrorists! This is about drugs."

"I don't want to argue with you. This is about Fede. Fede, your son and, incidentally, my nephew. The point is, what do we do now?"

Just as Mauricio could see in his mind his brother's protuberant eyes cast down in a blank and stricken expression, Horacio could see Mauricio's taut, severe face, admonishing and grave.

The next day Mauricio went to see Fulano. Fulano, like Mengano, lacking children, had taken on the role of proxy uncle to Federico, quietly keeping track of the young man – where he lived, who his friends were, and so forth. And Alberto seemed to have compiled more timely information than the others about trends in the metropolis – the good and bad neighborhoods, the turf of the gangs, the particular reasons for the surges and pauses of violence in the city. His friends assumed this had to do with what remained from his days when he automatically sympathized with the urban poor. Obscurely, this was also because of family who, Mauricio knew, lived in the poorest *barrios*, indeed bordering *El Gallito*, the most infamous of them all.

Once, after crossing the old, weedy railroad tracks that cut through the city, on one side, the older or original fount of the metropolis, on the other, the more haphazard *barrios*, then winding seemingly forever through more and more broken-down neighborhoods, which seemed less and less like urban space and more and more like a cracked,

potholed and cantilevered madness, Mauricio had accompanied
Alberto on a visit to an impoverished cousin, who lived in a doorless
corrugated roof shack at the end of a street with great broken
seams in the asphalt that simply gave way, in exhaustion or primitive
anarchic energy, to dirt. Periodically, Alberto brought the man's family
some food and tablets of medicine. Even Mauricio, a sophisticated
man, accustomed to seeing not just the better-off but also the poor,
was struck – not so much by the scene of poverty, poverty that was
visible every day to anyone who drove through the city's streets; no
one could escape the scenes of naked destitution. What surprised
him instead was his friend's genetic connection to a family who lived
in the vast lower depths. Mauricio noticed the little twenty-*quetzal*
propane containers that lasted about two weeks; on a corner was a
hearth with three large black cobbles; on the walls was a montage of
images: Jesus with the Virgin, a formal portrait of a young man in a
school uniform, Tweety Bird.

Greeted somewhat slackly by the man, Alberto was matter-of-
fact and sensible, and after a polite embrace and a little conversation
about other members of the family, he and Mauricio left. As they
drove away Mauricio glimpsed young men on the streets with close-
shaven scalps. Alberto paid no attention, but then Mauricio noticed a
baseball bat and a brick on the backseat of Alberto's car.

"What's that for?" he asked Alberto.

Alberto shrugged and turned to look at Mauricio.

"You know I was a Communist. But that doesn't mean I like
punks."

The day after his brother told him about Fede's difficulties he
found Alberto working on a bicycle in the backyard of his house. The
house was in one of the quieter neighborhoods of the city, cleaner,
with intact building facades, well-worn but functioning grates, locks,
and metal sliding garage doors opening to the sidewalk, and streets
with speed bumps. The *tiendas* seemed larger and better maintained.
Watching Alberto working with his ratchets and other tools, it struck
Mauricio that in some indistinct way his friend's predilection for the
bicycle had something to do with a preference, down deep, for order
and calm.

Mauricio briefly explained the problem.

"Federico's in a bit of trouble. Maybe, that is," he said. "These Arabs, these Palestinians, whatever they are, are involved in some bad business – "

His friend listened, his expression, as always, fierce but stolid.

" – drugs, and guns."

In quick acknowledgment of the danger, Fulano interjected a "Hah!" – the little gutteral plosive one of the few spontaneous utterances of the Guatemalan, everything otherwise seamlessly hidden by the automatic reflex of self-preservation. He said, "Fede would not be involved in this."

"Of course not!" said Mauricio.

"What do you want me to do?"

"*Hombre*. You always seem to know, better than any of us, what the *maras* are up to these days."

Alberto Fulano said, "I'll look into it."

Driving home, wondering what Fulano possibly could find out, how he could possibly help out, Mauricio called his brother and told him about Alberto's somewhat cryptic promise. The two brothers let the silence go on for a moment, each on their own reflecting that it was no use even to remark upon Alberto's courage and curious strength – the same virtues that had put him in a boxing ring but then hang up the gloves for fear of killing an opponent, and that had made him persist with his bicycle shop too long – virtues which were undermined only by the certainty he once had in thinking he could be a boxer, in thinking bicycles would be profitable, in thinking Communism, whatever that was, was self-evidently right. In the city, as everywhere in the Republic a fact that made Fulano such an improbable human being – there was no such thing as cowardice or courage. There was only intelligence and stupidity. If, for example, you resisted the gang members robbing one of the beat-up red city buses that blatted, wrenched, and careened their way through the urban bottomlands and high pineshadowed desolation, protested simply because of the injustice of being robbed when you were so poor to begin with, well, then! If, driving, stopped at a red light, a tap on your window was from a pistol and you didn't open the window, if you shook your head and tried to drive away, if you said *No* to the gun, well, then! On the other hand, if someone broke into your house, and you managed to shoot the intruder, you dragged the corpse into the street and left it there; otherwise you would have to explain to cops interested only in what they could extort from you for having the corpse in your home. Neither Fulano nor Mengano had been in their houses those terrible nights when their wives had been murdered but, if they had, that is exactly what they would have done if they had been able to kill the bandits.

Before ending the call, the brothers agreed that Alberto would not do anything risky.

A week passed. The city slumbered through one of those brief periods in which everyone seemed to forget that bad things could happen; it seemed as if the edge of existence was blunter in the summer haze, the only preoccupations those of normal aspirations and mortality. For several days there weren't even any newspaper stories about shootings and robberies.

Without incident, Fede went as he said he would to retrieve the rest of his belongings. He found the apartment above El Portalito empty – no drugs, no guns, no Palestinians. Just dust and an air of neglect. With his wide-eyed girlfriend who had insisted on accompanying him, he even had a quick glass of beer in the old cantina in memory of Che.

Okay – all seemed fine, for now, Fede told his father and uncle, a bit sheepishly.

But then there was no word from Fulano.

And, then, like little tympanum drum beats, he did not call to say he might stop by the Flanagan house, and he missed the next planned get-together with Mengano for a plate of street food. Inquiries at his usual haunts turned up nothing.

Fede was directed to visit Fulano's house but, after knocking on the metal door, and ringing the bell for ten minutes, with a definite intuition of emptiness Fede concluded Fulano was gone. Alberto even missed a long-planned escape from the city to Mengano's great house on Lake Atitlán where the soaring views of the water and the volcanoes had provided him, so many times in the past, a balm – as he reclined in a deck sofa, the wreathed lines accumulated on his dark face upturned at their ends, smiling.

The disappearance of an acquaintance, friend, or family member was as familiar as the smell of tortillas on the griddle. Like wisps of smoke dissipating, individuals vanished as if through holes in the air: this was the magical transcendence of life there, but it was a black magic! The disappearances lent the physicality of one's whereabouts a dreamlike quality; the streets, the trees, the buildings, the shouts of the children hawking newspapers and cell phone cards, the traffic ripping open moments of quiet, the sky, the volcanoes, the sun, the morning mistiness, the human lives occupying space, all seemed unreal, as if people, by vanishing, had never existed.

Some days later Mauricio paid a visit to the poor cousin. After many false turns and questions to pedestrians – receiving the inevitable, smiling wave, with a *"Directo!"* indicating the destination was straight ahead and easy to find – he pulled to a stop in front of a jumble of broken-down buildings and aluminum-roofed dwellings. The pathetic little slatboard shack looked different from how he remembered, but when he had been there last, of course, it had been in darkness.

Responding after several minutes to Mauricio's *hellos?*, the man peered suspiciously out of the doorless space and, after taking a moment to recognize his visitor, to Mauricio's question he said only, oh, *lamentablemente*, Alberto is dead.

"They found him in the ravine last week," the man explained, rubbing back his black cowlicked hair. "I had to go and identify the body, which was hard to do because he was so, you know, beat up and all. My wife was sick and so were my children so it was difficult to do this but the cops said I had to."

In a little warm breeze that felt chilly on his face, Mauricio found himself asking if the man knew what had happened. The man simply shrugged when pressed for more details. He could explain nothing about Palestinians, drugs, or guns. The fact that it had happened, however, was already moving on in time with barely a skip of a tragic heartbeat as Mauricio found himself hoping to bring something back to his brother and, Christ help him, to Guillermo Mengano, more than the short, terribly inadequate fact: *el murió*. A thought flickered in Mauricio's mind: how had the cops known to come to Alberto's cousin? But he dismissed any kind of conspiracy to kill Alberto for once having been a Communist – this was too long ago. He had to conclude the terrible thing had simply happened for no particular reason. Incredibly, stupidly, the man could only repeat what Mauricio could have surmised on his own about any random murder in the city – someone accosted Alberto, apparently in Mixco, the great, desolate, lightning-quick, lightning-perilous suburb to the west of the city proper, and demanded his wallet, watch, or cell phone. What had Alberto been doing in Mixco? The man shrugged, scratched his head, and then asked for some money.

Numb, Mauricio returned from the dismal drive and called his brother. After a half-hour or so of shaking his head, and a sharp word to Moises, later regretted, Horacio called Fede to instruct him for the time being to say nothing – having Mengano in mind. The grief could only penetrate so far into Fede, no matter how sensitive and perceptive he was, because he was young. But Horacio, who knew his son well, understood that Fede was truly sorry for the role he might have played in Fulano's death, however accidental or indirect.

Thereafter, for months, falsely sanguinary, Horacio might find himself in one of the little *barrio* cafés where he stopped sometimes before going back to the house. Without prompting, suddenly juxtaposed in his mind with the routine bedlam of the city would be a memory of Fulano. The moment then seemed to prolong infinitely with all the customary sounds and sights – coughing provoked by the black smoke of the buses, yells in the indifferent, preoccupied street, little stick figures clambering into clots as the dusk arrived – yielding nothing to explain the mystery but the ordinary. Once he watched a bicycle moving off in the distance until it was lost in the asphyxia of the treed streets, and Fulano hesitantly sprang alive again in his memory. Disjointedly, also, there were other memories of the reunions, and he remembered how the faint smell of cement dust replaced the mantle of sawdust that had accumulated on Fulano's shoulders when he had given up the bicycle shop in the neighborhood of the woodcarvers and, as if submitting to reason and reality, had bought the block factory.

The sudden dumb advantage of the living over the dead would strike him. The maxim was, if you wanted to commit a crime, even a murder, do it in the Republic because you would never be caught. If the victim was your wife, husband, mother, father, daughter, son, you would never find out what the last minutes were like, and few palliatives meant anything.

Guillermo Mengano continued to go to the bench by the parrot vendors, sitting by himself, ghostlier than ever. In the bounded but eternal transience of the rustling magnolia leaves, the ever-present stout, thick-waisted, *traje*-wearing Indian women stood by their smoking griddles, peddling tortillas and sliced pineapple and watermelon in little plastic bags. A helpless, bitter otherness was all that remained around a hard lump of pain. In contrapuntal fashion, like an organ playing with a violin, against the obvious joke that otherwise both ridiculed them and elevated them by their dismissal of it, Fulano's company had lent Mengano a transcendent dignity.

Almost a half-year later, on a late afternoon that presaged one of the almost comically grandiose sunsets the volcanoes could provide, Horacio received a call from an excited Fede.

"Well, Papa, steel yourself. For great news. Maybe troubling news, but great news. You're not going to believe this."

"What is it, Fede?"

"I think I saw Alberto Fulano."

"What do you mean you think you saw Alberto Fulano?"

"No, I'll change that. I'm sure it was him!"

"Fede. Slow down. Where do you think you saw him?"

"He was on one of the city buses! His head was all wrapped in a bandage! I ran over towards the window and waved at him. I was right by his window. I'm sure he saw me. Papa, you know how I always say that Fulano is like a flea trying to put on a big belt with a bigger buckle?" – Fede had said this, chiming in to agree that this short firecracker of a man always seemed to go off on exploits and enterprises that had little chance of success – "Well, I think the flea is still jumping!"

"Fede. Federico. It's impossible."

"No, I'm sure it was him, Papa! Don't tell me I'm crazy! I waved at him but even though I'm sure he saw me, he didn't recognize me! I think he may have forgotten who he is. I think he must have got hit on the head and now he has, what's that called – amnesia or something."

"Federico Alejandro. Please. It is not possible. Fulano's cousin went down to the police and identified the body."

"Well, I don't care. I tell you I saw him! That cousin of his must be wrong. Maybe he was drunk. Maybe he lied and didn't go. Papa, I was in the Trêbol – "

"Federico, listen to me. You must absolutely swear to say nothing about seeing Alberto Fulano, on a bus, in the Trêbol, or anywhere. If Mengano heard this you know what it would do to him. Do you hear me?" There was silence for a few seconds.

"Yes, Papa," he heard Fede say.

Fede's acquiescence contained a note of defiance. He seemed to accept Horacio's judgment in the matter but in a way that was purely Fede's: contrite, retreating from his assertion, but resigned in form only.

"Now, look, I believe you believe you saw Alberto. But you were mistaken."

After a moment, his son said quietly, "Okay. Okay... I'm sure you're right," and ended the call.

Horacio put the phone down and went outside. Facing east the air just before sunset was gray-white, ashy; to the west it was turning rosy. Faintly he could smell the great burning city dump which had caught fire years ago and could not now be extinguished.

He thought about poor Mengano, who seemingly was and would be, for the rest of his life, lost without the partner whose name completed the joke of their names and allowed the joke to be transcended. *But could it be*, he thought, *if Fede was right, could it be, by some miracle, that Fulano was alive, existing anonymously, in despair, without even his memory?* And he decided, *no, it was not possible.*

It was Fede, motivated by his energy, optimism, and compassion, all of which seemed to represent somehow a greater understanding even than his elders, who organized the search party: his father and uncle, along with Mengano, of course, who, strangely, did not have to be persuaded despite what the others knew was a wound so deep it had just about finished him off. In fact, they didn't tell him precisely why they were going on the mission to the Trêbol.

So they went. Below a densely polluted sky that turned blood-red at sunset, the coming dusk obscuring the smoke and the reason to worry about taking a full breath, this was the madness of the place: where all the buses from the country congregated, where the trucks chugging and blasting great clouds of black exhaust lined up, earsplittingly squeaked to a rocking vibrating halt, hands on horns without respite, where endless numbers of people waited, or ran, or walked, over the crumbling spidery metal pedestrian overpass, clerks and students, shabby construction workers, mothers with daughters with grandmothers, all seeking their fates, where care might descend to them in their wayward but tightly circumscribed lives, where everything was in transit, embarking, debarking, a huge pulsing arterial-venous flow out and back from the sick, broken heart of the city.

And in the busiest spot of this busiest of all *barrios* where all the streets connected, the *asistentes* coaxing and shouting to speed up the departures, to coerce the travelers onto their particular chariots, all of which had names belying the caustic vibrations of their chassis – *Ruby, Beatriz, Vicky, Maribel* and the like – where, as they arrived, a blind legless man was wheeling his torso on a trolley through the catastrophic bedlam of every variety of patched-together junk vehicle careening around the stalled buses – they did, indeed, find Alberto, sitting slack-legged, his pants ripped almost up to the hip, on the pavement where a bulge had formed of buses stopping and starting.

Despite a bandage circling Alberto's head, general emaciation, a missing left eye, and a doglike expression, somehow they recognized him. He was sitting on a particularly filthy part of the sidewalk, food in splatters, straws, little plastic bags that had held soft drinks, everywhere.

After barely an astonished halt but with the firm surety now that he had been right all along Fede gripped Fulano's arm and pulled him to his feet, which were bare and covered with scabs; the three older men at first were a little helpless to act and Fede had to look at them with an expression mingling a plea with some anger. As they helped him up, it was clear Fulano had no idea who they were or where he was. His face lacked something fundamental, integrating him as a person.

They took him to the best hospital in the city, where he stayed for two weeks, after which he was discharged to the care of Mengano. Although Mengano stepped up to the task of caretaker, because of an inability emotionally to bridge the huge span of such loss to such gain, he pretended it was the same old Fulano, sometimes acknowledging little actions with a vague but brilliant smile to some perfect observation.

The Flanagans and Mengano continued to ensure Fulano got proper medical care; this came to include a false eye imported from some Asian country; when it came and they discovered that, by mistake, they had ordered a blue eye and not a brown, Fede insisted it worked just as well and would give Fulano the distinction of being half a *zarco* – a blue-eyed person.

After a few weeks, bit by bit, Alberto began to remember things. To help him remember, Fede would deliver him to the bench near the parrot vendors, where Mengano would be waiting. But speech was a problem. For a time all Fulano could say was an approximation of his name – "Señor Flan, Señor Flan." But Mengano would talk to him as if he had just heard from his friend the cleverest comment, and shake his head vaguely but emphatically, saying, "Isn't that so, isn't that so?"

Gradually, Fulano was able to remember that he had, indeed, gone, baseball bat in hand, again and again to the apartment over El Portalito until, finally, one night, he found the Palestinians had returned. He asked the Palestinians, politely but intently, what was going on, with the drugs and the guns, explaining that he was a friend of Fede's family and that this was Fede's apartment, and that no "shit-business" – that was the phrase he used – would be permitted there. In turn, the Palestinians explained that they had only one more shipment to get rid of, and the buyers were arriving in a few minutes. As surety of this, they invited Fulano to stay with them; in fact, one could presume, the Palestinians might have thought the baseball bat would be good to display and they could claim Fulano was their bodyguard.

And that was how Fulano ended up, in a confusion of suspicion, slow to react, understanding and belief limited by an innocence when confronted with lash-quick menace, being clubbed from behind, beaten so savagely he lost an eye, driven to Mixco and left for dead after being rolled over the precipice of a *barranca*. It was a wonder he wasn't shot.

He could not remember how long he had lain at the bottom of the ravine, nor could he remember the pain he must have endured. One memory he did have was of opening his one eye to see a dung beetle trundle through the trash, struggling zealously with a big flake of manure. Fulano also remembered from his mental twilight smelling the milky soil, so abundantly fertile, so abidingly innocent, new and ancient simultaneously, mixing with the garbage.

The beginning of his salvation, however, he remembered better; once he opened his eye he found himself looking into the face of a ragged little boy. The boy, scavenging in the trash, climbed up out of the abyss and, a little later, the boy's sister appeared, making her way down the steep sides. With their help he staggered to his feet and clawed his way up the garbage-strewn defile. He remembered standing in the particularly desolate pollution of Mixco, face lined with dried blood from an empty eye socket. He remembered being fed and having a place to sleep for a few days. He also remembered, for some reason, how the young woman was animated and ripe, in a complete state of rut, given over to the needs of youth, clinging to her boyfriend who came and went, casting uneasy eyes at Fulano. When his caretakers got tired of him, as Horacio imagined, Fulano had been handed a *quetzal* now and then and then been coaxed, half-lifted, half-carried, onto this or that bus by an easily misunderstanding *asistente*, zealous to take the coin, and had ridden back and forth between the steaming cities of the south and west, passing in a mental haze through god knows what little crossroads shack towns.

As more of the bits and pieces came out from rasped phrases, it was easy for the others to conjure a heroic scene: their friend facing off against the drug gang, striking out against the vandals of society, the robbers of the city buses, the incorrigible tattooed predators who once were victims but now were just another enemy of civil society. But privately they understood that it was not so much that, crazily, futilely, Fulano was striking a blow for Good against Evil. Rather it was that he was, indeed, if not a little unhinged, then different, and he had always been so – but no more different than one of the many in the Republic fated by an inexplicable conspicuousness to be singled out and savagely struck down.

Mengano one day spent six hundred *quetzales* for one of the parrots, knowing how attached parrots can become to their humans. To his father and uncle, his uncanny perspicacity balancing his wonderful tact, Fede commented that the parrot represented to Mengano the surrogate hope that Fulano would regain full speech.

And with scarcely a word about it all, as if nothing had happened, Mengano began driving his friend over to the Flanagans' great-house to resume the weekly get-togethers. Fulano was given a special wood chair, on which the parrot gnawed when he wasn't perched on Fulano's shoulder, burbling and cooing, jealously watching for interlopers, and screeching, lowering his blue-feathered head to bite, splaying a webbed, clawed foot out when someone came too near. Fulano looked like an old pirate; the sight made Moises show his gap-tooth smile.

The Palestinians returned, without guns or drugs; apparently all of that activity had been a once-only effort with a different kind of contraband. While they were explaining this, seemingly quite openly, indeed, in almost a conciliatory way, they looked at Fede a little strangely, leaving him with the impression that they knew something about Fulano. When Fede told his father this, explaining that, of course, to spare his father's feelings, he would not move back into the apartment over El Portalito, and when Horacio thought of the kindnesses that must have been bestowed on Fulano during his time on the streets, and as little as that kindness might have been, Horacio ventured to say to the others, one day sitting under the parasol in the Flanagans' garden, as if seeking to put an end, with an epitaph, to it all, "Well, maybe I was wrong about the Moors."

At other times, Mengano brought Fulano back to the bench on 20th Street, standing over him, his fragile height, his paleness and white hair, all seeming almost to make him disappear – a most vulnerable protector. If there was an end to the incident it was shimmering, rocketed into the air almost, the sudden impact of the magnificent rejected and rejecting Now striking the two aging men as they looked out from the bench at the chaotic streets. Then, of course, the winds that came, the detritus of time built around Fulano's near-death, would cover it all up as if it had never happened, dying with whoever died – the lofty but vague pieties hypocritically offered that God saw to everything. For as mythical is its allure the darkness is mysterious in the Land of the Many Trees, the Land of the Replacement Parts; even as it is salty with the pith of blood, its forethought is misted because it has no end. And somewhere, out in the green-fronded bosque, are the hinterlands, where time, the map, and history all stop – though there are many stories, even from there.

THE FORGOTTEN MAN

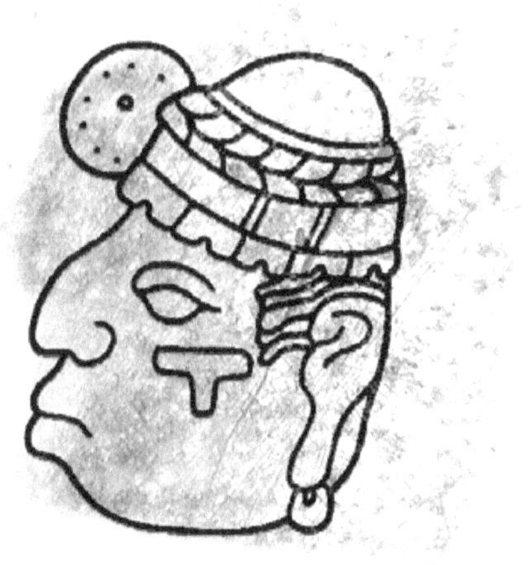

A large man with a close-cut graying head, handsome but for slightly pop-eyes, Carlos Kruger displayed a quickness unusual for someone his size. His physique and his movements, characterized by a fluid but impatient surety, matched up – no doubt because of long habits of the hardest and most severe discipline. Dressed in an expensive, slightly rumpled suit, a blue dress shirt with white collar and silk tie, his manner seemed both lethargic and somewhat apologetic. I sensed it was neither. He might have seemed hurried, or harried, but there was no doubt he was a forceful man, and absolutely able to handle whatever pressure he encountered in the various leading roles, public and private, he played in his life and in the life of the nation.

The fact that I was tired – make that exhausted, and at the limits of my tolerance – distracted me...such that when, repeatedly, I had to jerk myself back to the realization of just who it was now standing in front of me, waiting for me to speak again after a few words of greeting and wondering what ruses I had employed to get to him, I had to recall what he had said, twice, now: "*Mucho gusto...es bueno conocerle...* What can I do for jew?"

It is probably little exaggeration to say that my life passed before my eyes, standing high above the crazed capital of the Republic in front of the glare-protected interior of his suite of offices on an upper floor of one of the Capital's three "skyscrapers." At the same time, that this building was no more than twenty stories high imbued it, in my *extranjero*'s mind, with a kind of shame, pathetically low as it was by comparison with other edifices elsewhere in the world.

No matter how seemingly modern, perhaps, was the architecture – white stucco and stone, with an enormous government logo hung on its exterior midway – as one's eye followed it down this building descended right into the trash and hubbub of the Republic's manic, generalized poverty. The bottom of the building seemed shrouded by matted monkey pelt, a perception caused by palm trees with their coconuts twined and balding as if with pubic hair. There, at street level, coconuts littered the ground as if from profligate and unrestrained sexuality.

If I had managed to arrange the meeting on my own, despite the near impossibility in any normal universe of doing so, it would cross my mind later that – unbelievable to me, a *gringo* – someone else in my shoes might not necessarily live very long after the meeting. For, if good rumor was to be believed, death spilled from this man's hand. You might say that during the course of my brief conversation with Kruger, my recent life, that summer of failures so numerous I had forgotten most of them, their dismal details blending one to the next as moments of disappointment, disgust, and despair all passed before my eyes...for the death, at least, of my career was looming. Years, *years*, gone up in smoke. In fact, I was falling apart – at that precise moment, though, trying to hold myself together, forcing myself, almost psychedelically deranged by despair, to still appear completely fit for the noble task of guardian of the cultural patrimony of the nation – and which was also, to many – scholars and museums – the cultural patrimony of the world.

At the moment this review served a purpose. I needed to explain in the clearest and most convincing fashion my problem and rationalize the bizarre appeal at the back of my mind. To understand even the slightest bit of the wild tale I needed to tell him required familiarity with how things went down in a former banana republic – in international consideration no more than a postage stamp of a country, small on the map but full of volcanoes and post-colonial violence that afflicted its mostly Indian masses and who had no escape from the deep historical rut they were stuck in.

As it transpired, the meeting seemed to have come about by accident. If I was a superstitious type I might have laid it to the gods or to a *centavo* picked up that summer on the old magnolia-stained pavements of the Capital's rich zones – ragged destitution eating at the edges of these shotgun-guarded enclaves as my worries ate at my nerves. I had pulled every last string I had and I whiled away my hours on hoped-for meetings with the *gordos* – big shots – each meeting promising to buy my latest quarry a fine meal at one of the restaurants on the Reforma. They rarely if ever showed. The few who did come, at some point or other, quickly changed the subject and found some generic joke to tell, laughed uproariously, and then excused themselves, pleading *un compromiso.*

I had an acquaintance, a kind of colleague, who visited *xamanes* and who, in my opinion, took everything much too seriously down here. The last I heard he went a little off his rocker, which was understandable, to a degree, because the "scholar" racket is a crazy one, if you think about it, and you can wind up in some strange places mentally. His problem, I think, was that he didn't know how to just close his eyes to certain things. But now I, too, had become superstitious! I started praying to the gods, any god – the ancient rain god Chaak or Tohil, the lightning god – for help with my problem, a problem which, in despair of a resolution, had taken me back to a doctor-diagnosed depression and, unfortunately, to certain bad habits I thought I had given up, of visiting favorite sex clubs where, with a bit of the avidity that a white man in a brown country – rationalized as anthropological study – is susceptible to. Without excuses, I had nourished a few true loves to the point of the ridiculous. There was one fabulous tall *morena* from Bluefields, Nicaragua who always kept me waiting while she made up her face into an almost Egyptian-like mask, eyes ringed with kohl. Without the cosmetics she was a muscular, supple, pretty girl with woolly hair, the product in the colonial past of African slave and Central American Indian. With her, things came very close to being domestic. She let me fuck her without a condom – risky, but I trusted her because where she worked doctors checked the girls every month. And there was a tinkly-sunny tiny *Guatemalteca* with an extraordinarily shallow pussy who never complained that I was hurting her who, last I had heard, had married a millionaire Mexican; *good for her!* I thought. With the *morena,* so convinced was she by my attentions she started refusing payment.

From this height, sights that were familiar on the ground where *Septima Avenida* cut closer to the dirty white-tiled Burger King and then ran suddenly divided again – were unfamiliar, the unfamiliarity further distorted because of the interpolated *luxe* of the very different world Kruger occupied and that presented the most extreme contrast to all those people below. Kruger's world within the Republic was a small group of well-guarded, incestuously connected rich. They frequented little shotgun-patrolled malls, fine shops catering exclusively to the wealthy and offering the finest products – delicatessens modeled after stores in New York or Los Angeles, brand name clothing outlets – where spoiled sons and daughters of the tiny privileged class wearing stressed and pre-faded jeans shopped for the trendiest gear from *los estados*. I had acquaintances among this group and had visited their country houses and seen the latest consumer gadgetry – the most option-laden cell phones, enormous flat-screen high-definition televisions, expensive hookahs, all spread around or set into oversized Western-style interiors.

With Kruger, I couldn't help but glance at some photos of what must have been the "family" displayed on the polished black laminar surfaces of his otherwise bare office – the backdrop, a fabulous *finca* estate. The paterfamilias himself was surrounded by a tribe of sons and daughters – pop-eyed younger male versions of himself, slightly heavy, melancholy young women who apparently took after the wife. From the scant experience I had with him – a few minutes now, no more, already overly long for him – I was struck that, even in the photos arranged around the office, he never broke the grim impassiveness of his expression. The clear message was that he never allowed himself to be distracted even such that his face might assume a more relaxed look...a smile. The unavoidable sense, as well, was: *these are mine. Do not even think they can be approached or remembered or thought about in any way. If you do, something terrible will happen to you...*

Resigned to another failure in a seemingly eternal recurrence of failures, I was already thinking ahead, with some yearning, to when, driving to the strange old shotgun house I had rented in Zone One, I would be navigating as if to the very end of the world, or of my world, at any rate – deep into the interstices of the massive slum capital city. Closer and closer I would get to the quiet little potholed streets, then pull up in front of the scratched green accordion garage doors, scan the block a hundred and eighty degrees, jump out, unlock the gate, pull in as quickly as possible, instantly relock the gates and shove the slat bars into place – even in Zone One the dangers out on the street were all-too serious – shut off the old truck engine which only died, engine knocking, after interminable extra shudders and climb one story upstairs to an atrium still receiving late afternoon sun from the peaceful and hot blue sky. The relative quiet was broken only by an occasional dog bark and parrot's lunatic squawk from the neighbors' houses. Every step up in the old linoleum and cheap tile was a step of escape from my problem which, more and more, seemed like a fatal illness. Automatically, I would grab a beer, a *Gallo* ("Cock") or perhaps a *Moza* ("Black Slave Girl"), from the ancient refrigerator in the primitive kitchen. I would carry it up the narrow half-story concrete stairway, painted incarnadine red to match the *faux* pre-Columbian murals I had had an art student draw on the walls (the Republic ever-colorful), to my tar roof.

If I still had any of the opiate painkillers I had prescribed for me by certain *farmacias* on a no-questions asked "agreement" I would take a few pills, as well, and chill out. From my roof I could gaze down into my "back yard": a series of cantilevered trapezoids, like cages in a zoo, of the most rudimentary but quaintly mustered domesticities, each contained within their own twelve-meter walls. I could imagine the chaos outside and elsewhere in the city did not exist and my life was no different essentially from my neighbors. I could look down to their ground-floor open air spaces as if my life, too, was normal by proximity with normal citizen amenities: the ever-present *pila*, laundry hanging to dry, splatters of papaya, mango, watermelon, and seed husks beneath the parrot cage. Someone's television was blaring out sappy *novela* music. Someone else was frying food surrounded by clouds of lazy flies.

Behind and surrounding each indoor space were the high cinder block walls, the tops embedded with broken glass placed to deter pole-vault break-ins from the rear. If any further reminder was needed that I was living in a Central American country it was in the form of an occasional great tree growing within these rear walls, a palm, depositing its giant testicle-like bombs with thunks to be cut open and the milk drunk, or an enormous *volador*, absolutely straight and regal, with some leafage still festooning its upper reaches with *bosque* green, the tree that, in antiquity, and *per* its modern name, "flyer," launched ritual flights of performers who had wrapped themselves up in twine, climbed to the top, and then swan-dived downward, outward, whirling ever wider and faster until they reached the ground, hopefully having measured the rope correctly. My scholarly sources said the flyers leaped from the top only after they were completely intoxicated on *pulque* or hallucinogens. In possession of my own intoxicants, more than once, blackly I joked with myself about asking the undoubtedly befuddled but friendly neighbors to borrow their tree for my own swan dive... without the rope.

That summer, at the end of each day, despite the inevitable frustrations and the accompanying despair, such moments of repose were actually tranquil, and I could almost make myself believe that outside the gates and walls everything was normal. With this in mind, I would shut off my cell phone and try, simultaneously, to forget the latest rounds of preposterous meetings with corrupt *diputados* and ministerial functionaries who heard out the *gringo*'s passionate, reasoned appeals with the expression of a dead fish. When, after listening to my hyperexcited pleas for help, their faces changed to an almost comically serious solemnity, the straight faces containing a haughtiness and a glimmer of humor *who is this ridiculous gringo?* It was as if by shoving at them all the facts of my case in the most forceful but lucid way possible, somehow this meant I assumed either they were stupid – the overly specific explanation as if given to a child or an idiot. Or I was all but declaring that they needed moral prodding to convince them to do something they should want to do without the prodding, the insinuation of moral vacuity thus a grave offense against their honor and dignity – of which, of course, they had neither.

Because of my desperation, I even permitted myself from time to time to believe in the good will of these authorities, even though I knew their only concern as public servants was the monthly envelope of cash from the drug cartels – that this stipend was the real reason they bought the votes for office in the first place. Mostly, they heard me out, but, tellingly, had few or no questions afterward. A few of them, however, with what, no doubt, they believed was extremely crafty probing, asked if I was digging up any objects of value and if so how much were they worth and oh by the way where did I store them? With this line of interrogation several things happened: my heart sank, I felt even more like a complete fool, and I reminded myself to put extra locks on the *bodega* or warehouse holding our artifacts and, in the future, should deny I had any particular artifact of value not already turned over to the national museum.

That I was so exhausted and distracted scared me because, in Kruger's presence, I felt I was now, finally, close to some universal *truth* – he was one of the few people in the Republic who could make things happen – good or terrible. Emphasizing this even more strongly because a supposedly impossible encounter was really taking place, the *truth* was the pithiness of nothing less than that ultimate reality, the matter of life and death.

"Pues muy estimado Señor Ministro...es un gran *honor blah blah blah"* –

But even if, in my *gringo* Spanish, I was able to explain to Kruger my sad story, I was already anticipating leaving, defeated yet again, to return to the useless oasis of my weird summer domicile. There, with the sense of inconsolable loss – my career, my professional life, circling around the drain – I would fish out the key to unlock the room in the house in which were shelved several magnificent vessels – thousands of years old. Illustrated with free-form quill ink depictions of dwarves bearing cylindrical cups of foaming chocolate to portentous Buddha-bellied kings, of caricatures of grotesque underworld deities in diabolical dances, of the maize god and his blowgun-shooting protectors, every figure and line was drawn with the most exquisite humor and subtle nuance each and every scene incalculably *different* in novel and curious ways from ancient artifacts from elsewhere in the world. Under my supervision, workers had dug up these pots from tombs and temple caches. Marveling, we turned them over in our hands in the first sunlight falling on them for two thousand years. Given to me, from luck, and hard, hard work – "thrill" is too small a word for the intoxicating drug of my profession – headlines for the discoverer... and the erudite decipherer of the esoterica of ancient kings. As I held them in my hands I knew that soon these pots – worth hundreds of thousands of dollars on the black market in antiquities – could be gone to the thief and the international auction hourse or the mantel of a *rico* as if I had never labored to find them. Before the problems had arrived which I was now trying to explain to Kruger, whenever I removed one of the pots from its box my only anxieties had been about the earthquakes so common to the capital city.

Not that illegal sale of antiquities was anything I would be involved in – far from it! I was a certified scholar for whom the pots' value lay in the information they contained about the great long-dead civilization that had flourished within the borders of the modern Republic before the coming of the Europeans and the priests conquering, enslaving, and killing for Jesus, their king, and themselves. But almost every afternoon I could not resist looking at them, hefting them again in my hands, feeling their delicate weight and the cunning shapes, marveling that I – my research project, that is – had dug them up, and that they were evidence that I had, indeed, discovered a *bona fide* great lost city.

I had made it in to see Kruger because of a phone call on my behalf from his lover, a stunning *Salvadoreña* in her mid-thirties whom I had run into at a museum exhibition opening. She had taken courses in universities in the United States and professed to love antiquities and art objects from the extinct ancient cities. Not so mysteriously – since, counter-intuitively, it did conform to certain completely hypocritical signature issues of some in her social caste – she also claimed to hold human rights causes dear to her heart. In this, the land of genocide! Slender-waisted, with perfect honey skin, *Castellano* gray eyes, and a luscious, dimpled mouth – in profile, childishly budlike – Mercedes struck me as a type: a woman well-practiced in the arts of seduction, with the emphasis on catering to the needs of the *über*-powerful Latin male, in which looks, intelligence, and, undoubtedly, a large catalogue of sexual skills were requisite. On the pillared patio of the new private museum, candles fluttering in the evening breezes, her eyes caught mine and she smiled warmly and intimately through the crush of gabbing babbling invitees. With a glass of champagne in hand, she swept over to embrace me Latin-style, barely touching but permitting a close-up confirmation of the upper deck of her physique, her low-cut satin blouse unbuttoned enough to reveal a tanned, brown-freckled bosom, bunched globes delicately scented by sweet lemon. After the cheek-touch, she tipped back and favored me with a smile, little crinkles at the corners of her eyes, while in my mind was how fabulous a creature she was – overly sensible, as she stood on her toes for the clinch, of the press of her breasts and the exquisite forbiddens of her body.

Later on, I would ask myself just what about the situation had brought her outside of her comfort zone. Normally, I would have been suspicious of someone like her – too modish, therefore too connected to the oppressor class. In my profession connections *were* important, but you had to be very careful. The Republic was a minefield of perplexity, and of course at that moment I had no idea she was Kruger's lover! In fact, before I was made aware of this, what had sprung to mind was how I might hook up with her – a prospect instantly dismissed because, in general, the women down here were not interested in *gringos per se* but also because it could be dangerous for too many reasons to list even without knowing more about her. Besides, with a crisis looming that was possibly fatal to my career. romance with any woman was quite secondary. I had one thing in mind: saving my project. Nevertheless, for the next several minutes of chatter about my work, I definitely enjoyed how she seemed, remarkably – no, *amazingly* – to be directing all her attention my way. Except for when her cell phone rang, which was pretty often.

Exploitation of her looks in the social milieu of the privileged class – who could blame her? – was as manifestly clear as the cleverness of how she handled it. The fashionable hip-length jacket and expensive black slacks identified her perhaps as someone from the business world; I noticed how other people glanced at her either with too-obviously dismissive but invidious interest not necessarily cutting her dead, but so pointedly avoiding her it was as if they were holding clubs behind their backs but were afraid to use them. A few other attractive women more or less of her type and attire came up to us with automatic smiles; but it was evident she radiated some kind of power that distinguished her from the crowd. My sense, though, even in those first moments, was that whatever she did and whatever her connections were, they were not necessarily very admirable. The bottom line was that she was definitely on most people's radar, including some embassy officials, one of whom I knew pretty well, who sidled over to me, nudged me while she was on one of her cell phone calls, and whispered loudly in my ear, "Be careful of that one, son."

To my "why?" he replied,

"She moves in very high circles. And," he paused for emphasis, "she's taken...by someone you don't wanna be on the same playing field with."

"Who?" I asked.

Conspiratorially, jokingly, looking one way then the other a full one hundred eighty degrees, he whispered, "the Interior Minister," with an "only in the Republic" special wink that told me the "Interior Minister" wasn't just another government official in this case – or, as it turned out, just another interior minister. As he lifted another glass of wine from a passing tray, he added, "Ah, love. Who can explain it?"

Jesus, I thought. More intrigue – as if there wasn't enough already in the Land of the Replacement Parts.

But all right. Why should I be surprised that this woman had such a back story? Still confused by the attention she was directing my way, I remembered watching her face while she was speaking to one of her callers – realizing, with an inexplicable certainty, that it was the face of a woman talking to the man she loved. I could tell this not because she seemed particularly happy; no, her face bore, rather, a *hard* expression – the gray eyes narrowed, the face slack, the dimples disappeared presumably because of the gravity of the conversation. It was an expression, as I watched, that changed to one of forced patience, the look of someone explaining something, perhaps, to a petulant teenager, something that the other person just had to understand, for his own sake – the facts of life, as it were, and knowing that the effort, likely, was completely wasted. Only when I learned more did I ask myself how she could love such a man, and arrived only at that stereotype about the beautiful *Latina* drawn to the bad boy – and, holy Jesus, in his case one of the baddest, as I found out.

But love the guy she did – plain as whatever was plain in that country. Her brow wrinkled up, she rolled her eyes and then closed them, as if in pain at the impossibility of making herself clear. I heard her say something like "...*Despues nosostros juntos… Estamos… Si!... Si! cariño… España...*" – which, of course, without more information meant nothing to me except that, as a topic of discussion, Spain might come up as well as any as a lovers' destination. It didn't occur to me until later why she had said *fuga* instead of *vuelo*. Only later, as my mental state permitted, did I put the pieces together.

I had no idea why she seemed to know me – a mystery only partly explained sometime later. It was true that, that evening, I was a bit of a star, as some of "my" pots were on display, and at affairs like this scholars were the stars, particularly ones like myself, with a few big grants and a major project. One must understand that worlds of scholars and scholarship exist that rise to equal, in certain countries, the most exclusive clubs. In such a small country, it was true, even in such a benighted one, foreigners who brought in research grant money, discovered ancient cities and beautiful artifacts that, if they were not stolen and sold at Sotheby's before arriving at the national museum, regularly got headlines in the national papers, enjoyed acquaintances with cabinet ministers and, in general, moved about in pretty high circles.

So, at any rate, despite my problem, which, as I say, few at the party could have known of, I was feeling a bit in my glory that evening, fresh from the site and full of the heady exhilaration one in my profession feels from unearthing palaces and royal tombs and the bones of kings and suttee wives and so forth, all buried for two thousand years or more. Hence, also, my stupidly slow pick-up on things that evening. Amid the museum's efforts to make me, and a few of my similarly lucky peers, feel the gratitude of the nation, in the flickering *candelas*, parked near the colonial-era furniture covered with Indian folk-art cloths, *hors d'oeuvres*, glasses of champagne, small coffee-colored men and women mingled in constant streams all around us, smiling and saying *Caballero* and *Doctorrrr* and so forth. The *gringo* adventurers received the susurrating worship of the little conquered ones for showing off, to *them*, *our* booty from *their* most fabulous ancient lost world – Ordinarily cautious because connections, right connections anyway, were everything – as I say, I avoided people at these kinds of parties who, from appearances, were wealthy patrons of do-good projects who mouthed concern for the "indigenous" but personally had many serf-like retainers and inevitably were linked, usually directly by family, to certain other people very suspect in the terrible and violent history of the land. One might ask why, if museum exhibition parties drew some movers and shakers and at which I was congratulated by all sorts of officials from the cultural ministry and other agencies, so far I had gotten only brush-offs about my problem from *diputados* and reps of some lower-level ministry officials who, after the most strenuous contortions, I had been able to see. I was learning it wasn't *me* that was the problem, it was the problem itself. At big gatherings like the exhibit opening everything was fine and dandy; private meetings with specific and difficult requests were different, apparently, if the problem had to do with politics and land ownership.

In addition to the fact that appreciation of the *patrimonio cultural* was given lip service only and that nobody cared more than a pellet of macaw shit about the glorious Cultural Patrimony, part of the answer to that question was that the Republic, as an entity for which the citizenry would be expected generally to feel a sort of patriotic bond, was a Punch and Judy show. *There was no country*, no collective national entity but, instead, only certain individuals on the make for themselves, at all times, in all ways. First and foremost of these, of course, were the generals, politicians, big businessmen and the *dueños* of enormous *finca* .

At any rate, only shortly later and after doing some homework, did I find out that Kruger – the man she was speaking to on the phone, the man she loved – could lay claim to another notoriety in addition to being Interior Minister. That evening, apparently because I was a *gringo* of a certain type, that is, with a Ph.D. from a top university, it appeared to my both exhilarated but desperate mental state that the whisper even from the embassy guy, number two, actually, in the diplomatic hierarchy, was not worth more than a second's pause. And my new friendship, if that's what it was, with Mercedes, I decided was due to nothing more than that, as director of a big project turning up great stuff, I was empowered, at a party held to accompany the opening of a new museum exhibit, to proceed from inconsequential chit-chat to the moment now at which Kruger actually stood, in the flesh, impatiently in front of me.

The simple facts of the matter – if the thing could be simplified at all – needed extraordinary tact in the telling except to my colleagues (to whom, by the way, I could never ever admit to having met with Kruger). Idiotically, I thought, even when I knew who Kruger really was, I could not bring myself to call off the meeting. Perhaps it was the momentum of hope, perhaps it was fear that once I was on Kruger's radar the decisive step had been taken and there was no turning back, but, whatever it was, I had to go through with it.

At any rate, whatever capacity I once had for rational thought seemed to have disappeared. For the fact was that, since running into Mercedes, I had learned from onetime *guerrilla* friends that during the genocide that concluded the civil war in the country a few years ago, Kruger had been the head of *la Mano Blanca*, the most notorious of the *escuadrones de la muerte* – the death squads and which was responsible, all by itself, for thousands, tens of thousands, of murders.

The actions of the White Hand took place under cover of such official invisibility the fear multiplied even beyond the almost unimaginably terrible rumors, speculation running riot about torture and other horrific retributions even against a victim's extended family. The actions of the death squads existed in the darkness of the Republic's vitals – what counted, what mattered, what caused things to happen and not to happen...all spelled out in one word, "death." Anything associated with the "bad times," as the rural people referred to them, developed quickly the status of myth – the notoriously untraceable, anonymous, unmarked *panela blanca*, the white van, so often seen in the vicinity of snatchings, kidnappings, torture, and murder." At most, in certain *canciones rancheras* with double-meanings – a death squad *coronel*'s name inserted in a stanza – one sang a phrase or two with only the most trusted friends. All of these secret facts were passed over, generally speaking, completely *sub rosa*.

What had the White Hand and Mr. Kruger, Interior Minister of the nation – and former head of the most terrible death squad of them all – to do with me and solving my problem? Aware now that it was too late to pretend I had any other reason for seeking the meeting, I told Kruger that there was a man who was conducting a great *estafa*, a swindle of the already long-term miserable and shat-upon, right in the town where I was working, and whose big *truco* had completely brought to a halt my wonderful, good-works project – stopped it in its tracks – and was ruining any possibility of continuing, putting at enormous risk my funding.

Now, switching back and forth from smiling politely at The Man to looking as tragically and unjustly victimized as possible, I was still trying to figure out how to get to the point of why I had wanted to meet him. Because of the still fresh memory of Mercedes' lemon-scented bosom and her delicate clinch, with Kruger now I had an unpleasant sense of shared intimacy: he knew I knew that that beautiful, wasp-waisted, big-breasted blonde-frosted brunette with the dimpled mouth and laughing, level gray eyes was the owner of the fabulous body he knew carnally and whose braceleted arms, ringed fingers, scarlet fingernails and receptive orifices disposed themselves in such a manner as to accommodate every part of his large and hairy body. It ticked through my mind – I couldn't help it – how probably when he was with her he was grabby, *machista* forceful and demanding, unzipping his fly and huffing and puffing to quick orgasm on top of her.

I am taking my time describing the nature of my tragedy because it was so fantastic and convoluted that to understand it required complete suspension of disbelief. Despite the, still, to me, incredible nature of it, it turned out Mercedes knew of my problem! – and understood at least its general dimensions, because a friend of a friend of a friend or whatever had mentioned it to someone who mentioned it to someone who mentioned it to... Mercedes... and Mercedes... Bottom line: you know you're never supposed to pet a burning dog. Mercedes was most definitely not a dog, but she was on fire.

Like Kruger, my problem was not orgasms – he had Mercedes and if I had time I had my casual carnalities in the clubs. As I thought now how to explain the situation, as always it occurred to me that my problem had been long in the making – one might say without exaggeration, over a five-hundred year span, beginning with the Conquest! And, in most respects, I was standing in front of someone who could easily be construed as the representative type most responsible for the half-a-millennium of persistent horror that was now directly rebounding onto me. But for obvious reasons – who he *was*, the complete lack of interest he would have in most of what I could say to him – I put aside philosophy, history, politics, and esoteric scholarly interests.

I started off a bit too desperately, talking very fast, only realizing too late that I didn't know the luscious *Salvadoreña's* last name, or names, even though she had given me a card with all four of them on it – it was Mercedes de la Flor something something and which announced her profession, something to do with law or media or finance or some such all-purpose "business" (when she saw me trying to decipher the card's fancy script, she said in perfect, unaccented English, "Oh, it doesn't matter, everyone just knows me as Mercedes, anyway! And all I really do is try to help good people like you").

Halfway through the explanation I knew things might turn out horribly wrong. But having arranged to see him, it would be ludicrous, I told myself, not to have some important request to make. Now, finally meeting with the man who represented what I considered a last recourse, someone who possessed the most terribly compromised morality, Kruger was looking at me with curious intentness. He must have understood that I had not been shunted off to him as a mistaken act of the randomness of the diplomatic world. No, his lover, Mercedes, had phoned Kruger about me, not long after she had circled her arms around me and said she had something she wanted to talk to me about. Apparently, she hadn't explained to him the reason, though. So, mixed with a skill he must have learned long ago to anticipate and evade most matters that would come his way that were not associated with his real and practical business, it was up to me, absurdly, to make my case from scratch. off.

"Mercedes, I believe, called you on my behalf... " I started Cutting me off, without acknowledging her phone call, again in English he repeated only, in his surprisingly deep, gruff, get to-the-point voice, for the third time, a little roughly, now, "What can I do fer jew?"

I was thinking that, to most other people, my complicated problem required great patience to understand, such were its astonishing convolutions of ironies and malevolence. However, perhaps more than any powerful official in the government, *he* could understand how it was that I wound up in such a hole. I told him how I was directing a major archaeological project out in the *campo*, excavating an enormous ancient city – in a country that has been described as one giant archaeological site – and some recent events and actions by certain individuals, certain most unhelpful, "bad people," as I put it, had stopped the project and, therefore, the good works I was, merely attempting to bring to fruition not only for the cultural patrimony of his great and wonderful country, but for the impoverished residents of the nearby *pueblo* – giving employment, for example, to nearly half the entire village.

With Kruger, of course, I went far less than the whole nine yards on the scholarly stuff, sensing he may never have encountered someone like me before, someone with an Ivy League pedigree in a scholarship of interest basically only to the Ivory Tower and the super-rich collector, although he may, he just may, I hoped, have sensed that that Ivory Tower was the same one that produced people in the political and business worlds with power and influence he would appreciate. As I was talking, he stood impassively, rock-solid, giving away nothing.

"Obviously, you are aware, Mr. Minister, of the F.R.G. and the ex-PACs..."

Stone-faced – or was he startled, and was concealing this? – he looked at me as if taking my measure now as I presumed to describe an issue that he had to understand far, far better than I ever could.

In as correct but anguished a tone as I could summon, I told him I was gravely troubled not for my sake but for the project's. A blatant and criminal exploitation of completely impoverished *campesinos* was greatly damaging my project. A man, Ruffino Barrios by name, was promising compensation for service during the so-called civil war in the paramilitary *Patrullas de Autodefensa Civil,* also known as the PACs, and he had completely commandeered the project offices - including our computers and other expensive equipment. Long lines of these men were passing through the site and our offices to fill out false paperwork and pay Barrios "processing fees." I did not mention what I also knew to be the case – that many of these now old men – as often as not, multiple amputees – had been forcibly impressed, on threat of immediate execution by gun or machete, into the very death squads that *Señor* Kruger once organized and directed.

Apart from the brazen expropriation of my project, the swindle was that no actual compensation claim could be submitted because the compensation merely was a promise in the national election campaign then going on. And the government had gone on the T.V. and radio to announce, in advance, that if compensation were to be approved for the men in the paramilitary patrols, it would be against the law to charge fees to process their claims.

I did not feel the need to remind Kruger that the compensation promise was one of the planks of the far right political party created by a former general, initiator of a *coup d'état* and the dictator-president during the civil war who was also known as *El Genocida* because of his role, *personally,* in the killing of at least twenty thousand people. That the general was, also, a self-proclaimed born-again Christian was one more astonishing twist in yet another unbelievably pathetic and disgusting fabric of lies the Republic seemed so reliably capable of weaving. Previously, *El Genocida* had, somehow – with loony backing from American anti-communists *cum* Bible Belt televangelists – created a rightwing political party, the Republican National Front, or F.R.G. Ruffino was, of course, an F.R.G. member.

Mr. Minister, I said now, thanks to the kind intervention by our mutual friend, Mercedes, how very privileged I was to be telling such an important and honorable – blah-blah – individual who had the weighty cares of the nation – blah blah – on his mind about my little problem. Earlier, I thought I had observed what seemed a certain expression of understanding on his face which was both dismissal and – perhaps – amused impatience. Now Kruger's impassive face seemed, without otherwise changing, to darken a little, which reminded me that, far beyond whatever dishonorable knowledge he knew I now had about his mistress, I had passed into dangerous territory. While I could almost hear him concocting the yelling or complaining words he would use with Mercedes for setting up the meeting with this *gringo* and although, from his completely unreadable expression, what I thought I was likely to hear was yet another brush-off, I found myself thinking, almost idly, was *I* setting myself up for some kind of *real* problem simply by talking to him?

Even worse, on the subject of whacking, I reminded myself that what, incredibly, I was really asking him to do he might already somehow have assumed to be my request. And, in retrospect, I think the question already had worked its way up in his own consciousness no more than ten seconds into my account what I was really asking, if I indeed had the nerve.

And that was how, amazing even myself, I heard myself saying, like an echo in my head, or like it was someone else talking: in all candor, sir, *Señor Ministro*...might there not be some way to, well, ah make this Ruffino ah be kind of just ah…well...*removed*... as the obstacle to my wonderful project! and which had already proven itself to be of such benefit to the local people and to the cultural patrimony of the nation...but which (I repeated) would only be possible...with, say, well, ah....his...er...*disappearance*? At this point I think I produced a little pained chuckle as if the insinuation of the request was completely out-of-the-question – absurd!... even though I was, well, kind of serious...yes, indeed, I was serious...though it was all kind of ridiculous...

If you were to ask me, at that second, was I in my right mind? I would have to say, for the love of Christ, no! For, in point of fact, and make no bones about it, what I was asking the former head of the most notorious of the death squads, now the particular government minister with his hands on all the police and national security forces in the Republic, to do was to have

Ruffino "disappeared." At that second I felt a bit lightheaded, hollow – as if the conversation had not happened at all and I still possessed some scruples.

But did any of this startle him? I couldn't tell.

I stopped my recitation. We'd entered an area of fog – certainly of things of which one did not speak, at three o'clock in the afternoon, in the office of one of the highest officials of the government.

Maybe, I was thinking, he was impressed I had some *huevos,* or was he a little amused by such a *gringo*? I couldn't tell… Somewhere, though, in all of these unknowables, this *stew,* I suspected that Mercedes, herself, was percolating – *she* was the issue, *she* had come to *me, she* had set up the meeting with Kruger…and *she* had some reason for finding out about my problem to begin with, and suggesting that her all-powerful lover, a man whom it was probably fatal even to know! might help.

Since he still was saying nothing, merely looking at me – could I detect a sardonic inflection of the brow? – I felt obliged to continue talking, and elaborated, persuasively, I felt now, how it wasn't necessarily that Ruffino was, at the same time, cheating hundreds upon hundreds of the most pathetically poor people of money they didn't have to begin with that was so bad – here insinuating to Kruger that I was not some commie sympathizer – but, what was worse I was sure, I said, was that there are so very many criminal-minded people out there, and he couldn't be expected to catch all of them, right?…and, as for *me,* Mr. Minister, I had no particular feelings, one way or the other, personally, about Ruffino Barrios…no… It was only because, as all my grants and awards and so forth demonstrated, the project was important to the nation, to the glorious ancient history, the glorious cultural patrimony, of the Republic…and (I stumbled on) this fellow *was* committing blatant crimes…

To be fair, I continued dreamily, one *could* make the case as *El Genocida* (I didn't call him that, of course!) had done in interviews with the national press – in such a way that even certain newspaper columnists could agree, that the ex-PACs *should* be compensated for their military service.

Even then, *even then!* I realized I was finishing my recitation without giving vent to my outrage and sense of violation – these emotions stimulated by the fact that I knew how *unreasonable* it was of me to expect anything above-board could be done – that my unwillingness to accept that this kind of crime, this Ruffino and what he was doing, was part and parcel of the fundamental insane lawlessness of the country....

I also realized that even though I was talking to a mass murderer I had to avoid making him lose face.

And abruptly then I stopped talking. For the sadder story, actually, behind even my sad "problem," complicating my perhaps quite justifiable desperation, to the point of asking Kruger to do something, *something*, about Ruffino Barrios was, simply, that I did loathe, despise, and detest the fellow.

For it *was* personal to me. A big-bodied fellow with a paramilitary buzz cut, Ruffino walked around with a gap-toothed smile of self-important phony benevolence; the smile never seemed to disappear, indicative, to me, of how self-laudatory he was for concocting such a wonderfully clever scheme. In fact, as I learned from the townspeople, during the conflict he had been a commando in the PACs – the worst of the worst because the commandos were the ones on the ground directly giving the orders for the tortures and slaughters. He broadcast, by his haircut and the camouflage pants and vest he wore, that he was still now in some nebulous way to be connected with the bad elements in the military – the land-stealers, the enforcers, the killers. In every conversation I ever had with Ruffino, conversations always in which, pretty quickly, with barely controlled rage, I would point out to him the damage he was doing to me, to my project, to everyone! he, in turn, would just smile a little...not malevolently but maybe like someone who had just put a pin through a butterfly.

In calmer moments, when I asked him why he had picked my project headquarters with which to run his scheme, he was admirably candid – he happened to need the official-looking space, with the computers and filing cabinets and so forth in order to make his project look legit! Sickhearted, shaking my head as if in disbelief that anyone would want to do such a thing, when I asked him when he and his *guardaespaldas*, all toting shotguns, would clear out, smiling broadly and even with the little sympathy the clear winner may feel for the pathetic loser, he would raise his hands as if in surrender to necessity. He couldn't say – maybe in a month, maybe in a few months…maybe much longer.

So the sorrier story was that I was using this awful history to try to save my precious project not only for my own career, but also because I absolutely could not abide this man, Ruffino Barrios, and the scheme he seemed to be getting away with right in front of me. What he had done to *me*, then, was to drive me out of my mind... If ever I was going to need the consoling arms of the sirens of the sex clubs, if ever I was going to need the beer and the opiates that terrible summer, this was the time...

And *Ministro* Kruger, the former capo of the notorious *La Mano Blanca*, now the Interior Minister of the nation, must have realized in spades how desperate, indeed, how self-traduced, I was. For, as I was winding up my speech, stumbling and stammering, he was looking down and to the side, as if he had seen enough men in his life before reduced to similar bottom-crawling amorality.

During my tirade, he seemed not necessarily to want to hurry me despite, no doubt, a busy schedule, including, perhaps, an appointment with the fabulous Mercedes. But during the last minute or so of my plea for help, Kruger seemed physically to grow in front of me, as if he had gotten heavier and heavier as I spoke.

I finished, awkwardly, in mid-sentence, as if I were choked up with outrage, out of breath.

Waiting, I suppose, to make sure I was done, looking at me again – through me? – with a look both distant and final in his eyes – the look of a military man – he asked, in a rasp, "What diss man name?"

Readily, instantly, with scalding shame, I provided first and last names – and was prepared to spell them out.

But finally, mercifully, to end the little hallway meeting – it all had taken no more than fifteen or twenty minutes – he said, curtly, "I will look into diz matter for jew..." And then he was walking heavily off through the door to some other office, where I saw him signal perfunctorily to somebody.

A military attaché type, icily formal, stepped out, almost snapping his heels. Examining me up and down, he then firmly took me by the arm to guide me back to the elevator. There he paused, told me to wait, and went back inside the office where Kruger had gone. A few seconds later he reappeared, with Kruger at his side, along with a photographer with a big digital camera who stepped in front of us and, motioning for us to stand close together, took several pictures which he showed, obsequiously, to Kruger, who grunted approval of one or two. At the time this was just one more mystery and, if I had the time to think about it, I might have looked for an excuse, if possible, to avoid having the pictures taken. But it had happened so quickly, and there was no polite way, anyway, to excuse myself.

The factotum shut the door to the private offices after Kruger went back inside and moved me toward the elevator again. As the elevator arrived, the fellow asked if I might want one of the photographs "for my remembrance." I recalled then a rumor I had heard that Kruger might, in future, be running for the presidency. Oh sure, I said.

"We will send one," he said, accommodatingly, in English. As the elevator door closed on his austere smile, I wondered, stupidly, just how Kruger's office knew where I was to be found to receive the photo, and answered my question immediately: of course they knew where the project house was! Of course they knew where I was probably at any hour of the day!

With these thoughts running headlong through my brain, still wearing the idiotic smile I had managed for the attaché, as the elevator smoothly descended I had the sense that I was floating in unreality. I felt both stricken and relieved, in a way, to hand over the Ruffino problem to someone I was sure could fix it – and covered in moral filth, because of *how* he would fix it. I felt like a conniving bad guy in a bad movie.

For it struck me, then, absolutely forcefully, what had just transpired, with every detail now lit in the most sinister light: Kruger standing there in front of me, now and then fingering the leaves of a ficus plant, listening to my petition for, what? another hit – the easiest thing for him to accomplish – turning my enemy, Ruffino, into a headless torso. Like Jekyll, I had my Hyde – and he had come out. Incredible, but true: no longer was I a guileless academic, a scientific researcher only concerned with his data – his potsherds and maps, his drawings of sculpture – no longer scholarly papers and conferences with bored, joking colleagues...

Paralyzed – as if transfixed by a nightmare – I recalled how Kruger had arranged himself somewhat impatiently, even brusquely, in front of me as someone who knew and acted on the necessity of force. That, by Mercedes' phone call, he had been more or less forced to see me only increased the futility of my panic. For, filled with a sense of complete helplessness, I couldn't now just ride the elevator back up to tell him I had changed my mind and wanted to call the whole thing off.

I did have Mercedes' card with her phone number, so I could call her to ask her to ask him not to kill Ruffino, but even a phone call to her seemed ridiculous, out of the question. I wished I could reverse time, had made the wiser choice, and the meeting had never happened... I could picture myself laughing that even the thought of killing Ruffino had ever occurred to me...

As the elevator door opened in the building lobby, with heavily armed guards in place seemingly everywhere, I felt myself resorting mentally to the poorest of coping mechanisms: denial. But I knew I was denying what would be forever imprinted in my memory and that I could not erase it, nor even reduce it.

I exited the building into the hot, diesel-polluted air and the routine chaos of the streets of the Capital that always seemed so noisy yet so muffled of protest against hopeless and pathetic poverty. Shaking my head at what it appeared I had just accomplished, I stopped and made myself contemplate how I had arrived at the conclusion of a long, dark trial – the verdict comprised in the person of Carlos Kruger – and how my own moral scruples must have been abandoned some time ago when I had been led, too confidently, *over* the brink of success such that there came along this fellow Ruffino who was managing to destroy everything I had worked for. And now there wasn't even any moral ambiguity I could claim for myself; what was done was done, there was no going back because what had been discussed was murder, and even the discussion with Kruger must have been a crime.

I was also shocked by how easy I had been able to condemn another human being to death. I wanted to find a cool, dark, quiet bar somewhere and drink a bunch of *cervesas*...followed by tequilas, and then, oblivion in the project house. In a haze, I found the truck, paid off the crumpled little guy who had watched it for me, and gunned off north of the Burger King as if I were fleeing from a crime scene. My thoughts sought the safety of absent-mindedness, as if everything was still normal and nothing had changed...taking in again as if remembering from a long time ago where, by the vagaries of the city, the neighborhoods seemed less threatening and the pace of things, despite the raging poverty, slower and easier.

Feeling a little sleepy – drowsiness, I had noticed, seemed to be one of my self-protective reactions to crisis – I even pretended to myself I was enjoying driving into forgotten precincts and smaller neighborhoods with nothing remarkable about them except a precious anonymity for people who were simply trying to survive with a little bit of comfort and stability, trying to keep the embers of remembered gentility still warm. In my own neighborhood there were some surprisingly neat, flower-bedded little parks, tended by souls paid a tiny amount for their effort; there was even a synagogue, though why on earth God's chosen people would have picked to live here was beyond me: the high, brick walls of this compound even bore what looked like ancient Semitic script, giving off a most strange sense of the far-off Middle East in this capital city of a Banana Republic...the capital city where one was constantly assaulted by the crudest glimpses of poverty and attempted accommodation to it.

Passing the synagogue, I could almost hear the shofars blowing.

Needless to say, I am not Jewish. But I felt like the wanderer, Ahasuerus, and I hoped, perhaps, to rest among the cedars of Lebanon, for an hour or two... I remembered how, at times during that terrible summer, I had been tempted to knock on the great metal doors of the building and present myself as a Jew in search of community in a city where there was none. Now, I wanted forgiveness. I would have traded the ordinary desolation of the project house, full of the lengthening shadows of my defeats, for the chafing and worrying that had already begun.

And I felt very old. Completely beyond rehabilitation as either scholar or human being.

A day or so later, despair and guilt giving way to anger – at myself, at someone, anyone, at this terrible wreck of a country that sat on priceless antiquities everywhere – I did call Mercedes, realizing as I heard her voice that I was powerfully tempted to fix on her the responsibility for the whole thing: *she* was the one who had ensnared me in the unbelievable moral dilemma.

As soon as I said hello, she asked how the meeting went. Calm but savage, I told her what had happened, of my own culpability in arranging the murder of one Ruffino Barrios...which happened because of her setting up the meeting with her lover. She said nothing for several seconds. As if she were there in in the flesh and was looking at me I shook my head in wonder and disgust.

"You wanted to meet Carlos. I merely set it up," she replied, reminding me, all too correctly, that the desire to fix the problem I had with Ruffino was so great I was willing to do anything... Because I was too tired to think of how to shout at her, I told her that, for some strange reason, I had been photographed with Kruger afterwards. As if to herself, she quickly said, "Ah. I asked him to make sure of that."

"You did *what?* Why did you do that?"

Before giving her a chance to answer I gave vent to some dawning suspicions. She listened, and then I heard her laugh. She laughed so hard I thought she was crying. When at last she spoke, her voice was a bit hoarse, flat, as if it came from far away or as if she were now removed from the whole situation.

"You know so little," she then said. "You know so little about Carlos. You are a baby too."

"*Baby!*" I answered. "I was never the head of – " but she cut me off before I could say it: *Mano Blanca.* I heard her voice, now much crisper, in my ear.

"*Ahora, mire* Mister Pot-man, Mister-Doctor-*Profesor*, just as Carlos helps you, you help him."

I was speechless.

There was another pause and I thought she had hung up on me. But, no, she was simply waiting for me to realize *her* situation.

"You helped him," I heard her say at last. "He is going to get into some trouble soon. And you can help him get out of it just with some photos of the two of you together. Sometimes you *profesores* can be important to us. You," she said mildly, "are an important *profesor* down here…, at least for the moment…"

I was too incredulous to be hurt that all Mercedes considered me to be was some kind of tool… but, in spite of myself, despite a huge fatigue, despite the fear about what I had gotten myself into, I was intrigued…*fascinated.*

"Mercedes!" I said. "In what conceivable way could I be important to someone like Carlos Kruger?"

Crisply, as if repeating things I should need not to be reminded of, she replied, "*Señor*, apparently you have done a little asking about – among certain most unreliable friends of yours, I emphasize to you – and you think you found out about the Minister of the Interior's possible, I repeat, possible, involvement in certain…unpleasant occurrences in this nation's history."

I listened.

"Well, although I know Carlos – I know him very well – "

Indeed, you do, I thought to myself.

" – and whatever truth there may or may not be, may not be, I repeat to you, with regard to these allegations, first, *Señor*, I suggest that you, do not do what you all do" – she obviously meant all of us *gringos* "– much too often, in my view, especially in a country that is not your own. I suggest that you *not* jump to conclusions. And just wait patiently for a resolution to your problem."

She suddenly sounded angry and her voice dropped its normal coyness – only at the end of the clipped English did the

Spanish accent reappear. But then, after another fairly long pause, as if she needed a moment to gather herself back together, I heard a big sigh.

Cowed by the performance, her anger, sincere or not, and unable to deny to myself, let alone to her or to anyone, my own responsibility for setting in motion the hit, I lied, "All right, Mercedes, all right, you're right, completely right, I should not jump to conclusions. I accept that. And, look, I am happy to be of help to you and...Carlos. The Minister. No matter what happens."

I could not bring myself to ask Mercedes how or when Ruffino would be disappeared, as if staying clear of the details might mean the whole thing would just go away. Also, the thought had dawned that the hit might never actually happen. So I said, "But what problem does *he* have and, again, what possible way can there be for *me* to help *him*?"

I heard a little extra exhaustion in my voice. I could see her again as if she were in front of me, her poker face as she said, "That I cannot explain to you at this moment."

Suddenly straining to sound warm, even enthusiastic, though as if it should be completely obvious to me, the obtuse *gringo*, quite the *idiota*, she changed the subject, manipulating the phone call back to the positive.

"Let me say this. You, Doctor, you, have your problem... your problem out there in the countryside, the *campo*...where no politician, no cabinet minister, not the president of the Republic, himself! ever goes, because they all are too scared to go. Because of the troubles one can get into there. You, you – *que maravilloso, que bueno, señor, que bueno, verdad?* – you have this project which you make for the good of the people, for the good of the cultural patrimony of the Republic... You also know many officials in your embassy, important ones, by the way, no...? And the newspapers report on all your great successes with your digging and your pot-finding and all that – "

"You want me to be Kruger's beard," I said slowly, flatly, interrupting her.

She didn't understand. I explained.

"Oh," she said, a bit nonplussed but, perhaps, amused.

"Okay... If I understand what you mean, that is basically correct. Which brings me to another thing" – her voice lowered, became very serious – "*Cariño*, dear friend, this is what I am making for you to do. I am arranging an interview with you by some of our leading reporters. And all you have to do is what I believe you *should* do, because of what *he* is doing for *you* – "

As if she were still in front of me I could guess the seriousness on her face.

" – which is to mention, simply call attention to, if you like, the fact, the true fact! that, alone of all the people you asked for help, only one person, *one* person, Mr. Minister Carlos Kruger, not only offered to help, but *did* help."

"By disappearing someone?!"

She laughed, shrilly, then said, quickly, "Of course not. And we mustn't speak of such things in such a way. *Ever.*"

Before I could remind her that the kind of help I *had* asked for and that he seemed well to understand did boil down to just that, before I could even ask, not believing I was having the conversation I was having, for details about the when and where of the newspaper interview she said she was arranging...before I could ask, again, how such a little thing as a newspaper interview with a paltry little *gringo* like myself, could help Kruger with whatever problem he had, she excused herself, very politely, very formally, saying she would be in touch soon, and hung up.

Alternately cursing at myself, at Mercedes, at Kruger, and at the crazy country at large, with the bitterest and blackest feelings, I indulged for a few days in fairly serious drinking along with some visits to the clubs. The days passed in a blur of late night pretty young faces and many, too many, *aguardientes* and *cuba libres*, after which, in the wee hours I drunkenly raced the truck back up *Septima* to the project house and its rooftop overlooking the calm domestic spaces of my neighbors.

About a week later, Mercedes did call, as she said she would and then, in most businesslike fashion – not letting me ask questions or vacillate – she told me to go to an upscale coffee shop in Zone Ten where I would meet with "certain people." Then she mentioned some names and affiliations too quickly for me to remember. In the meantime, hoping against hope that the situation out in the *campo*, at the site, at the headquarters, might miraculously somehow have changed on its own, that Ruffino might be done with his scheme and left the little town on his own, I contacted some of my informants in the town.

They told me, no, Doctorrr, the situation was, if anything, worse. The lines were longer than ever, stretching now all the way, a full kilometer or so, from the long broken-up driveway by the old German-built coffee processors and warehouses to the steps leading up into the project headquarters. And Ruffino had more and more "staff " lolling around in my chairs, at my desks, in front of my computers. The report was that the offices were a mess, trashed.

Like a zombie, I went to the rendezvous Mercedes had arranged. Though something tickled my brain and then clicked, I was surprised that there were three *reporteros*, one each from the two leading dailies, but a third from Spain! This fellow seemed a bit confused about why he was interviewing me – until upon his slack, black-suited, rotund figure and rosy-complexioned face I could somehow see the radiant impress of Mercedes' perfect child-woman's face and her precious figure – a fragrant, gorgeous flower pressed between the leaves of a book.

It turned out he had been sent to the Republic to cover a completely different story but, well, he lamely said, this one seemed too interesting to pass up. Primed, obviously by Mercedes, the "story" was my work, and the interesting perspective an important scholar like myself had on the tragic threat to the glorious cultural patrimony of the Republic – and on the lack of help I was getting to save an important ancient city out in the *campo*. Without prodding, I found myself providing exactly what Mercedes wanted me to provide, intimating that there were, nevertheless, some in the government who had understood the stakes and were helping, giving me real hope, at last, of a solution. And really the only one who has been of help, I said, offhandedly, is Carlos Kruger, Minister of the Interior. The reporter from Spain didn't seem surprised by this, but the other two were interested. Willing, apparently, to take the

Spaniard's lead, they followed up with some back-andforth between themselves about the likelihood of Kruger running for president in the next election cycle.

What ensued was a surprisingly easy inflation, with my participation, of Kruger not only as a fine Interior Minister but as a profound friend of scholars like myself trying to rescue the glorious ancient remains of the nation and – I don't know where this came from – of the *indígenas!...los olvidades...*and the (non-existent) *medio clase* – such that Kruger must be considered a greatly underused resource in the country for all sorts of matters relating, as well, to human rights, and dignified help for the impoverished of the countryside. A great future candidate for the presidency! we all agreed. The two reporters from the Republic made no mention of the fine gentleman's *Mano Blanca* past.

Now, what I did not know at the time of my meeting with Kruger, and which I only found out later, from an absolutely devastated Mercedes, *pobrecita*, was that – as if he was already hiding behind the hedges! – at the same time I was having my fatal meeting with the guy, final preparations were frantically underway in the Kruger household, preparations that had been greatly accelerated. What I didn't know was that, at the very second I was perhaps reaching for just the right balance if there could be one between noble pleas for help and a request for murder, porters were putting their shoulders to pushing immense and heavy luggage to the rears of big SUV's inside the gates of the high-walled Kruger compound and his wife, Doña Beatriz, and their teenage children, Adolfo, Carlos Jr., Elizabeta, and Rosalaura, were packing the last of their personal effects prior to a permanent getaway out of the country.

But this all came out later.

The weekend after my meeting with the reporters, a big spread appeared in the two dailies, not only as a front page profile, but continuing in the style section, as well, about the museum exhibition. There I was, standing with the embassy officials and the cultural minister, there were "my" pots. And there also was the picture of me standing with Kruger in his office after our meeting. The caption cited Kruger's "long interest" in the cultural patrimony of the nation and of his great love for and pride in the "indigenous peoples' contributions" to the nation. The article also speculated on Kruger's possibly resigning in order to run for the presidency.

In the weeks that followed I heard nothing of Kruger except, as had been hinted, a little item appeared in the papers that he had resigned from the government. However, the article said, contrary to previous speculation, he was not running for president. The explanation was that he was weary of public service and wanted to devote more time to his family.

With nothing else to do – not even bothering any longer to check with my informants about Ruffino and the ex-PACs, as if by not checking, the head-in-the-sands part of me could deny the bombshell I had primed would actually go off – I reviewed old news files on Kruger's record as interior minister. I was amazed to learn that the former head of the White Hand had apparently served not only without controversy in this important government post, but had tried to bring about some important reforms. Mainly, though, there were only humdrum references to commission appearances, advice to the president, and "robust" actions he had taken to modernize the security functions of the country.

A new president was elected. Kruger disappeared from the radar. But there was nothing to suggest anything suspicious. In other words, it was a normal kind of a disappearance. It dawned on me that Carlos Kruger clearly wanted to be forgotten. It was thought by some, cited in some post-election article about former officials – I recognized the names of the interviewed, a tight circle of the governing class, as well as a few of the more influential *diputados* – that Kruger had remained in the Republic. In this he had to be considered different from other former federal officials unlike the overweight red-headed former chief of the federal police, Fleischman, this latter public servant notable from photos in the dailies showing him with mouth always hanging stupidly open, trying to look tough with police visor cap mashed down on his oversized ginger-haired head – who had escaped just before the election with as much money as he could stuff in his excess luggage, following the rule with former government officials that when their tenure in office is over and they no longer have to appear dignified and righteous about public duty they can just hightail it out of the country with everything they can steal from the public till. One former president stole several hundred million dollars from the social security fund – bankrupting it – and bribed his way into Mexico. Of course, they had to pick a country, in Europe or South America, less likely to extradite when the thefts were discovered.

It is in the nature, of course, of quite dramatic things to happen with no warning. If, for example, as in my case, I was waiting for something to happen that would be good but only because of something terrible, one day, precisely two months after my meeting with Kruger, I got word Ruffino was...could it be true? gone. *Gone.*

I heard this from Don Avellino, the grand and grizzled old first president of the coffee cooperative in the little town – one of several larger-than-life characters out there who were all as sharply cut and memorable as if they arrived full-blown from central casting in the Hollywood they had never heard of. I always took Avellino's calls even though they almost always contained no information of any use to me.

Astonished but, horrible to say, not surprised! what I had dreaded, I had to conclude, had happened. I asked Avellino on the scratchy cell phone connection what he knew about Ruffino's disappearance..., but then the line clicked dead. This often happened when talking with someone in the village because their cell phones ran out of time and they didn't have the money for a new card.

With Avellino's dropped call – and, of course, after trying repeatedly to get him back on the phone, panic mixed with dread reaching overload – I thought again of my *cita* with Kruger. For the terrible thing apparently had happened. In my mind, Kruger still stood, bulking large as an Interior Minister, in front of me. He had to be the most concrete, the most formidably real and constant, personage yet in my experience in the Republic, at least of the official kind. Oddly, however, he was becoming shadowy. I could no longer quite recall his face nor his manner during the meeting. This was, as I understood it, because my mind was playing tricks – trying to diminish the whole awful affair, beginning mercifully to erase the details. The meeting with him *had* happened, but it was as if different people had been present.

Nevertheless – not for the first time –it still resonated in me that this man of terror, who had caused the deaths of so many people, who *had* been standing right in front of me listening to my petition beside a ficus plant, standing there somewhat impatiently, with the sense of a bit of forced acquiescence, as if he had been cornered – was not someone one would want to corner, not in the idlest of one's dreams. Seeking the unseekable, access to him, generally, was unobtainable because of the nature of his power and influence; if not for the photographs I could have denied ever meeting with him. Because the access was dependent on so many back channels and hidden ways I would have needed, without Mercedes' help, to squirrel myself through, if I knew how easily one could lose one's moral compass, how easily I could assert that I had never compromised myself because, I could claim, I'd never met the man... But, still flickering in memory, undeniably, there he stood, listening to me stammering out my plea.

But, not able to deny it, not for the first time, as if thinking what Mercedes must have wondered herself, *I* still found myself wondering: did Kruger think of the mothers he had killed who had tended those he also killed, their children, of those whose entrails, on his orders, had been ripped out – native women whose most customary daily chore was the washing of clothes by beating and rubbing them with a smooth stone and hanging them above a *pila*, of a straitlaced Catholic woman who started wearing black when her child disappeared and there was no word, ever, about what had happened – the son or daughter was there one day and gone the next, and the sun shone on each new day as she did her errands and saw to her round of tasks, the routine especially cruel since, if not for the disappearance nothing else changed...

And not only was there no acknowledgment that the son or daughter was gone – probably, her accurate imagination delineating it – after the murder the body had been thrown in an unmarked grave, with, perhaps, no more than a stunted tree standing sentry. And if not for a few photographs of a serious young person dressed in a school uniform there would be no proof the child had ever existed.

Ruffino had a mother somewhere.

Carlos Kruger *was* a bad man. A *very, very bad* man. And so, apparently, was I.

Even had I not known about Kruger before meeting with him, I had become familiar with how things went in the Republic. I had attached to my mental processes an alarm apparatus – an internal mechanism by which I had learned to remind myself that, down here, it is both a small world and an enormous one and anything is possible at almost any moment, including mayhem or maiming or mutilations or murder of the most brutal kind, even, or particularly with respect to, someone *like* Carlos Kruger... These things struggle to be remembered because they are never mentioned. Certain people may want to be forgotten – the perpetrators, the drivers of the white vans, the drivers' paymasters. Kruger had, in fact, stood squarely in front of me, not hiding, at least from me. Even if, already, as I say, in some mysterious process, like an image on an old photograph becoming fainter and fainter, he *was* becoming shadowy in my recollection, as it hastened away from me.

Incredulous – disbelieving Avellino's few words that Ruffino was no longer in the village, still somehow denying to myself that he really had been rubbed out, frantic to know for sure! I realized I would have to go out there myself, a trip I had avoided making since I felt a bit unsafe with the long, long lines of one-armed or one-legged men, with their desperate faces, their angry, exhausted eyes, shuffling in front of and then through the project headquarters, with its computers and desks and whatnot, with a benevolent Ruffino taking from them and carefully smoothing out and counting their wrinkled, soiled bills.

I drove out to the *campo* one peaceful sunny morning soon after Avellino's call. Mercedes came with me; she was now a representative of some combined government-private industry entity. I wondered if she had tagged along because I had become close to her most intense desires and hopes in life – we were both combatants of a sort, not against each other, but helplessly bonded because we were both veterans of conspiracy.

She was very much like a crushed flower – prompting me to bring up the news that had been out for several days about Kruger's flight to Spain, not all of it, but some of it, wanting to pull this from her, guessing from her meek demeanor she *would* answer, why he hadn't taken her with him – to which she sighed and then, after a long moment during which I sensed both a tear-out-her-hair heartbreak and yet a fierce resilience, she said, "He did not want me enough."

I couldn't stop myself.

"He did not take you to Spain, where I helped him escape by helping to launder his reputation by providing some nice newspaper stories about how he loves the *campesinos* – "

"*Sí.*"

" – which helped pave the way for his holing up in a country difficult for extradition whatever crime he may have committed..."

"*Sí.*"

"...the nature of which may or may not become known at some point..."

"*Sí.*"

We drove along in silence for a while. "Mercedes," I said.

"*Sí?*"

"Mercedes...who are you anyway?"

I had wanted to say *what* are you? But I wasn't feeling rude. Apparently perfectly misunderstanding the point of my question – even, I believe now, the implicit horribleness of consorting with a mass murderer, to say nothing of being in love with him! and of suborning me, with my eager-dog anxieties about a little gringo project, to enlist as my murderer and then be a launderer of someone with the most evil reputation – she crossed her legs, lowered her sunglasses back over her eyes, leaned back in the seat and, after another pause, lengthy but well-timed to convey a most matter-of-fact, unconcerned, reasonableness, said, "Oh... let's just say I am a friend also of the president."

President of the Republic or of Spain? Or the United States, perhaps? I didn't ask as it probably would not have made any difference... The way her accent produced "friend" – *frand* – somehow reinforced for me how she was, after all, foreign to me. Or I was, and always would be, the foreigner in the Republic.

Racing, now, I bounced over deeply potholed back roads carved out a hundred-and-fifty years ago in the heyday of post-colonial profit, finally getting close to my beloved little village and my wonderful archaeological site. The enormous coffee fields, with banana and avocado trees providing shade, the still-untouched mounds – representing ancient structures – mounting now on either side of us, filled me with happiness despite what I was sure I was going to find confirmed.

It started to rain and, suddenly, the natural world walled us in with a sweet, piercing wetness, everything green, all at once, radiant in the gloom, the sense unique and so peculiar, so marvelous about the *campo*, of, for want of a better word, *life*. Taking care not to skid on the wet road, the rains just subsiding, the sky lightening ahead, I turned the final corner where the bullet-holed town sign stood. My heart was pounding both in jubilation and awful apprehension. Truth be told it was my own heart of joy, my own heart of darkness I was approaching... Despite her broken-flower pathos Mercedes glanced curiously at me.

I felt like *I* was returning to a lover who had told me everything was over between us – a love that was the closest, most intimate, yet, at the same time, the most surpassingly beautiful, that I could ever hope in a few lifetimes to have. And it was a return from beyond the grave, a love that miraculously – if it really were true Ruffino had been whacked – that *lived* yet, an impossible dream become real, again, palpably so, right there in front of me... Scholars *can* have their delights, their dreams come true... And that is what my project had been for me.

And then there it was, the little primitive village, fresh with the limpidity of nature – even the many rudimentary cinder-block evangelical churches somehow part of the village's charm, even the old rusting German buildings which were evidence of the gouging for profit in the soft colonial underbelly of the nineteenth century. For these vestiges of another time provided passage back into a state of things as remote yet fascinating as if they belonged to another, enchanted world.

I drove up the final battered few blocks of the cobblestone street of the village that stood on top of my holy grail, the ancient city. Full of trepidation, I pulled into where I had always parked, close to the front door of the project headquarters, an old plantation building constructed by the indefatigable Germans when they were owners of the enormous coffee *finc* . I stepped out of the car and Mercedes – fabulously beautiful, still, if not more so, because of her desolation – got out, more slowly, and stretched.

It was as if nothing had happened. My joy was high as I greeted some of the little brown workers. I even hugged a few of the men; the others tittered. Then the crowd cleared a little, as routine, as always in the little village in the *campo*, dictated.

All quiet, all calm. Though I could tell already, I walked around a bit and found, blessed heaven, indeed, no lines of ex-PACs. No Ruffino! The project *guardián*, as phlegmatic as always, ostentatiously pulling out his key, let me into the project offices. The equipment was there, used and trashed during Ruffino's occupation, but even the computers, the fax, the scanner, and so forth, all seemed intact.

Avellino showed up, all indignant – his natural frame of mind – this time presumably because I did not immediately come and find him. He saw the beautiful woman and, without waiting to be acknowledged and introduced he went and plucked a flower from a hedge and presented it to her, bowing and saying, "a beautiful flower for a beautiful woman," which, after glancing, eyes wide, at me as if to say, *what's going on?* Mercedes accepted with a little nod.

And at this moment the *Prensa Libre* vendor was passing and something compelled me to stop him – force of habit, also a curious premonition. And there it was, right on the front page: Kruger was being sought for arrest. It had been thought previously, and incorrectly, the article said, that Kruger had remained in the country, retiring to his estate when his employment with the government ended. The article stated that he had not even been a speck in the public's attention for months. But then his "nefarious flight" was discovered, when the warrant for his arrest was delivered to his large private estate in the Capital. Inside the walls, overflowing with bougainvillea and topped by spirals of barbed razor wire, rumored to be patrolled by Dobermans and protected by Israeli-trained security services and bodyguards with Uzis and so forth roaming the grounds – all was empty except for a caretaker and watchman.

In the months immediately after the new administration was ushered into office, if anyone thought about him, it could have been assumed he had remained in the country. It might have been that he had disappeared as modestly and humbly as he could, so that when the next administration was in office he might simply have been letting the new ministers move into their offices and assume their duties without interference. It might have been assumed he was traveling, innocently unaware of the arrest warrant, which had been drafted, according to the article, while he was still Interior Minister – but not delivered because he still had immunity.

The accusations were very serious, although, if one considered Kruger's resumé, not really so unusual – the charge was "extrajudicial killing." He was accused of arranging for the murders of a bunch of gang members being held in the maximum security prison in Escuintla. *Goddamn!* I thought, suddenly faint-headed. So he *was* still a killer. And I had just walked around myself verifying that Ruffino was gone! It didn't matter to me that some penny-ante con man, who had managed to nearly destroy my project, was not alluded to – somehow Kruger's role, and my own, in killing Ruffino *would come out.*

I was trying to read this, rushing through it for more detail. As it happened, after I grabbed the newspaper from the *Prensa Libre* guy and found a seat for myself on the concrete steps in front of the cooperative's headquarters – another of strangely German alpine design – and I was flipping, no, flying through the pages of *Prensa,* a slightly clingy Mercedes sat down on the steps beside me. I didn't even bother to show her the article. Avellino was still there, standing nearby looking wounded. He sat down next to us, one step up. He was always finding and stopping me so I was always thinking to myself, *unhand me, graybeard loon!* And shame on me – I was at this second unwilling to stop reading to listen to him, since he always needed twenty minutes of my time to make sure I understood whatever it was he felt obliged to tell me. But this time, he was quite aware, as I was quite aware he was aware, of the rudeness of this inattention, and also of the worse rudeness for not properly introducing him to the lady beside me, in modish jeans and fine leather jacket and aviator sunglasses – that is, introducing him with all his titles and honorifics.

But he was patient. He huffed and panted beside us, since I was so evidently gripped by what I was reading, not yet making clear that he felt insulted because that would have meant a truly righteous indignation was called for that he was not yet ready to rise to. Even Mercedes, perhaps insulted, now got up to take a walk. I had told her how beautiful the village was, despite its awful destitution. Avellino looked like he was ready to offer her his arm if only I would introduce him to her.

Finally reaching the end of the article – Kruger and his family had, indeed, been tracked to Spain, and an extradition order was being sought from the court – I looked around for Avellino as I had an obvious, *the* obvious, question to ask him. Apparently, he had lumbered after Mercedes, already assuming the role of her protector in the wild *campo*. Frantic – where was he when I needed him! – I reflected that because I had met with Carlos Kruger, I, the *gringo*, with the help of a beautiful woman, had made for myself some trouble, oh some little trouble, trouble that *gringos* don't want to run into, don't want to know about, shouldn't know about. I remembered how, because I met with him, I *had* had the rather capacious sense, ironically, more than a little bit sickeningly, of "freedom," the freedom that comes, as natural as breathing air, from wealth and power in the Republic. Now, as jubilant as I was to be back in the little town, I felt sick.

Dread made me philosophical. Even if, now, somehow, it would come out that, before his flight, Kruger, the already bad man, had arranged for the killing of a man at the behest of a *gringo* scholar, it would come out that I was no different from Kruger and his tiny class of the rich and powerful – well, I *was* no different. I was trying to defend *my* rich possession, the site, as if it were my *finc* . There are many fatuous personalities, egregious *corruptos*, who might have explained this to me beforehand with much laughter after many *cervezas*. But a few of these, a *reptil* here or there, who was nevertheless willing to be candid for a moment and drop the pretense and/or truly, in his mind, wished actually to be helpful with my Ruffino problem, would have brought Kruger's name up, sooner or later: "by the way, Doctorrr, have you thought to speak with the Interior Minister? Or have you thought simply to hire an assassin?"

At any rate, I felt I had learned that I was not far from adopting these necessary and sufficient rationales on behalf of the "good and decent life" that permitted such solutions provided in answer to the question, "what can I do fer jew?" ... the necessary and sufficient rationales in and of themselves for defending what the "good people" possessed – *finca* , giant flat-screen T.V's, great black SUV's, and murderously well-guarded compounds in the Capital, as well as delightful country houses, servants and all, on Lake Atitlán. I thought now of that shimmering body of water cupped in a giant caldera, itself nestled in the string of active volcanoes stretching west into the lofty and primitive highlands where more Indians than elsewhere in the Republic still live, but that now was the playground for the powerful and wealthy, the businessmen, the politicians, and the generals...their plots and mansions parceled out among on what had been Indian land, leaving, it seemed, only the most marginal steep little hillside plots for the destitute and bewildered *campesinos*. I thought of *them*, stunned or numb, like pack animals, baskets of scavenged firewood propped on their heads, who lived out their short and miserable lives at an unfathomable distance from the Carlos Krugers and from me, who lived on the other side of a divide, so great that someone like Kruger *was* just a shadow: invisible, forgotten...if only because to remember someone like him was to put one at risk of death.

Mercedes returned from her little walk. As if the first offering was not enough Avellino labored over again to the hedge, plucked another flower, brought it back, and said to Mercedes, within my earshot and obviously for my benefit, as well, "Allow me to introduce myself. I am Avellino. A K'iche'. Now I know you are not one of us, Mrs-Lady, an *indígena*, as you would say, or even an *indio*, as some of your friends might say, a word which we don't like...but I must ask the beautiful lady to accept this flower, a flower for a flower... And I must ask the beautiful lady..." – oh, here we go again, I said to myself – "...if she knows the story of the K'iche' and the Kakchiqel, for this is a most important story to us, to us, the *indígenas* of this country...how we, the K'iche' people, five hundred years ago, fought Alvarado, but the treacherous Kakchiqel, otherwise brothers to the K'iche', turned and joined Alvarado and fought the K'iche', and they are, therefore, forever our most terrible blood enemies, most terrible blood enemies," he repeated. "But, but!" he then said, glancing at me to make sure I appreciated the gallantry, "if you were one of us, that is to say, beautiful lady, if you were *indígena*, I feel you would be K'iche', that is to say, one of us, that is to say, one of the real people, the original, the true people, the people of maize and blood, the K'iche' people..." and he pursed his lips in approval of the words.

Avellino made his speech to Mercedes and things settled down – in my confusion and euphoria, despite my fearful impatience about Ruffino and what had happened to him, I had made enough amends in whatever ways, in body language of regret, and placating comments, to stop him from rattling the cage anymore in which I felt he had put us. I explained to Avellino what I had been reading about and why – skirting the substance completely – in other words, that a friend of the lady's was in some trouble.

And now Avellino crowded in to read, slowly, painstakingly, the *Prensa* article, mouthing the words and repeating them to himself...

"A bad thing, Doctor. A very bad thing. Very, very, very, very..."

I said to myself, thank you, gods, the old man is not going to explain such timely matters again as the treachery five hundred years ago of those dogs, the Kakchiqel. But instead of nonsense, just saying stuff to keep me there with him or to show the villagers that he had the status to advise the *jefe gringo*, instead, showing me once again in one of those rare confounding times that he was *not* simply the foolish blustery old guy he seemed to be and that I had jumped to conclusions, as I had done so many times before about him as also about the entire benighted Republic, instead, he nodded and, looking past me, rheumy bloodshot eyes half-blind with glaucoma, unshaven, unprepossessing self fully on display, tapped me on the knee.

"Doctorrrr...," he asserted, trilling his r's beautifully. "... the truth is...everything, you know...goes, passes... Men go...so it's the same with me, with you" – he poked my chest crudely – "I don't know your Mr. 'Interior Minister,' this Mr. Fulano, this Mr. Mengano ...! But nobody, *nobody*," he emphasized, "does...not.... not...GO!"

I wasn't sure what this had to do with anything, but hoped he wasn't referring to Ruffino. I believed then he was because he became even more self-righteous, almost belligerent, as if accusing me of something – the *gringo is* guilty of everything, though, of course, even though some of them, like *el Doctor, el Jefe*, don't mean any real harm.

"I, too, Avellino, will go someday," he said, then, crossing himself piously.

Amused in spite of myself – for I had heard it all before in some form or other from him – not letting on but, rather, nodding as if in acknowledgment of his profound perspicuity about all things, I let myself ask him,

"'Go.'... Where, Avellino? Where do people go? When they die?"

"Oh!" he said, sitting back and putting his hands in front of him as if to ward my words away or in surrender to something, but at the same time prudently keeping to himself things that could not be shared with a *gringo* or, at any rate, with anyone not a K'iche', "that is something we K'iche' don't talk about." He said this and then closed his mouth right away, as if I had said something offensive. But I saw my chance. To say I was afraid of the answer I expected would be one of the significant understatements of my life.

"For example, Avellino, where is Ruffino?"

And here he looked straight ahead, not at me, confused, obviously unable to figure out exactly how to respond. But then he half-turned to me and, tilting his big head down to one side, all he said was, "Doctor!..." as if I was pulling his leg.

But even these most profound matters of life and death took second place soon enough. Just as I sensed he was about to ask me what I had done to get rid of Ruffino, Avellino's new wife – Ruffino had already outlived two wives – came silently over, holding their little baby (and, again, I reminded myself how remarkable was Avellino, this old man, how remarkable the somehow ever-resilient life one ran into, now and then, in the Land of the Replacement Parts). His wife was not more than a teenager and darkly beautiful in the most Indian of ways – bejeweled Roman nose, dark eyes, glossy black hair braided beautifully – as was the baby, with snapping black eyes and a look, somehow, of wonder and judgment, both.

She and the baby needed Avellino now. He got up with another big swat on my knee and stumbled heavily off. Then I reflected that Kruger would be, was perhaps, fortunate to be forgotten – or, if he was remembered, or would be remembered, it would be without a name, and then only as one of the numberless bad men in the world who afflicted the *campesino*. The men who were remembered were the K'iche', and the traitorous Kakchiqel, the latter only remembered because they were The Enemy, and beloved as such. Avellino's own new wife, for reasons his bluster never fully addressed, happened to be Kakchiqel.

Another who *was* remembered, apparently, was Ruffino. Since he had not answered my question the first time, when he tottered back – in impatience or grief or suffering Mercedes had taken another walk – as always unable to give up the chance to buttonhole me, *el gringo-doctor-jefe del proyecto* – I asked Avellino, again, fear cutting through everything, if he had heard anything about Ruffino.

"Ruffino!" Avellino said again in surprise as if hearing the question for the first time.

"Oooooohhh!...You don't know, Doctor? Go to Mazate, just go ask in the street of the sneaker salesmen..."

What?! I asked myself. Immediately I thought: *was this where they found Ruffino's body? Why in god's name did they find his body in the street of the sneaker salesmen? Although, in a country where bodies are found all over the place all the time, why not?*

Mazatenango, which I had often joked was the "Paris of the Republic," was a city I happened to detest almost more than any other

(Escuintla still topped the list of the most awful). At certain times in life, all roads seem to lead to these places, end-of-the-world places that are one-way destinations of doom: The End Most Awful. So it might make sense, somehow, that Ruffino ended up there, with no return, because he was dead – certainly in a way one had to consider a bad, or the worst, end – probably as a headless torso.

Always rankly so hot the sweat poured out the moment one drove over the hinky little bridge into it, it was not a big enough city – perhaps no more than fifty thousand people – to have any little niches, little oases of respite from the turmoil, a nice neighborhood (to refer to a tourist "downtown" would be preposterous). It was only everywhere the same impossibly compressed density of people, people, people, kids in torn tee shirts, filthy laborers, young mothers with kids, and howling, screaming smoky vehicles, everybody and everything making an insane racket – radios, horns from trucks and buses, eardrum-shattering engine revvings and accelerations...hollers, shouts, yells... There was nothing, truly nothing, that relieved the eye or heart looking, hoping, for some escape.

It was full of commerce, of a sort, so one commendation might be made that the spirit of enterprise there was strong, though it was of the "small business" variety, with inevitably suspicious-looking, rude, indifferently insolent, nobody clerks, selling the cheapest stuff: machetes, electrical parts, paper-thin, lumpy, cardboard-stuffed mattresses, *panaderias* with strange, already stale rolls, *farmacias* with blank-faced "nurses" wearing ridiculous pastel medical cloaks, appliance stores with a hundred cheap pink-screened image-rolling televisions turned on to the same *noticias* or *novelas* or badly dubbed American action movies, and, of course, the ever-ubiquitous *pinchazo* services, *llanterias*, and auto repair hovels. "Mazatenango" – "Place of the Deer," where the sight of this timid animal, appearing in the jalopy madness, would cause collective cardiac arrest if the fat and glucose levels of the citizens had not already made for so many dead-men-and women walking – hence, was my own personal suggestion for worst city in the world for how it dazed and shocked, confronted as one was with its eschatalogical fumes, its end-of-days visions. Except, again, for Escuintla (the citizens of the Republic like to name their cities after pathetic, vulnerable animals – "Escuintla" meant, "Place of the Little Hairless Dog").

Mazate, as it is called for short by its denizens and by the chicken bus *asistentes* hawking their routes from the front steps of their chariots, converted American Bluebird school buses, does briefly taper off around its outskirts to torn up streets, endless, half-finished construction or half-finished demolition, cyclone fences, rail yards, and rough-grassed soccer fields, invariably with teams, in uniforms, playing at sunset skillfully and all-out. There is a kind of *parque central* with the comically crude sculpture of the decapitated head of a deer – made of what looked like papier-mâché – stuck on a poorly finished, ungeometrical, concrete platform, and there is, also, of course, a central market, where poultry carcasses, strips of fly-humming meat, all manner of fruit and vegetables, and a great variety of grain and beans in big plastic bins are for sale in the nooks and crannies of tiny smelly warrens.

Embarked for this, my own personal Paris of the Land of the Replacement Parts, I held on fiercely to the tiny bit of information from Avellino about where I might find out what had happened to Ruffino. I was not to turn more than twice to the left after the *viraje obligado*, and then not more than twice to the right, where, after going *directo!* a few more blocks I would find myself more or less exactly in the little precinct of the sneaker stores: where in dusty bins and dim interiors of stall after stall selling athletic shoe wear of the knock-off, fake-branded, fell-off-the-truck kind was located. And then, from the sudden profusion of shoe stores all around me, this time, directions seemed accurate – a rarity in my experience in the Republic.

I found a spot to squeeze in the battered old project truck, horns, of course, constantly hectoring me as I did so. My mind was a blank. There was no scene I could anticipate except the anti-climatic confirmation that this man, Ruffino, who I hated and had just about brought me and my noble project down, was dead and that somehow I would learn this here – from a poster? A reply to a question? I got out and started walking up and down the block, ignoring the sullen or, sadder, sincere solicitations of young guys selling sneakers. There was nothing but chaos organized around sneakers. I didn't know what I was doing, or how I was supposed to find out what had happened to Ruffino, and I felt crazy in the midst of the craziness. Then, *then!*

...He was not dead.

My first thought was that, normally, seeing a citizen of the Republic holding a shotgun produces a chill. But not this time.

I saw the fellow, in the sweaty haze, as if an instant of time – the instant right *now* – had blanked out all of my nightmares. Or a time machine went back, then forward again, and slowed down to a dead halt, at *now* – like a fairytale, because the story was finally revealing itself to *not* have the awful, awful ending I had tried to prepare myself for. For there he was, wavering a bit in my sight from the heat, but as solid as living flesh and blood can be, his unmistakable blocky body, crop of shortcut black hair, and gap tooth. No smile though.

He was standing idly more or less in front of one slightly larger sneaker store, dressed in a ragged, makeshift uniform, confusedly manhandling an old and battered-looking shotgun. The sight of him impacted with the force of a shotgun blast itself: he had not been "hit," "disappeared." No, but it did seem that his world had been taken away from him.

From his glorious swindle days I saw that he had been reduced to being a bodyguard for a sneakers store. Turned out from the warmth of what, in his mind, was such a perfect scheme he had, instead, fallen – and what else is new? – to the most normal fate of millions, become only another lost and hopeless nobody in an inescapable nowhere – the overweening reality of the Republic for the teeming masses. Just from looking at him now, the hit I thought I had put on him through Kruger, that had so haunted me, turned out to be a fate worse than death for this dreamer of greater things for himself. His dreams of wealth and self-advancement *were* thoroughly and completely gone. He *was* as good as dead. At rock bottom.

Through a tangle of screaming, gum-chewing students looking at sneakers I walked diffidently over to him and said "Hello, Ruffino." A bit startled, he recognized me right away – I saw a flicker of scared confusion in his eyes. In my mind, then, it was obvious he would have preferred not to see me nor speak with me. Ever.

I couldn't think of anything to say except to ask, almost as if I was going to pat him on the back in sympathy, but unable to avoid cutting to the heart of the matter, a bubble of good humor forcing the incredibly relieved question out of me, "*Ruffin* !... *Hombre!*... Ruffino... What *happened* to you?"

He gave a little shrug as if to ask, "what happened about what?" and then gave me not his normal big, patented, self-contented smile but a distinctly lesser, half-hearted one. Completely gone was the braggadocio, in its place a surprise dulled by fear. I continued looking at him – longer than was polite. Again, he shrugged a little wistfully, I thought, trying to smile...

"So you work here now?" I asked.

He shrugged again, cradling his shotgun like a stick doll. It struck me – I knew this little factoid – most of the lowliest store bodyguards had no ammunition for the gun because they lacked the money to buy the shells. So he was probably deshelled, too. I noticed he wore no socks with his sneakers. I noticed also the sneakers had pink laces.

Continuing to stand there with him, polite restraint limiting my movement to the most unconfrontational and inconsequential possible, as if we only casually and accidentally met up, for a full minute while the noise of the street cycled from loud to soft to overloud, I could think of nothing else to say, no question to ask him about what actually had happened to his swindle, to the lines of hundreds of hundreds of broken men and widows, waiting to pay him, in my project's offices dressed up to look like his, the illegal "processing fees" for compensation for service, as PACs, in the killing fields.

Of course the obvious question I could not ask: had he been "persuaded" to give up The Swindle with the accompanying suggestion to vamoose it pronto out of town? I certainly didn't think Kruger's men would fail to kill him if that had been their instruction. Later, I would query Mercedes about this and her tired, lazy answer was that probably it was because Carlos was already on his way to Spain and had not had time to do more than mention Ruffino's name to some people; it had occurred to me, as well, that, given the arrest warrant for "extrajudicial killings," Kruger might just as well have asked himself, without having to think about it for more than a half-second, why should he do some *gringo* this particular favor when the shit was hitting the fan? But I couldn't think of a way to phrase any of these questions without giving away that I would have been behind it. Although Ruffino, I don't believe, no matter the bastard he was, possessed enough cynicism to suspect me of such deviousness. He couldn't even read.

I didn't ask what had happened to the "fees" he had pocketed from his dream scheme – big money even for a bigger schemer than Ruffino; obviously, he had no money now. Nor did I ask, an omission which might well be construed to be rude, where he was keeping himself and how he subsisted, as the abjectness of his circumstances was so clear.

After a minute more just standing there, I did find myself, weirdly, patting him on the back – in sympathy? in congratulation for being alive? Then I said goodbye – actually the mindless *hasta pronto!* Or maybe it was *nos vemos*, just as silly, because I very much doubted we would ever meet again. He made an effort to smile again with his old disdain – with what I detected as slight bravado, underlain by fear – and kind of waved his shotgun – peacefully, of course. As I turned and walked off leaving him behind in the afternoon heat and racket of the little street, sneaker business flowing hot and heavy all around, I got the sense he wanted to ask me for a job. But it seemed another indication of his absolute abasement that he did not do this...

Notes to self. You have, and probably will continue to retain somewhere in your mind, the images, imagined but ingrained: the shocked-stupid face of the shot-dead *campesino*, or the luckless union organizer, or human rights campaigner, or the bespectacled "Marxist" professor, trying to run away but so terrified he finds his feet are tripped-up or stuck as if he is standing in hardening concrete...or, if not shot then and there, as a "warning" simply having his pants yanked down and his dick lopped off with a scalpel-sharp machete blade in one short, quick chop, then shoved stumbling away by calm, absolutely businesslike, masked men who drive off in a *panela blanca,* somewhere deep in the *campo* or in the late night of the trashy outskirts of a city...after the pink otherwise of sundown, and health and life, turns to gray and, finally, black...

But *you* are not a murderer.

If you had known that a mindless and terrible dread would eat at you, chill you to the bone, for months, picturing how it would happen – a decapitation while tied to a chair, or, on the knees, a simple bullet to the back of the head, then the toppling of the body into an unmarked grave out in the *campo* somewhere, the man no longer with his smile, in his place no man any longer at all but only a little animal of prey, heart trip-hammering, unable to control the bursting of the bubbles of neurotransmitter in absolute panic and the involuntary release of bladder and the bowels as it approaches its sudden evisceration – if you had known any of this you would not have met with Kruger, not even have listened to the beautiful, distressed, conniving woman setting up the meeting for you.

Funny – you think now – how there were really three desperate people, each for his or her own particular reasons, and at the same time, a fourth person, Ruffino Barrios, not desperate at all at the time but, to the contrary, smiling as the soiled bills kept passing into his hand for him carefully to smooth out and add to an already thick wad. No – no matter how much you wanted, how you *had* to, get rid of the guy, to make Ruffino Barrios disappear... *you did not do it*...you did not do what you, in fact, intended to do...

So it *was* all quite like a dream, which I had thought of, at the time, before the complications and implications hit me, as a wonderful, hazardous accident, a last minute reprieve for my life and my career and my pots and my great ancient city, granted by virtue of a last-minute meeting... It was like a dream that I had been standing inside the inner sanctum of a Very Important – albeit terrifying - Person, a dream in which it turned out it was all a mistake that I had really wanted to see him. And even if it was not a dream, it certainly was all a terrible mistake because, no matter how innocent or naive I *really* was – not capable of believing what I might believe about this person – the story I had been rehearsing to tell the man seemed suddenly both amazingly correct for him to hear because, yes, he *could* solve my problem. But with a "final solution."... The whirlygig of logic: circular as in circle with a bull's eye, the bead drawn by three people on the smiling fourth.

But it all passed. And it was no dream. The sunset in Mazate, as I left, as always at that time transformed the roiling clouds of diesel pollution from pink to orange to red to translucent filmy gray to black, night coming on swiftly. The Golden Hour changed the running, the screaming, the hawking of the vendors, the nowhere-people okay for being nowhere, unconsumed by the burning surface, the meet-ups for nobodies in routines of utter destitution or before destruction in the shadows... the streetlife, for a few minutes, seemingly satisfied with its lot, just minutes into a mellower place – no matter the never-fulfilled hopes of the citizenry, left with a portion of peace: they had made it through another day and there would be another one after that. I knew that the less bad man had been remembered. And dealt with! Guarding sneakers with a shotgun for which he had no shells. And because Spain will never extradite him, the worse bad man will be forgotten –

Ah, love. Except by a beautiful woman named Mercedes de la Flor Something Something.

La Embajada

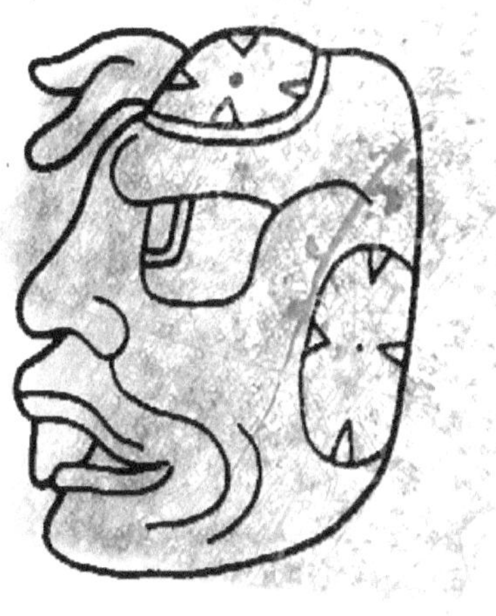

He went to La Embajada to buy a woman. Then he lay down in the dark road to die.

He lay down in the rutted, potholed lane, far enough out from the bay of the road where the wheels on the passenger side would be most likely to hit, but close enough to the side of the road so the truck would come too late to see him.

Now his various juices pooled out through his body, flat on the asphalt.

Although he didn't know it, the asphalt where he lay was, by international standards, nothing but a little country road, even though as drawn on maps in unbroken double lines it was a major thoroughfare.

As he lay in a stuporous haze, trying to orient himself; in the corner of his eyes was a thick black line. He realized this was the poured cement ditch, angled and pitched to sluice away the flooding rains, closest to him at the side of the road. Since he was liquid he sat up, sense delayed by intoxication. Beyond the ditch was brush and stinging *chichicaste* strung with barbed wire, on the other side of which was trash, a tiny *milpa*, and an even tinier corrugated slat board shack with one exposed light bulb on near the door. The neglect and isolation of what must have been someone's plot of land and house vibrated slightly like a hallucination.

Even more than simply being alone, now in the road in the dark *campo,* he was invisible, though he also felt he was outlined in sparks as if from exploded firecracker strings, as if his thoughts sparked little fires or as if he was lit up and visible to anyone who might be near. But there was no one – only the road in which he lay, which seemed receptive to him, faintly warm, serenely sure of its own continuance. Little breezes now and then touched him and the road at the same time, allying them, as if they had a pact.

If he was lucky whatever came would crush his head, though he didn't think this out fully, but just lay back now as if he was tired, wanting to die but liking, because he was so drunk, being able to lay down on the asphalt. He felt, in a way, as if he had fallen down from some height, maybe from a tree, and he could see the rising crown of limbs and long hanging vines of the trees across the road as if he had just dangled there. He felt sleep coming on.

A huge sorrow woke him immediately with the image of his dead son, his slack mouth and open eyes. Expelling air through his nose, making a little sound that sounded like a snicker, in the drunken fever of grief he tried but could not say his name: Manuel Lopez Estrada... Caan. But a snake constricted in his throat: the resigned face of his mother, the pained smile of his father, both dead for years, came into his mind. He remembered his mother in a worn and faded once-vivid *traje* and his father wearing *ladino* pants and work shirt, having given up the indigenous *traje* early on, the striped trousers and blouse of their village. These memories of *indio* life that had been shunted into a corner inside him from years ago lay now at the end of a tunnel formed by the pot-holed road in which he lay, in places arched over by great ceiba trees and palm and magnolia that emphasized, illusorily, the *campo*'s remoteness, untouched by, untouchable to, change because it didn't matter to anyone anywhere in the world. The memories of his boyhood always made him feel he was at the bottom of some primitive animal world where children played in dirt alleys by fallen coconuts, now and then a howler monkey screaming. In a smear of vision and time the perspective was heightened by being able to see the towering parasitically vine-tangled palms now in the present blind and oblivious world, pervaded palpably with the sick-sweet salt smell of rot, piles of open garbage, banks of trash under trees or lining rushing streams through a riot of plants.

In the hours after the baby had died, he realized that since his childhood many things had happened of unimaginable complexity. Though the sun appeared at dawn and then disappeared behind the mountains just as it had when he was young, everything else had changed into a landscape recognizable only because it was what he saw, now and the day before and the day before that, no more than a three-day sequence aborted then by exhaustion, but otherwise a complete mystery: links between and causes of events, actions and circumstances were obscure, like the mists after the afternoon rains slipping the hard outlines of what was so obdurately hard for him to navigate, day-to-day, hour-to-hour, or which, like the sun-radiance when he walked every day in the dirt by the road from his hut to and from the sugar cane, confused by the barbed wire: how did this pasture come to be? Who put up the fence? Who owns this cow? A blanket was thrown over everything and all that was needed to return things to normal was grasping the edges of the blanket and pulling it away, but the blanket was not a blanket but a solid layer of air pressing down on all things, escape from which was absolutely impossible.

Now, head placed on arms, elbows akimbo, laying in the darkness in the road in a waving fever slowed by drink he was terrified that because he could not say his name he would die nameless, would die a day after the infant had died, of something that had made the baby unable to eat but only shit, had died as he and his woman stood by, helpless, had died leaving him, the sire, with no good gesture available within a very limited suite of gestures; the woman had collapsed on the dirt floor of the shack, a huddle of useless *traje* and unbound black hair.

To the terror of namelessness he could not react or to being a black blot fanned by the soft breezes, a blot like a giant moth's outline blacking out the night, so his being, composed of mortal liquids, coursed through him to make one mixture of his waters and juices, his blood and sweat, the milky sap in him that had made the child.

He had gone to the whorehouse several hours ago. In his head was a white-hot haze, as if he had some great awakening, some idea had sparked, stoked by fuel for a fire. He was aware his face was flushed already with several pints of *aguardiente* – bought first at a *tienda* from a woman who showed her disapproval by the sharp way she took his money, though his face was frozen, downcast, and all he saw of her was the sharp taking of his money and the returning of his change. He didn't look at her afraid that if he did he would grin automatically because of the image he would have presented to the woman, an *indio*, like her but a fool, a failure, no, a monkey. He was aware his face was childlike because he could not grow hair on it. He also felt that if he looked at her she would somehow know where he was going, to La Embajada or someplace like it, where he could buy a woman. If he could have put it into words he might have explained that his son had just died and he had been completely helpless to prevent it and having a bit of money gave him a certainty of action. He could direct someone to do something because the very nature of bills of money required an exchange, the bills exchanged for something else, and if they didn't want to give him what he was offering to buy from them, he wouldn't pay, although in fact he would pay almost for nothing because he would be afraid his money would not be accepted.

The night before he dreamed he was walking through the center of an ordinary backroads town. In the dream it was alternately hot and dry and then, what seemed only a second later, cool and wet, as if the cycling between the two seasons, monsoon summer and hot dry winter, had been bunched together and quickened almost to no time. He came to a boundary of sorts, with a *viraje obligado* sign just like there was coming into the nearby large city, Mazatenango. In the dream, however, the arrow obliging the driver to turn only in the direction indicated wrongly pointed left instead of right. As if taking a cue from this, after making the turn, all streets thereafter inevitably, strangely, turned to the left, interlacing like a web of veins, or roots in the earth, leading left, again and again, as if turning onto themselves, but into many different *barrios*, stifling and rank with heat, radios playing *ranchera* and *salsa*.

Even though the dream city was full of little passageways, alleys and arcades, the entrances and exits from tent-covered side streets seemed tubular in shape and every face he saw was a caricature of boredom or gloom. He next found himself in a *barrio* of sex clubs and he was walking beside young women on their way to work. He felt the urge in the dream to tell them something was wrong, that there was a great out-of-control fire somewhere close by. This fire, he knew, was enormous, and was composed of the colors of noon and sundown, as if the surface of things was burning, all in an unpremeditated present, frozen forever in ending. But when he tried to speak to some of them, the girls merely shook their heads and brushed past, their profiles suffused orange by the fire, imprinted against it for a moment before fading. In the dream, as quickly as the rains changed to stifling heat, in an instant day changed to night, without warning, and the night was laced with elaborate soft blossomed vines like on the massive walls and hidden gates of the estates, behind which lived the owners of vast sugar *fincas* whose fields stretched on forever toward the salt-aired coast.

The next morning, woken from the strange dream and hung over as usual from fatigue he was up before dawn and, with a last glance at the dead infant lain out on maize husks, he took his machete and some tortillas lying half-burnt on the hearth's griddle and hiked to the cane fields as the sky began to lighten. The *jefe* had looked hard at him because he had come a little late. He felt helpless – it would do no good to tell the man his son just died because if he didn't show up for work another would take his place and then he would have no work and no money at all. Then he spent the next fourteen hours focused on slashing the thick green bushels of sword-like shoots and stalks, the labor, as it was every day, so exhausting he felt he had no body left, his body one great clenching ache dissolved to a vapor of sweat.

After he finished and got his pay, the sun was almost down, the dark green blades of the plant imprinted in his vision when he closed his eyes, and he hiked back to the edge of town in the long, late rays. In the lightsome twilight other people were on the streets heading home. He was heading past the junction where buses stopped, sides vibrating or rattling in great panicked heaves, the driver from his magisterial height behind the wheel now and then impatiently flooring the gas pedal, revving up the engine, emitting plumes of boiling-hot exhaust that wavered raggedly and filmily into the dark lavender sky.

Strangely, then, though he did not know why, he realized he was reviewing his world, as if coming to some decision about it or judgment of it. As he made his way heading straight through the intersection he saw, still a good distance away, the incandescent lights – the brightest sign by far down the street – though he didn't need the lights to lead him there, because it was, somehow, deeply and intimately familiar although he had never gone inside before. Now, with queasy stomach he went toward the lights as if toward a dirty bandage in the night, a bandage the men who went to the bar would need after going there. The flashing lights – raw, brazen, bright-hot –

mixed in his mind disease, nausea, sex, blood, semen – enwombed in the almost comical mournfulness of the countryside.

As he approached the whorehouse, the night brightened – at night La Embajada by far the brightest place on the block – and he thought if he had carried on east to the Capital he would pass little *milpas* slanting high up on mountain sides and tilting steeply above the great *finc* 's level lands. Then, interspersed, would be pine forests behind which, evident from the terrible foul smell, were rubber trees in great dark groves and a processing plant; he had tried to get work there but they weren't hiring.

If he didn't turn and continued straight and passed the whorehouse, beyond was Mazate, the choking crazed city, by bus just a half-hour away. And as he approached the lights of La Embajada he thought he could just keep on walking as if all along his destination was elsewhere: if he went further along this road he would end up passing some *llanterias*, open spaces of rusting machines, cinderblock walls, some kind of *maquila* owned by strangers, *Koreanos* he thought, and little roads not much more than paths running away from the road towards little collections of huts and houses, squalid settlements in that accidental space between *maquila* and *llanterias* – nowhere.

But he knew he wasn't going farther but, instead, tonight, was going bad. He wasn't just walking anywhere. His son was dead and when, as would happen, which was often, he stopped thinking about this because it was too hard to think of it, he felt he was betraying his son and himself, which was worse because he could not even say his own name.

It crossed his mind again how the women in La Embajada were big – unlike the small, small-boned Indian women. In this they were apart, alien, mixed blood. And a constant income provided for them. They didn't worry about not having enough, but their isolation by idleness was sin and disaster in itself. The trade they practiced permitted them to eat well, and the result in consideration, also, of mixed generation was that they were giantesses. One of them he knew looked *gringa* – white skinned; she had a rough, uncaring look. She plucked her eyebrows and wore metal lipstick that made her mouth liverish.

With a drunken lurch to the side off the curb he hesitated just for a moment, dizzy, and though he felt guilty and ashamed he ignored the guilt and shame, and the whorehouse squared up now in his consciousness not as a deliberately chosen destination but, instead, as inevitable and, with the confusion it occurred to him that he didn't understand the name of the place. He didn't know what an "embassy" was, although he had heard the word, from where he didn't remember, although he thought it was a *coyote* or other people talking about visas for *los estados*. Not knowing what "embassy" meant, nor why this bar with the whores bore this name except that it suggested, as a joke, a portal, or the beginning, or end, of a journey, made him feel, again, stupid and worthless.

But, sullenly – because sullen was how he thought he must look, like a bad man – he stood in front of the hanging plastic strips below the glittering little electric bulbs, hearing now extra-loud the quick percussion of the *salsa* music inside. Again he forgot about the infant as an automatic and familiar complaint came into mind, forced to be ready with coarse joke and falsetto titter if he saw another field worker he knew, agreeing they had just worked a week of six days, dawn to dusk, slashing sugar cane with machetes, and tonight a man deserved bright lights and a leg pressed against his as he drank. Now he noticed, as he stood outside, the multitudes of moths, varying in size and shape from tiny furry-winged ones to green-bodied lacewings, flittering and flickering in the blinding light of the bulbs and flinging tiny tendrils of dust or whitewash powder. Some leathery-winged giants clung to the rough wall anchored there as if overcome by a combination of surrender and supplication before their end.

Then, putting a mean expression on his face, he parted the hanging plastic strips and went inside like he was going to some *fi sta*. In a sliding unfocused glance he saw the inside, orange-lit, and sat down at one of the little tables, deafened by the music, receiving an instantly dismissive glance from a big whore, whom he had seen in that unfocused instant lifting a chicken bone to her face which was orange from more little light bulbs hung and pulsating on chains inside. Two other whores he hadn't seen turned away as if to say, we don't want your money, man. He gazed down at the cement floor. He felt he should nod his head in time to the music which had changed to *ranchera* – fast-slithering, blattering horn and accordion with tenor male voices pleading, professing absolute, undying desire, the exaggeration of which sounded, though he could not put it into words, threatening if you could not believe in the avowed sincerity.

A kid came over and he said, half-croak, half-whisper, "aguardiente." The boy didn't understand, so he cleared his throat and repeated himself. The boy went to the counter and spoke to the whore who turned around and reached for a bottle of *aguardiente* and gave the bottle and a glass to the boy who brought these over. The whores ignored him and he felt again the sadness so overwhelming he might be laughed at seize him and, with a great effort, he stifled what would have been out-of-place, uncontrollable howling and crying.

He unscrewed the bottle and poured himself three fingers-worth and then, as if pausing to debate for a second, raised the glass to his lips and drank. Shoulders hunched, he wiped his mouth and glanced down at his dirt-crusted shins, exposed in the short *campesino* pants. He looked to the side, as if deep in thought, tutored by the music's great loudness.

Four men came in through the curtains, laughing falsetto and talking loudly. With appraising eyes they looked at the whores and then they looked real hard at him but disguised the instant evaluation – *one of us? no?* – with feigned indifference or a disjunct of hostile, hot volatility and male camaraderie. He saw they were not laborers; from their tattoos he guessed they were *maras*. He turned his head away from them and stared, as if absorbed in the label on the *aguardiente* bottle showing a *traje*-dressed smiling young *Castellana* woman holding up in her white hand a tiny bottle of Quetzalteca with a label of her again in the same posture, the image repeating itself infinitely inward, each time in tinier and tinier scale, beyond the point where you could follow it; seductively calming, it was meant, he felt, to remind the drinker of the immense depth and subtle complexity to life. Because of the noise the four men were making – laughter, slapping of hands, table pounding, getting up and sliding the plastic chairs with a *screak*, then sitting down again – aware through his drunkenness of vague menace, it occurred to him he might be in some danger, as he saw by certain gestures and the whores' eye rolls letting him know very clearly they didn't want his money.

And so, as if he was making the decision out of weariness not to buy a woman tonight, he pushed back out through the plastic curtain and stood by the pulsating brightness and the flittering moths. It was at that moment that the logic struck him with the relief of clarity to kill himself.

This was how, without much sense of making his way there, he found himself stretched out in the pitch dark of the road. As if in deliberate and conscious thought, as if consulting with someone familiar – another self – he drew himself up on one knee in the road just as the one good headlight of a vehicle in the opposite lane corrected itself laconically, vibrated, and then, a second or two later, an enormous truck slammed past, the whack of the vehicle's rush of wind rocking him back, but not making him fall.

This made him want to laugh and, stretching out again on the hard asphalt and rolling to make sure he lay down now in the exact place where the tires of the truck had just been a succession of images appeared, without sense or logic: first, a fat, pale woman whom he thought was the fat white whore but then he realized must be someone else, the woman on the Quetzalteca bottle, because she was looking straight at him with concern, and then, the rippling of a curtain's plastic strips, and then he found himself, shaking hard, and he caught a glimpse of someone's face, and realized it was his face, and his expression was extremely startled, a caricature of terror.

An afterimage appeared of how the truck had slammed its tonnage past a second or so ago, but then it was not actually a truck but was, instead, a gigantic dog, grime-encrusted fur spotted and colored yellow, a dog so enormous that, at the same time he saw the huge black tire humming in rotation he saw the dog's legs revolving in perfectly articulated motion. Then, another image emerged as if set in motion irremediably by his decision to die, and this was of a large dark-skinned woman who, though he could see her only in profile, seemed to be studying him with a massive condemnation and melancholy; she was a witch whom he recognized from the village next to his. And then he knew that he was seeing what one saw when one was dying: hell; as he realized he was, indeed, not far from a crossroads, where one could go to hell, pass down through a portal like La Embajada's strips of plastic curtain...

A huge truck or bus, he couldn't tell, shifting its headlights which were revealed as the orbital plates of a jaguar skull, the fenders jaws devouring the space, was roaring at him. When it was immediately in front of him, he pulled himself into a sitting position and propped himself up on his knees. He saw himself then in headlong fall suddenly from the verge of a precipice, a *barranca*, or volcano ledge – in the gray darkness there were stinging fumes swirling around from vents in the ground making it impossible to breathe, and to the side he could see the glimmering red slow-moving lava streams. As he was falling he saw beside him, on either side, like guides or guards, and somehow he knew they were *tzontemoc*, two blunt-headed, crop-haired figures whose spiral eyes turned toward him and away, and he knew he was falling forever down, through crazed streets of cities at sunset, then shadowed by night, slowly, slowly toward the bottom of the underworld, toward the point where the sun, in its journey through hell, lay exactly opposite to where it stood over the world at noon.

He was asphyxiated as the air was pushed at him. As the truck hit him this journey seemed as it should be, and he would fall down to the bottom of bottoms, through earth and mud, past the rubber trees, which made round soccer balls hollowed out to hold a human heart, to the dead sun on whose back he fell – dropped from the back of the gigantic dog. He had in that moment the dim foreknowledge that either he was going to be evacuated from existence soon, one of millions of others of no consequence that his death, as his life, made no difference to anything, or, if he could grab hold of the green snake tail of the sun, he might be reborn, as maize, as he hoped might have happened to his dead son, fearful, on the other hand, that the darkness might be too complicated for anyone to escape from it –

El Obelisco

A New Age

Proving we live in a great age of progress, the capital city of the Land of Many Trees, the Land of the Replacement Parts, is formally divided into "zones," although the farther one goes away from the old central zones the more haphazard are the trapezoids until, finally, they lose all sensible shape. The security of law, the delicacies of culture, the wonders of science and technology are particularly evident – though with the gloominess of the protections necessary for entrenched wealth – in the two rich zones, Nine and Ten, the veneer quite modern, even contemporary, with travel agencies, patio restaurants, bars, clubs and some fine international hotels. But everywhere else is disordered and retrograde. Chaotic jalopy traffic spews great clouds of diesel fumes over broken streets and dissipates in the air at seven thousand feet. Street vendors sell pirated goods and cut-up fruit. All those others who subsist within the seams of the city like insects teem over the thrown-away fruit, skin the color of wet cardboard.

But it is a city. And so it seems until one passes through neighborhoods on canyoning lanes of streets and roads so battered the visitor wonders which takes up greater space – the smooth or the potholed. Hauled down so far you might laugh at the ridiculousness of it: the only way to your destination is to dislocate all your joints as you try to navigate, juddering violently, through what passes for the urban.

When the sky is clear and the sun radiant on the high hedges of white-flowering trumpet vine, the afternoon rains leave coarse green grass. Shock-headed palms shiver or rattle in the buoyant and dry winds. Until accustomed to it, the *gringo* is lightheaded from the altitude.

Beyond the two rich zones – perhaps the sign of an inverse world – the Capital's infrastructure is inside-out, visible in the form of exposed wiring. Every building except, on the one hand, the meanest corrugated-roof-and-slat-board shack without electricity, and, on the other, the brand-name international hotels in the rich zones and a modern, tall office building or two near the national palace in old Zone One, is clotted and arteried with crude, jerry-rigged cables plugged into dangling extension cords, or stapled or draped on cratered exteriors of whitewashed faded plaster, cinderblock walls, and metal doors. This pattern – electrical spider and spider web – stretches into neighborhood after neighborhood. So much for the exigencies at first glance – there are many others – and the Republic is not the only place on earth stricken by terrible events, not the only place on earth that witnessed genocide, though that fact alerts one to a chill that bends one's perspectives and preoccupations inward, and which few outside the Republic's borders would understand.

Nevertheless, exposed or not, electricity *is* available for many and it is possible that fewer and fewer families have to rely on the little propane tanks, the size of envelopes, that last, on average, two weeks. In addition, the great works of progress do provide, two hours each day, from subterranean drains, the benefits of hydraulics, although the water is full of fecal matter and using the tap requires thorough drying afterward to disinfect the hands. But *agua pura* can be bought in twenty-liter plastic jugs at reasonable cost. And in the streets, on the buses – converted American Bluebirds repainted, given a woman's name, dashboard retrofitted with the driver's personal objects of devotion, always including a cross, the Virgin and a stenciled Playboy silhouette – many people seem happy, slapping backs in greeting, laughing; others seem serious or cast down, and it seems that in every second or third person one sees in yellow-tinged corneas the milky film of hepatitis or the amoeba.

But one might say that the Good has arrived, for it could not be much better, given the ever-imminent alternatives. The Republic is not at war, millions of citizens have vehicles of a sort, markets sell strings of meat (flavored with flies), soap, plastic hairbrushes, shoelaces and other sundries, and cell phones and pirated DVD's are everywhere. There are – never mind the high stress and degrading tension of the hair trigger ready to kill – office buildings with metal detectors framing doorways with trays for the businessman to check his guns. Also, the many sex clubs are full of impressive technology, and those citizens with televisions can see on other countries' stolen channels commercials for the latest conveniences.

The Monuments

El Obelisco is a tall geometric spike whose facets might represent the different directions. It stands at the top, or bottom, of the Avenida de la Reforma, the Great Way that divides Zones Nine and Ten. In certain specifics it is the idealistic heart of the city, where the ragged demographic of the Republic, intent on betterment, passes. An American fast food restaurant, right on the crazed Boulevard Liberación but maintained to international franchise standards of cleanliness and with a new black asphalt parking lot – unseen elsewhere – is testament.

Below the spire in the air flaked with ashes from the inextinguishably burning city dump far to the south, contrasted with its clean lines and with a now-and-then sunny calm, is a barely-contained chaos rising through and above a bedlam of pollution and honking. The monument stands well higher than the Montículo de la Culebra, the fifteen-meter high long grassy ridge topped with an old Roman-style aqueduct. Near the grime-walled little national zoo (where the "zebras" are painted donkeys), near the cartoonish turreted yellow museum with its unvisited casements and displays of dusty artifacts, trains of people walk to and from the obelisk, where the city buses come to a halt with shudderings and squeaks and then rev up and depart with great rupturing gusts.

One might have asked those who pass by if they know the obelisk was built by Ubico, the *caudillo* dictator of several decades ago, to commemorate the independence from Spain of the patchwork twist that is Central America. Whatever its history, known or unknown after so many light-speed years and stories ended, the obelisk's past shivers like the fabric of a plaintive ghost, incomprehensible to the life threading around and beneath it.

Isolated by a little fence around the coarse grass plot on its island in the roundabout, the modernist spire suggests an indifference surpassing the inattention to its own history. In the intermittent quiet, in the hot blanching sun, in the polluted winds, in the soundings down the avenues, this inattention is evidenced by the rustling of the fast-food paper wrappings and other trash accumulated against the fence from the commerce of the streets, visible and invisible – transactions of boredom, cold, heat, despair, tragedy, and murder, along with quick scurrying huddles under eaves from the thunderous afternoon rains. In what might seem an obscene contrast with the muffled caustics abutting the lives spilling around and below it, the spire projects, distantly to be sure, a sense of lofty gentility, of settled urbanity. And – true – some ten or twenty long blocks east along and off the Avenida las Americas, behind six-meter high walls overhung with scarlet and purple bougainvillea like jewels livid against the dark green leaves, are great private houses with razor wire looped on the tops of the walls, which warns: Trespassers! If you so much as think about climbing these walls, you will die like the dogs you are!

For all its seeming irrelevance, everything that passes below the spire encompasses and transcends, although this, too, one feels through a remove. Because – and moving into finer resolution now – for all the smallness of the life cast off upon which the monument inflects its gaze, and certainly as far as another notable monument, the black *Torre del Reformador*, which mimics the Eiffel Tower, and, then again, as far as the gigantic embrous city dump, that life stretches far, comprising a world compacted within the larger, frantic lives both miniscule and, hence, swollen by panic and which reach their end after what has been, viewed from afar, a brief time filled mostly with tension followed by the inevitable.

By contrast, the *campo*, a few kilometers ride on a chicken bus, is menaced only by the coming and passing of generations – bubbles of stories within stories, empty or full before they burst against serenity. In the *campo* there is less the burning surface of things, although, interestingly, two thousand years previously, enormous beds of obsidian – product of volcanic fire – just to the northeast of the Capital, provided the mainstay of commerce. Then, life perhaps was more relaxed even as it depended on firefused grit.

Elsa

Each day consists of three-hundred-and-sixty degrees around, though boxed and squared, as well, from the lines of buildings – warehouses, dusty shops, two- or three-story office buildings, and old malls built upward for a few stories of honey-combed trinket-sellers and primitive markets.

Imagine elongated time warming toward fullness but, within this, a racket of distress and opposition. Under great eucalyptus and highlands pine, Elsa waits for the bus on the Reforma's charry island strip. She appears chaste and serious to the passerby pale-faced, verging on or just past forty, parceled out to the urban chaos.

She roots in her purse for a handkerchief. She feels the beginning of *la gripe*. A prospect has appeared. She has an interview for a clerical job advertised in *Prensa Libre*. She wears her one good coordinated outfit – a red blouse and skirt that look clean and pressed but, also, worn: white under-threads show in the creases.

Her face, too, is taut, pale, her legs are numb. She is aware of a little slack pouch that is her belly.

Bouncing and shuddering, squeaking and rocking, the red, frayed, old metal-stressed bus will come with its hand-hold bars shiny-smooth from millions of gripping palms to take her to her interview. She imagines herself, the busy staff person, using an adding machine, typing, turning a rolodex.

Standing near a woman in *traje* with a vending cart selling cut fruit, as happens whenever she waits for the bus, a voiceless threnody mingles with the charging and subsiding traffic about the dangers of bus transit because of robberies by the gangs. The dark red of the *Coobusco* bus is the same color as her attire. The threats are a sore that doesn't go away. Today she read in *La Prensa*: a victims' assistance group has been created, the *Grupo de Apoyo Mutuo*, and the government has been petitioned for pensions to the widows and families of the slain drivers. *Ah well... And then...?*

But Elsa has to manage. She takes care of herself and her mother, or was doing so until a week ago when her mother finally died. Now she has to manage for herself. So she is out on the Reforma where, as usual, she feels a tinge of imposture, small but so distinct it could shame her from existence if anyone cared to notice. She knows she really does not belong on the Reforma. Indeed, in the pollution-fuming busyness of the street she stands not far from the *gringo* embassy, a concrete-bunkered, many-windowed block-long edifice with its flag hanging over well-tended gardens behind high, fortified fences. The individual representatives of this out-of-reach life are photographed for the newspapers or pass infrequently, with stirs of tension, in high-hitched turbo-engined SUV's – *los ricos, los gordos*, businessmen, military, politicians, all with shotgun-carrying bodyguards, as well as the occasional *gringo* tourists, in scruffy jeans, gazing around at everything, or in a hurry to somewhere pretty. By an immutable law of physics they belong to a species with the power and ease of a life that dwells somewhere high and far above hers, giants bending to look down at the dollhouse-sized existences of people like her.

Even as her mind and thoughts are consumed by the most normal and inconsequential little promptings and reminders, reactions to this or that interpreted as either harmless or threatening in some way, faraway memories recur – perhaps once a week when their darkness is sought or seeks her. A memory then can seem as close as the faint smell now of her sweat – her city of birth, Retalhuleu, near the Pacific coast, swelling in the rich heat, the suffocating mugginess produced by the conjunction of flatlands given over to hundreds of kilometers of sugar cane owned by great *finque os* as anonymous as clouds, and interspersed with little shack-stalled crossroads hamlets, and the ocean, fringed by its black sand beaches: the *campo*. And such memories are somehow like the lush growth of plant life, jungle greenery stopped sometimes quite uncertainly or indefinitely before it passes into little communities – wild verging to human despoliation imperceptibly in a continuum that makes the panorama of the Republic something somehow beside-the-point, monkey-populated, yet, nevertheless, enormous in scale. A familiar image at times returns within Elsa's most secret self, smoothed over now by twenty-year revisits via the same memories, of her law-student fiancé, shot in the back in the street, in broad daylight, in Reu.

The long-dead Eduardo: there was a festival for the saint of Reu, with parades. Why the police focused on him during the celebrations, and turned and shouted at him, he didn't know. But he ran – not because he was a *guerrillero* but because he was suddenly, unaccountably, afraid. His memory, of course, is fixed in those moments with him shortly before his murder, and it is only the passing of time that permits any kind of peace. Nestled like fraying fibers into these thoughts is that something was different about his death. The soldiers have always been the ones to be afraid of – teenagers in camouflage and high black boots, with remote or vacant eyes, slinging rifles – not the easily bribed blue-uniformed police who, with their visor caps mashed on their heads, look like comic apes. Twenty years ago, during the bad times, she was too scared to go to the police to ask questions. The *orejas* were everywhere and informed on anyone for whom they nursed a grudge... She remembers it was a windy, hot afternoon, and that it was very hard to get to his body lying in the street, his feet sticking out under a coat. In a second these memories disappear like a vendor's melted ice. The air suddenly seems freezing though the armpits of her blouse are stained with sweat.

The countless complications of life like beached jetsam struggling to swim in the dry ocean of the city, sighing with traffic, radiate out from everyone and everything around her, further and further into zone after zone, packed, she sees in her mind, with the same faces, seamed and worn by the same tiny struggles, complication within complication – old balding women consoling themselves with fat little grandkids, children with brown teeth sucking from straws stuck in little plastic bags of Coca-Cola or Fanta, abject and tousle-haired laborers with expressions mixing exhaustion with a determination so fierce it is unconscious, instinctual only.

A motor scooter's Uzi-*brrrrruup*, then the thundering passage of backfiring cars, become one with the forethought of the afternoon rains.

Can't let these clothes get wet.

Resignation strangely leaves her feeling as if she could float away. She will never be hired for the job advertised in *La Prensa*. Since she has no more money, the prospect of eviction from the shotgun apartment where her mother just died fix the image in her mind of hauling her suitcases out onto the wide pavement amid the deafening noise and chaos. Elsa had lived with her mother and still lives behind a green painted metal door that lets out directly onto the *Trébol*, the "Cloverleaf " – the confluence of roads where all the buses into and out of the city arrive and depart. Just outside the door is instantly shocking noise and bedlam. The buses, the traffic, the people everywhere are borne from the great beating heart of the *Trébol*, which pulses its blood out into the slums of the metropolis and then pulls it back in again from other manic, battered precincts. Situated immediately on the larger conduit with its arteries on and off it for great halcyon journeys, or block-long commutes, the apartment has been where she and her mother have lived through the cycles of night and day, slept, woke up, ate Bimbo white bread and drank weak coffee – her mother liked it laden with sugar – left to do their little food shopping, waited for the mail with the occasional check in it from the man who had kept her mother as his mistress for years, worried when this didn't come, suffered in silence with each other, put together dinner, went to sleep. Her mother had cancer of the uterus and the terrible pain was evident in her stricken eyes and sunken jaw.

As she did this morning, Elsa still comes, automatically, in her flimsy pink robe to peer through the eyehole of the green metal door to the life outside, ever-fresh garbage on the sidewalk, the slightly reduced din and clamor of horns, shouting *asistentes*, and sirens, from a diseased totality – a whole too large to take in, which becomes, at night, firecracker bombs, tires squealing, persistent banging, *musica* fragments... *Helado helado* drone the little boys selling ice cream cones. In the street's bay, legless beggars, head-scarved whores, cheap eateries with cantilevered, lopsided pastries, windowless *carnicerias* with yoyo-ing flies, and people, always amazing hordes of people, waiting, running, for their buses: the Republic's citizens in their every variety of dress and drama. A little girl she sees now and then this morning was clutching an armless plastic doll retrieved from the gutter, the gutter that has been imprinted in her little mind. The child, who looked about three years old, was filthy but pretty, though her strangely porcelain-white skin – was her absent father a *gringo?* – was smeared with candy or ketchup. Chestnut-red hair, looking as if it had been set with curlers, framed her little face, set and defiant.

The sameness of routine, the familiarity of Elsa's home, had finally left when her mother's cancer grew very bad, but both women had known for a long time that the apartment had very little to offer as counter to the impossible sovereign difficulties of survival. As emphasis of the trick of hope the bottles of medicine were still on the kitchen counter this morning and had reminded Elsa since her mother's death of the falsely cheerful sunny breezes that were blowing every morning outside until the afternoon rain came. When her mother finally died, face uplifted in speechless agony on the thin mattress, Elsa had gone to the precincts of the city near the public hospital that were given over to numerous coffin sellers. She had enough money only to buy the cheapest pine box. But she had a plot in the national cemetery where her mother now lay, delivered there after some wrangling with a man with a pickup.

Now, the only possibility that has occurred to her if she is not hired for the clerical job is to leave the city and return to Reu, the slum city near the Pacific coast where she was born. A miraculous ending sometimes presents itself, of coming back to her dead lover – not that he isn't dead but that his mother might welcome her simply because she was her dead son's fiancée. The rest of the plan is unclear because she cannot quite imagine how she would survive. A return there, two days of bus travel to the west even by the bus service one step in quality above the chicken bus, the picture so obviously false it is like a mezzotint of a solemn grandparent hung on a cracked plaster wall. Sometimes the miracle takes place in a well-tended garden with yellow-billed toucans and brilliantly-plumaged scarlet macaws in cages or on roosts, where the one-time presumptive mother-in-law, white-haired but enthusiastic, embraces Elsa. Stay with me! Stay here with me, she croons.

The reality, she knows, is that a return to Reu would come to nothing. Eduardo had lived with his mother. An unassimilable picture of the reunion interposes: why would the mother have anything to do with Elsa? In place of the fantasy comes a cold tremor of terror at the disdain that would greet her. A remnant of dignity-in-suffering stiffens her even though she gave up, long ago, belief in the Church.

¡Fíjate! Useless to dwell...

A taxi passes. A man, a *gringo*, looks out, face lit up in the too-bright, falsely confected sun. Probably just arrived from a flight, he is on his way somewhere she cannot imagine. Verging on forty, arrived at that middle age much too soon, the operatic solo is that she, by contrast, may be contemplating the end of her life. The *gringo* cranes around to look at her. In a blur she can see what he must see: suppliant white knees, calves, and ankles – legs neither too thin nor too fat, a little matronly, but shapely – incongruous, female, a prey animal.

Sara

There are other monuments, more peculiar than the *Obelisco* – monuments few people can explain. There seems no reason for their existence or their particular forms. Now used as a cell phone tower, the *Torre del Reformador* Ubico built also to honor President Barrios and the Great Progress he brought a century ago in the form of European business, which built empires of coffee and railroads to cart the beans to a port and then across the ocean. Time passes, progress moves slowly. In the Republic, coffee disappeared as an affordable drink and only now is available as powdered instant.

The *Torre* straddles the center of a roundabout on lightning-fast *Septima Avenida*, some thirty blocks north and west of the obelisk. If both the *Obelisco* and the *Torre* were bell towers, they would peal out absolutely lofty messages – not to her, but above her.

The *Torre*, by the all-metal construction a crude miniature replica of the Eiffel Tower, lacks the intended industrial-modern shock, looming, rather, like a seventy-five meter black spider. At night in a sweat of anxiety one maneuvers one's vehicle fast up *Septima Avenida* around the tower as quickly as possible because, in the pollution-warmed darkness, carjackers and motorcycle stickup crews rely on just such an obstacle to pull up beside the traffic-slowed vehicle, with a sudden tap on the window and a bullet in the head if one resists. *Séptima,* with only a thin island but both sides running one-way, is preferred by thieves as an escape route because it proceeds without impediment up to the northern gang *barrios* so dangerous the police never venture there.

The metal tower marks the division on *Séptima* between warehouses and blocks given over to sex clubs. Their function is invisible during the day, when they are only unidentifiable buildings shuttered behind grates. At night, big neon signs and marquees burn, slashing the darkness, sinister but somehow humorous. Other sex clubs are identified only by little green or orange bulbs above dark steps and doors.

Several hours after Elsa waits for her bus, arrives without incident for her job interview, is told they had many applicants and the position is filled, and makes her way back on the red city bus to the *Trébol,* to the green door by the ice cream vendors and the whores and the chaos of the bus transit – like a frantic storm without wind or rain, just human outlines with shadowy routines – outside the *Club Platinum* men in suits with flashlights wave drivers into parking slots. Inside, leaning over herself in a plastic chair in a back room with steps up to a stage curtain, Sara uses a big pair of scissors to trim her pubic hair as close as she can. Boom-box maximum-volume disco is hissing in constant sibilance, obliterating every other sound. Unlike Elsa, whose life is static, frozen, poised apparently before a swan-dive end, Sara's life is only a dream in motion mingled seamlessly with constant desperate actions and stuttered calculations.

The seconds of time passing in Sara's life are hemmed in by rules made of some unbreakable material. If she had words for it, she might ask: can one be dead from exhaustion? Hours, days and weeks pass with only staggered fragments of detail. Without warning, what returns for a few seconds is a clear imprint of mangrove roots standing in lapping black water flecked like beer and fed by trash-clogged ditches: the ocean lowlands of Blue Fields, Nicaragua, from where she came a few months ago.

She remembers one day in the club when she felt she died without the Church to protect her; the first time she took money from a man to let him fuck her. This was the last time she felt a tension stiffening her as, reflexively, she resisted his hands and his body on top of her; he was a short, squat man with a big chest, who averted his face from her. Since then, a strange dizziness, free in feeling, but as if she is constantly drunk, physically alive but inwardly shrunk, has remained with her through days without definition.

Whistling with feedback reverb the disc jockey's voice announcing her dancer name cuts through the bass and white noise. Snatching into place the white stockings and wrapping around her a little spangle-skirted leotard, she gets up, kneels to strap on thick platform shoes and, avoiding stepping into papaya pulp and what may be rice, plantain, and beans, splattered on the floor – another dancer's dropped plate of food – clatters over to the stairs that throb so strongly from the bass vibrations they seem unstable.

Clacking up the steps she stops for a moment behind the parted drape, she hears her cue, containing a lie, given her months already of dancing: *"Ahora, caballeros, por la primera vez aqui en el Club Platinum…les presentamos una chica muy muy fabulosa, la maravillosa, una dama increible…*Miss *Saaaaraaaaa!!!!"* There is an adrenaline consistency to it. Like thirty-round-per-second machine guns the revolving strobe perforates the darkness with pink and orange, red and pearl, the lights revolving more or less in rhythm with the shocked whispers of the singer. She tries to wipe away the exhaustion to maintain a picture she has made of herself, a little girl dancing to hyper-excited, gutteral, growling voices of "acid" or "heavy-metal 'roke'" – so loud it clears everything from her mind so far away from it all. She has done it all so many times over the last few months that actually pushing through the little curtain is something she cannot remember – she only remembers being out there. In a way the sequence of actions seems out of time – the persistent sense of burning up on the surface of things.

Out in the buzzing feedback, the wheezing and gasping much clearer now, she kicks, then lopes on the high catwalk raised to chest level above padded black leather booths just visible down where the customers sit, nursing drinks. The noise from the music speakers – with sharp gasps and sighs as if someone is being assaulted – calls awkward attention to the near emptiness of the club as if the absence of clients is a rebuke but also, strangely, a benediction of abstinence. For the whole day and evening there have been only a few customers, which constitutes a direct threat to her and the other women's survival. Repercussions will come from the management – adjurements that she and the other women are not pleasing enough.

Dropping to her knees, she throws herself forward as if bucked from a horse. She writhes on her belly, then immediately gets up and, a mechanized doll, dances double-time – an innocent, skipping imaginary rope down the catwalk, alternating with spinning and then striding mannishly, snapping her mincing feet with abandon, squatting, knees splayed. On the television monitors hung from the walls behind her are silent close-ups of penises parting hairy sheathes, of lipsticked mouths plunging fast, up-and-down, on huge veiny glistening tumescences.

In the middle of her set, she reaches that moment when multiple reflections of herself in mirrors facing each other perpetuate the fact that she dances alone on the stage. She has long passed the point when she realized that she isn't really being looked at much; after a few performances she found the customers looked at her and then away. The men don't stare but only glance at her occasionally – seemingly embarrassed or preoccupied, nursing their drinks as if they have all the time in the world.

Because days cycle past with so little definition, she no longer thinks what she thought before – what men who come to the club encounter because they are, with varying degrees of urgency, at the end of some abrupt continuum of action or need, which will involve, if she is bought, mechanical pumping into her and, usually, if the man is not too drunk or impotent, will end in his come on her.

Because it was explained, she knows how the clients – politicians and businessmen of the Republic but also Japanese, Koreans, and, every now and then, a *gringo* – arriving at a narrow front door beside a kind of toll-booth, are stopped, told to raise their arms, patted down for guns, and then motioned inside by shotgun-wielding guards, some of whom are like gruff, jovial conspirators, others who simply watch, expressionless.

Sara remembers what she wondered about a few months ago: how, as the customer comes inside, he finds himself in a huge grotto. His eyes must adjust to the gauzy dark. He is met by the big smiles of other staff, who fetch drinks and escort a girl, in string-bra and tight shorts, to his small table. She is not thinking any longer what she wondered about a few months ago: how, after the clients are snagged by the big, welcoming smiles of the staff, they cannot help but see how frozen or indifferent are the faces of the waiting girls. She is aware now only subliminally how the customers are both welcomed and negated, turned into ciphers with money, how the staccato excitements portend misleadingly a descent out of oneself into another self, to a place in which all can seem exploded but contained, impenitent, possible but impossible the payment of money for flesh the fundamental transaction.

Now, it all seems very old. With her thin arms and shoulders, her midriff bare and her legs sprouting like white sticks in the leggings below the flimsy skirt, she maneuvers behind the frozen fantasy she has been fitted into to look like a preteen girl. With a final deep squat and, on all-fours, a writhing crawl across the stage, she is not thinking of anything much; she is so drained she feels she can't raise her tongue from the floor of her mouth to speak. She cannot smile as she is reminded each day to do. She knows exhaustion is her immediate combatant. She erases expression continually from her face.

But, finally, almost done, she feels anchored within a dark, cozy box. Her shift began twelve hours earlier. For her last appearance, numb, with a sensation of floating, she skips quickly and with apparent abandon up the catwalk toward the little curtains and the steps down from the lights. A thought comes – as if to a subsidiary consciousness, the thought metamorphosing instantly into and out of the savaging sounds from the amplifier

– projecting ahead to leaving the club in a little while for a place off a street of trash that is indescribably more primitive. Skipping over to the curtains, one platform heel misstep away from falling, lightheaded, she knows at some level *her* body, *her* self, feeds the fantasies – though the men, of course, do not realize, would not think of it, do not care to think of it, how close she is to erasure from existence.

Out of breath from high kicks, from skipping and swirling around the pole, nose running – she has a cold she cannot get rid of – bare back and panty-clad buttocks facing the cavern now, Sara holds the little skirt and string bra in her hand and clatters stutter-stepping in her platforms through the curtains into the flimsy labyrinth of catacombs behind the stage. As she clatters back down the steps, other trap doors of half-thought are opening and closing. For some time sleep and waking life continue, one to the other, almost seamlessly. A recurrent dream finds her in limitless darkness behind some drapes, and she asks herself, *Where am I?* Then, in the dream, she is back in the cavernous room, and that is where her home is after death, with its flashing strobe. Sometimes she thinks that just before death – the end of her story – she will become completely disoriented, and the line between life and death will be vivid, continual dreaming. But as soon as she thinks this, panic rises frantically: again how tenuous is her hold on existence, how the story of her life could end soon, but, then, how going back to Blue Fields, if she could get the money for the trip, would be a return to "nowhere," as even she spoke about it before she left.

Stripping off the white stockings, her skin goosepimpling, she puts on jeans and tee shirt. She remembers to use the *baño* before leaving because there is no toilet where she lives.

Earlier she noticed a man, a *gringo*, while she skipped up and down the runway. She could not see most of the room because of the roving spotlights and the flashing strobe, and his face was just a brief upturned dim white then red. In the radiant cavern, the luminous green neon of the bar, the blue and red of the liquor logos, reflected in mirrors as she was reflected, otherwise blocked out most detail.

Almost as soon as she first saw the man she forgot him. Now as she makes her way toward the front of the club to make her escape, she sees he is still sitting in his booth. She thinks she remembers him spurning one of the other girls offering *¡buen servicio!*

She is almost past him, but the man motions, braking the momentum of exhaustion. The *gringo* wants her: *how can he? I am dirty, I stink, you do not want me.*

Not fully aware of being on her feet, about to black out, she stands for a second beside him, then manages to perch on the edge of the booth, not looking at him, leaning her ear to his mouth as he says something.

The Gringo

She later understands that he wants her and not the other women who came over to offer themselves. A Stateside manager for some *maquilas,* to him she is a slim, lithe, perfectly proportioned, pony-tailed sylph. In some bizarrely easy transmogrification, as she skipped up and down the stage in her little top and skirt with white leggings, she is a high school girl. Every now and then her backlit form was an amorphous bottle, fusing into front-lit clarity, then turning away with a glimpse of legging-pantied crotch: a wedge of possibility opening to him between her white-stockinged legs yielding, the fast, dreamlike prospect of intimacy with a little girl waif. His money is the switch to start the erotic machine of elongated-foreshortened time, a door ajar to bypass all impediments, transcendence bought by the hour or the night. Somehow she understands this. It is all very, very old.

When she reappeared later and is walking past, he waves at her. But, as if she cannot believe he wants her, or, possibly, he thinks, because she is tired, reluctant for a second, she then comes over and sits down. He tells her how pretty she is. Unsmiling, she looks at him – eyes dark, vague – then looks away. Protocol requires summoning one of the male staff to bring overpriced, watered-down "champagne," but she does not bother with this.

He repeats how pretty she is but she doesn't seem interested enough to respond.

He asks her how much and in a few husky monosyllables she tells him the prices – for one hour or all night. He nods.

Swallowing the last of his beer, he follows her out past the guards. The shotguns the guards are cradling seem capable of expression, with punctuation marks – as if what is happening is playacting a fatal rendezvous with someone at the other end of the world...*the end.*

But they pass on without restriction, and when they get into his rented car, she directs him to a cinderblock motel in Zone Three with cracks in the walls. Inside, behind a counter an old woman with a face so completely wreathed with wrinkles it seems she is smiling even though she isn't carefully counts his money and hands the girl a key attached to a small wood tablet.

Up narrow linoleum stairs and down a hall they come to a door. Inside is a small room with banana and coconut-green frond patterns painted on dark thin wood-paneled walls. A queen-size bed with unmade sheets takes up most of the space. The room has a subterranean feel, at once clinical and obscene, with a faint but distinct smell of shit.

He offers her a bottle of *rón de Botrán* he bought earlier that day, but she merely shakes her head. He takes off his clothes and sits on the bed. With no ceremony she pulls off her tee shirt and strips off her jeans. Her olive body is scrawny but her legs, though thin, are strong and ropy. On her ribbed chest the dark tips of her breasts snag his eye. He lies back as she sits on the dirty sheet and then slips next to him, turning just a little toward him, closing her eyes. Evidently she feels cold, so he puts his arm around her shoulders, passes his other hand down her leg, coarse-stubbled and goose pimpled, then, holding his breath, touches the wire and bristle of her mound, then the little rubbery slit.

After no more than thirty seconds of half-hearted response, just rubbing her palm on his leg, she passes off into a dead sleep. Intimidated by her exhaustion he does not try to wake her up; he is a *gringo* from a civilized country, a manager in an international company and, though it occurs to him, he will not make a stink about it or force himself on her. For a minute he tries to examine her body but she has pulled the dirty sheet around her and he can only lift up the sheet a little to peek at one nipple which shows itself like a carcinogenic mole on her ribcage...

After what seems just a few hours she wakes up.

It's early. The air is gray. He must have slept although she doesn't know this. She feels him lying next to her, partially covered by the sheet, senses he's awake and is looking at her. Her limbs are foetal, her face turned away. He leans over to look and she knows he sees lines scoring her forehead and how she is not a child.

Still drugged with sleep, with no ceremony, insisting on upholding her end of the deal, turning toward him she lifts her pelvis. Still partly within the stream of heightened moments begun at the club which seems, now, very long ago, with a few misaimed thrusts, her stubble scratching, he partially enters her. Then, deciding not to try to explain – because clearly even if she cared for the sake of some professionalism she is too exhausted even to feign enthusiasm – he extricates himself from her quickly lapsed embrace, gets up, and puts his clothes back on.

He pauses awkwardly by the door. Awake, she wonders about him: why speak at all? Of course he won't see her again and she knows he knows this and this time with him has been a pinprick in her routine. She hasn't looked back at him, and she turns away to go back to sleep as she hears the door open and shut. As she lies there, she mentally traces him as he exits the hotel into the sun and the hot, brass air of the noisy streets with their psychic gorges and pans of rippled asphalt, clamor, and smoke.

A half-hour later, still lying in the bed, she thinks he must have made his way in a taxi back to the tourist zones and then to the airport. From the brief time with her she thinks how probably stamped in his memory will be the badly clipped nub of her pubis and how exhausted she was and the revelation of how near to the edge she seemed. Did the fact that her life was already over the edge make him sad about her?

An hour after the *gringo* left, Sara gets up and stuffs her things back in her bag. If she overstays there will be a late charge. She counts the bundle of bills the *gringo* peeled off for her – enough for her rent and for several taxi rides to and from the club. Dizzy, nausea blooms at the prospect of going to the club but then she realizes she might just be hungry.

Downstairs, she walks quickly past the booth occupied last night by the old woman. A young man with slicked back black hair, reading a newspaper has taken the old woman's place. He looks up and is about to ask her something but she has already exited into the street, the light bulb brightness of sun overhead, the sun which reminds her, from a mental distance, how, for many who do not live her life but share parts of it, the air often seems as heavy and dark as cinder blocks, straining and groaning with weight: pushing on with the necessity to somehow stay alive. Nearby, next to some oil drums, a street food vendor is preparing tortillas with bits of crumbled white cheese, ground meat, and scallions. Her stomach lurches.

When Sara arrives back at the club, another dancer sitting on the curb tells her there was a police raid because of a tip that there were undocumented persons working there. The other dancer, a *Salvadoreña* with a sallow face and mottled bad skin, tells Sara one of the guards explained that the owners of the club must not have paid the bribes.

Sara wakes up an ancient, unshaven taxi driver. No one, not her family in Blue Fields, not the other dancers, not the men who buy her, know this, but for two months she has lived in a tiny space uptown, which for some reason seems downtown, to which she navigates when her shift is done – day ripped into night from the early afternoon beginning of her shift when she disappears into the club, to the well-after midnight when she leaves – in a taxi with shocks long gone, turning off a broad avenue that represents the city's section of the Pan American highway, called in other places the Avenida Roosevelt, and then over rutted and ripped asphalt into inky dark, the seat with its ravaged upholstery wheezing and squeaking, the vehicle bouncing desperately. Late at night the street is silent which, however, does not make where she lives seem like a refuge – adjacent to a *faux*-postcolonial era pontefract, somehow looking like papier-mache, a kind of warehouse, perched a little above the precincts sleeping below in the chill of devolution. For some reason – probably because it is so small and insubstantial – it makes her think it is a little like a fast food child's play place which the American franchises offer even here in the Republic.

Paying the *taxista* with the *gringo*'s money, as if sleepwalking, guided by automatic memory, but still with inner alarms to be on alert for the *maras* – muted after two months without incident she makes her way to a hidden wood stairway, haphazardly constructed and with no guard rail, one full story up to a window to which she has attached a broken lock. For two months the broken lock has been enough – she now believes – to deter intruders. The window has no glass but, rather, is covered with a dented mesh grate she pushes inside.

Inside, she shivers, though it isn't cold. It always seems as if she is crawling into a little circular hole but, once inside, at night, away from the club, for a few hours, she has been able to picture that she is back in Nicaragua, under a lean-to shack's corrugated roof, near mangrove swamps. But inevitably a vehicle coughs or the sudden flatulence of some engine erupts in the quiet as a car revs up and squeals away.

Although millions of people like exhausted insects in the city are lying somewhere, the enervating air – dirty puffs of What Is – flows over a knife-edge, always awake. Combined with the frequent panic that she is so near to being nothing that the details of her downside-up life whisper to her not to notice them, she lies on her mattress on the floor beside a small pile of clothes and a foam-plastic tray with fast-food remains, chicken bones. She gazes at the smiling cartoon chicken on the greasy paper bag the food came in.

Sara! – a voice inside her yells.

Since she is here so rarely at this time of day, she realizes something is missing. At night, from somewhere a pink and then green light like long-legged crawling spiders reflects with regular on-off intermittence, onto her ceiling. Sometimes, idly, she has wondered about these lights but has been unable to locate their source.

As old as the ancient city's desires and wastes, despite her exhaustion she knows she has to think: what will she do? *Pues...* With the *gringo*'s money she could leave and go back to Nicaragua. Mentally she maps out the route: first on the city bus to the Trébol...another bus to the outpost north of the city...another bus for Puerto Barrios... at Puerto Barrios a boat to Nicaragua... another bus to Managua...in Managua a final bus to Blue Fields... and then the seamed, surprised but not too-surprised face of her mother. She feels a shame she'd thought she was long past the possibility of feeling: she doesn't know, can't possibly remember who the father of the baby she is carrying might be.

If she could sigh, she would sigh. The wall she hits: she does not know what she will do... But there may be a man whom she might convince that the baby is his.

Escape

If one endures, if one survives, life in the Republic follows fable: *caudillo* presidents, Catholic saints and miraculous cures, *Maximón*, the cigarette-smoking trickster *indígena* folk saint one makes devotions to because of his whimsical black-magic badness, *San Pasqualito*, the skeletal saint bedecked with jeweled necklace and rings on bone fingers one prays to because of his white-magic goodness. And the Narrative still transcends everything else. Just as in the outer world, everyone, everything, needs to tell a story.

And where life and experience are third-hand and seem quite hopeless, smoke, proverbial symbol of danger, producer of the half-light, is ignored – false glad-handed away in the eternal rushings and sighings of the traffic-polluted air. Up close, at street level, the citizen-philosopher might observe the great sadness of matter. For the surface here is burning, degradation approaching unadulterated transience, a young pretty woman glimpsed in profile nothing so much as fuel to burn, face resigned, gone in a constant quickening, a constant perishing. A burning surface, the moment the *All* – she feels this, or thinks it, but wordlessly, voicelessly – the flesh whether viewed or bought in consortiums of sex clubs, their signaling switched on at night, little green arcs or orange slashes or little light bulbs or big marquees completely hidden during the restless dry-then-wet autumn days...

The regularities imposed on the lower, the bottom-lands successfully keep the chaos of the Capital of the Republic pent in. As a result, there are routines everyone follows religiously. At the Trébol, in the dusky golden hour before the pollution becomes invisible, training onto and off all the buses that travel to and from the *campo* and the Capital, these routines are performed innocently and automatically, like someone who, before going to sleep, combs her hair and brushes her teeth. They are, as well, sucked into the drama and chaos of the everyday in the bottomlands but are allowed, in the chaos, to find their own trajectories home. It is these regularities that the monuments of the city seem to smile on, *El Obelisco*, cold or even frigid in the warm air, and the *Torre del Reformador*, a little closer to the routines waxing natural in the pollution-warmed evening because it is black and spiderlike, beacon for the sex clubs and their women for sale. And there are other yet stranger monuments to this or that *coronel*, and the running bull by the National Defense Institute – a febrile torpor. And yet further still, easily in reach of the fearful mind, deeper in the *barrios*, are other, wilder monuments – shanties and piles of smoking garbage and the worlds of the gangs, where a primitiveness and absolute and basic freedom, with its own inordinate rules, mingles with the anger of desperate men, hot as a blowtorch, in color, platinum.

If there are objections within the city's confines, the world at large does not see. Customary signs of distress – smoke, for example – draw no notice. The gargantuan dump that caught fire twenty years ago burns on, an inextinguishable beacon of an inverse state, its ruinous smoke casting a pall into the upper reaches of the towering eucalyptus and pine that adorn the highlands valley at seven thousand feet where the city spreads itself out. In the golden hour the smoke reaches into *barrios* tucked over and into deep *barrancas*, running along cracked concrete and asphalt until the streets wear out, then, in the violet dusk, through precincts of worse and worse slum shanty neighborhoods that verge on, then enter, the primeval of a candy-land of Nature, where no one goes because they are the mysterious home turfs of the most feared of the gangs, the *fauna* of this jungle the ones with tear drops tattooed at the corners of their eyes, each tear representing a young woman killed in rites of gang initiation.

Stories have endings as they had beginnings, although, to the visitor to the Republic, the natural symmetry is unclear. Cries of despair at the inability to escape are faint but one can hear them as if posthumously. And one might ask, in amazement, how this peculiar physics works and which is plain as day, and by which an entire sub-world, a sunken world, rages at street level, profiles at sunset suffused in orange, on their way to ending too soon but, still within the skin, in slow-burning anguish? If suffering equates with reality, how can this geographically smaller world, but with infinitely greater volumetrics of pain, fit inside the outer world? The bottoming out of life in the Republic falls quite deeply below the other.

The Outpost

Nine hours later, the sun, showing its power, cords down through the afternoon. All is powdery mirror surface, suffused. In Zone Thirteen, after an inexplicable, seemingly interminable delay the *gringo*'s flight is finally taking off. In his window seat he knows soon he can look down over the vast smoking serried city in the basin of the great valley as the plane banks, circling outward and up.

In the opposite direction of his flight, out of sight, on the roadway into the Capital there is an outpost, a high cliff overlook to the sun-reddening city extending below and which one sees through the stanchions of a billboard advertising a brand of car battery and displaying a giant bikini-clad model smiling with white teeth with the legend, *¡Haz un buen conexion!* placed like a banner across her crotch.

Because of the busyness of the spot, a little settlement of food sellers and lean-tos has built up over time. While people eat they enjoy the view through opalescent air and space. From this distance the actual coloration of the Capital – the roofs and asphalt down in its *barrios*, often separated by the canyons of deep *barrancas* – is copper, tin, and gray, muted by the brown pall of pollution, but fiercely bronzing now, like someone stretching her arms and yawning. The city below looks postcard-innocent, empty of harm or danger.

The place has about it a cheerful rowdiness. Buses shriek to a halt, some riders getting off and others climbing on, and then, engines roaring with a party spirit, shuddering with catarrh, the driver revs up the engine, farting huge gusts of black exhaust, and angles back out onto the pitted road. In its separation from the city, the sense here is that this can be where your story has taken, or will take, a real turn for the better – or, of course, more likely, hopefully not, that once more night comes and somehow you sleep, still stuck. The physical situation of the outpost enables it, with its high, high lookout over the city, on the one hand and, on the other, its proximity to the road as way station – away from the city that passes up between volcanoes and into the *campo* – to seem equipoised between metropolis and countryside, at exactly a meridian point where every good prospect not only seems possible but, in the drowsy, insect-buzzing, bird-twittering sunlight, prescient of new beginnings. Here, as on a fault line, the pull to the Capital is roughly equal to the push to leave it.

There are even some fabulous villas built into the hillside, invisible from the road and its bankments of wild vegetation, but clues to their luxury can be glimpsed only at just the right angle in the wild, unpruned hedges through high metal gates and a driveway overhung with immense pine and eucalyptus, the soporific aromas mingling of sweet sap and cat stink. But these bastions are not as forbidding as the ones in the rich zones, Nine and Ten, as if one might expect, even this close to the city, the manners of some country gentility.

Under the strut supports of the billboard by a few picnic tables vendors, as usual, are frying meat. A skittish dog with emaciated ribs stands trembling, guilty pop eyes lolling to a dropped tortilla. In a cage by its owner, a man selling *recuerdos* – the inevitable paintings of the *Volcán de Agua*, *sabanas* with Indian patterns – a green *loro*, now and then, emits a monosyllabic squawk as mysterious comment. One of the vendor women plies her business here. To some she is "Maria," to others, "Blanca," but her real name she hasn't admitted because there is no reason to do so. Her squat, thick-waisted form is wrapped in a *huipil*, the once brilliantly red, blue, and green starred-and-zigzag patterns of the *traje* identifying her as coming from Santa Maria de Jesús, a town resting just at the verge before the slopes steepen up the volcano. The Water Volcano is a monument not built by men, but can be claimed as a national monument, even because of its destructive force, because some long time ago, a hundred years or so after the blond Pedro de Alvarado conquered the Land of Many Trees for Cortés and the Spanish king, an eruption triggered a massive mud avalanche that wiped out the colonial city, the first capital, which caused the resetting of the capital to the great valley basin even higher up and to the east.

Though Maria/Blanca comes from Santa Maria de Jesús, in reality this way station for buses overlooking the city is her home. During the week she sleeps on a bench in one of the little lean-tos near the billboard, returning to Santa Maria on weekends. Now, with practiced movements, she slips her knife in and out of a pitcher of gray water and cuts up more pineapple, mango, watermelon and papaya, puts the pieces in little plastic bags, and hangs the bags with clothespin on a string hung between the poles of her cart.

A small boy shines shoes near Maria/Blanca's cart. His face, arms and legs are brown, but his hands to his wrists are completely black from shoe polish. His monument is his shoe stand, a little step with leather stirrups. Now and then he climbs it, stamping his skinny legs on it for some reason – as if testing its sturdiness for purchase.

The sun is still hot and bright, making one squint or turn away. The air stirs here above the city which spreads out far below as an enormous belabored toy morass. Delicate fingers of smoke curl up gradually from different zones, from different *barrios*. It seems very far away. A few people are eating, bent over, spearing the food, ignoring the vista.

A bus, its roll-scroll of destinations on the brim of the windshield reading PUERTO BARRIOS, its name – ESMERALDA emblazoned in elaborate cursive on its throbbing sides, boards its passengers, and, chuffing exhaust, lumbers onto the two-lane highway. In a seat toward the rear Sara sits, a bag on her lap. Her face is not made up and few might guess her life as it has been in the city. Still finding it almost impossible to stay awake, she anticipates the salt air twenty hours later at Puerto Barrios, and dirty brown water, foam-flecked like beer. Premonitory of Blue Fields, banks of mangrove will face her across an eroded channel emptying rust-red into the bay, where she will wait for the boat. The roots look somewhat like the metal tower near the strip club. She thinks of another monument, the white spire of the *Obelisco* at the top, or bottom, of the Avenida de la Reforma and of the electric Pepsi sign which seems to her carny-like and very far away. Looking out the window on the taxi ride to the Trébol, she has finally connected the colors of this sign to the flicker on the walls and ceiling of the room.

The radio is playing *musica ranchera* accordion at top volume. Up front, wedged between the pole and the driver, the *asistente* sucks in his breath as he counts a wad of soiled bills. Half-full now with other passengers, snorting and shuddering, the bus picks up speed. Under the driver's laconically prideful direction authoritatively with each wrenched gear shift he messages it is *his* – the bus chuffs past the roadside trees. Whitish volcanic ash embankments replace vegetation, in turn falling away to thatch-roofed huts. All becomes a blur. To the right, intermittently visible through the trees, still, is the Capital, visible one last time before the bus levels out and then passes down away from the volcanoes in a sea of antique-gold air, inlit with blue.

Sara does not know if her story is beginning again or will be a repeat of others. Remembering as if about someone else, she thinks again of how she is pregnant, of how she may have the baby. If she can't find a man to be the child's stepfather, her family in Blue Fields can take care of it and her at the same time. A child will be taken care of and, therefore, the mother. Despite the acknowledgment that her prospects are very poor, somehow she thinks now that her life may not be over – that, for a long time, it has been merely crazed. There are endings and beginnings. In fact she spends no more than a moment permitting the thought that everything may not be over and that there may be a future: she is still too numb to think too long about this.

At the outpost, chassis vibrating violently as if trying to shake off the chill at eight thousand feet, another bus, MARIBEL, has been waiting. The *asistente* has cranked the scroll. It now reads, RETALHULEU. Seen through the bus windows, below the overlook's brown and green fallen or chopped vegetation is the faint brick color of the far-off city. Its life seemingly stalled, all the sores, complications, impossibilities and contradictions of its streets and *barrios* rendered almost whimsical, the urban sprawl appears to be extraordinarily frail and delicate from so high up and far away.

Elsa leans against the bottom sill of a window. Earlier, she had swallowed an icy despair and allowed a burgeoning hope to fuel determination. With this she felt, antiphonally but still, somehow, positively, that with the rejection of her city life she is, in a moment, almost breathlessly segueing to a new life, set free from the events of the previous ones. In this strange euphoria, she feels somewhat as if the weight of personal destiny, something momentous and irrevocable, is upon her. Tall trimmed hedges, a toucan with great long yellow bill, a macaw with scarlet-to-russet plumage, make a dreamy, sun-spotty vision. She remembers a polkadot *falda* she wore when she was Eduardo's lover, and of sitting on his lap at his mother's. Eduardo had a catbird in a cage and it would sing in the chirps, clicks, warbles, and whistles of other birds.

The driver revs up the engine again, sending out great black acrid clouds. The *asistente* whistles, waits, crooks his arm again and again like a robot built to lure in more passengers. But there are no more for this bus, which passes now an old, two-tone, red-and-white Japanese-make car parked to the side just ahead of them. To some it seems strange, this car not parked at the Outpost but just here, roadside. Turning the wheel hard occupies the bus driver's mind, and he doesn't notice how this car he just passed jerks forward, accelerating wildly out of the dust, spitting stones from the road shoulder. Nor has he seen the skin-head and tattooed torso of the driver and the other shadowed passengers waving pistols at him to stop – the driver is preoccupied as the bus huffs and struggles toward a sharp turn up the road, and the beginning of a cliff falling hundreds of meters immediately to the right of the deeply potholed macadam.

Pistol shots crackle loudly and the door glass shatters. Elsa sees then in a slowed eternal-present the driver suddenly slumped down to the right. A slow, growing rumbling of acceleration directs the bus toward the edge of the road cliff. The last thing she sees and hears are yelling and more pistol shots beside and then behind the bus, yells and curses; she is thrown violently to the back as the bus angles awkwardly, but quickly sidles over the edge, eager to go vertical.

All of this has happened within earshot of the Outpost. The sudden ruckus erupted with what sounded like the muffled, then spit-crackling, of *cohetes*, the newspaper-wrapped homemade firecrackers. Instinctively, immediately, Maria/Blanca and the little boy duck down.

More shots crack out and a screaming is heard, which then stops all of a sudden. A red-and-white Japanese car races back down away from whatever had happened up ahead. Banging wildly over ruts, the mufflerless car guns, careening away from the city. Still crouching, in warning Maria/Blanca hisses sharply to the little boy, who is slowly standing up.

Some minutes later, on Sara's bus, a few kilometers down the road, coasting through the embankments cut into millennia of cream-colored volcanic tuff, sun flickering rhythmically and pleasant with shadow, the driver accelerates out of a curve, yielding to the momentary pleasure of travel because of the movement that presses backs into seats. Volume turned up even louder, the radio is blasting *canciones rancheras*.

Just as the bus is picking up speed, the driver brakes, pitching everyone forward. In Sara's mind, only half awake, have been images of Puerto Barrios, the sun drowsing on the water. She is still not fully awake when the bus stops, but she rouses herself enough to sense that everyone else on the bus is wide-eyed and quiet now. One woman has put her hand to her mouth. Unable to rouse herself to full alert, Sara pulls herself up and glances outside. A red-and-white Japanese make car has angled ahead of the bus, blocking the road. A sharp voice on the driver's side, near the driver's window, issues a command, just a few words. Sara makes out that the man has a tear drop tattoo by one eye.

There is a battering on the door, and the truculent driver is too slow to lever it open. The bus rocks as the door is kicked ajar. Sara tries to wake up fully now but she still cannot. The world around her rockets up. It seems flames are reaching up around her. She sees the white obelisk, which she did not understand; it seemed civilized to her, in some way, mounting with a dismissive but exhausted grace into the sky. The flames almost seem friendly as if, in a sudden fusion of things ending, carnal or warmly sensual, the entire past has hurried into the future, meeting NOW, when everything reunites, finally happens, all is made plain, all is consumed. She looks up at a teenager who is pointing a pistol at her. His eyes are wild, hot, both seeing and not seeing as he fires into her head.

For those carried on the tide into the city, it is for whatever restorative busyness one might, counterweight to fantasy, seek to find in the city's traffic, its sibilant soundings and backfires echoing, through the extensions of more and more degraded and debilitated precincts. An impassive, physical reminder of the possible, the *Obelisco* marks the end or beginning, the top or bottom, of the formal, central avenue that is the Reforma, with its dreams of grandiosity. Darkly complected with passing wealth, intended to be stately in the sense of the carriage way it once was, the Reforma also, of course, manifests a crazed feeling that clings to its interstices and to the intersections off onto smaller, potholed arteries into the two rich zones, Nine and Ten, and its townhouses for the wealthy jerry-rigged with razor wire.

If one is in the vast city, the tide might be out of and away from it, towards the motorcycle-riding youth's untamed and uncollected *campo* where the two-dollar-a-day laborer might hope to find something or someone lost. Going out of the city, to the south, which feels contrarily to the north, along the Boulevard Liberación, on an overpass hangs the giant Pepsi Cola sign blinking in a spider crawl its rapid pink and green. In the late afternoons, in the bright light paling before sunset against the sign, the sober sky seems lit-down rather than lit-up. Navigating through underpasses and over the worn nubbles of traffic strip-merges one proceeds out to the much greater hub of the Trébol where the bedlam of smoke, density, and noise are easily ten times that circling around the *Obelisco* and where the turmoil of the city breaks wide open, revealing that Chaos also has its own routines, where so many lives pass in transit, where, in the ruts of the Republic's vast bottomland, existence is defrayed. The winds, jocose, whip up to a middle-land at the already forgotten nexus of the blood-red sunset, the burning surface.

When, or if, on the other hand, one has the chance to leave the Capital, the vista is of blue smoke trailing up patches of high mountain maize plots under an immemorial thunderhead heaven. Endless sugar cane approaches the salinity of the coast – sugar approaches salt, salt favors sugar. *Proportion is all...* In all of this, *indígena* lives find no record in history: there is a great illusion of freedom in passage to the *campo*, manifesting in the lazy *salsa* radio, the sombreroed laborer asleep on the roadside after walking all morning, and the occasional interruption by the bucolic youth who has managed somehow to buy a motorcycle and is tearing down the road securely inside his own bubble of faith in Life's continuance. This young fellow might lean over a second, swerving around a bashed-open coconut, thinking idly in the wind whipping steadily against him, ripping at his clothes, about the great lake to the north, so beautiful, so beautiful – a candied myth where the *gringa* tourists go – cupped and tossing in a gigantic caldera of volcano once so enormous it gave birth to smaller volcanoes ringed around it, fitfully insistent with their fire, ashy faces tear-streaked for the mother.

Passages
Not Even to
the End of
the World

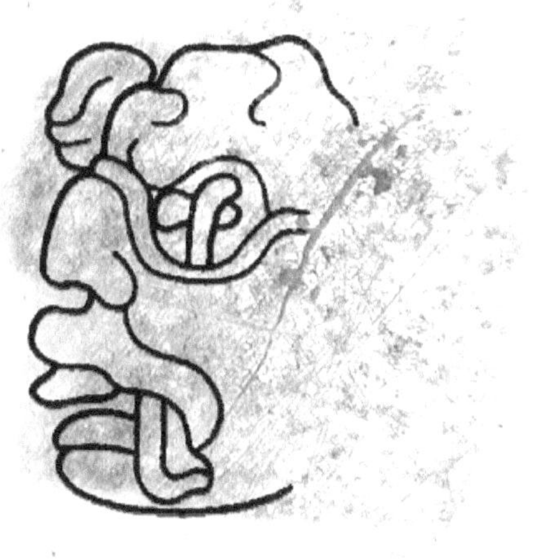

W as it a premonition? Some weeks ago he thought he could see through his hand – to the little muscles and tendons attached to the knuckle, the fine finger bones. At the same time, for some reason, a stray fact stuck in his head – how the opposable thumb distinguishes human beings from the other animals...

The dark red city bus roared up and rocked, squeaking, to a halt beside him. The last lurid rays of the sunset alighting on the upper half of his body, from the waist down he partially disappeared from view in the translucent acrid gusts of the diesel fumes. Trash eddied up from the slopped pavement.

The great city was the orb of an eye, opening and closing...

The door flung open, the driver already was levering the gears and revving up. As if expecting more customers and unhappy there was none the *asistente* took his coin. Beaters and jalopies with one headlight skittered past. Moons and planets.

The *asistente*, by rote, yelled out, in a hoarse, lilting atonal song, farther destinations – ignoring the poor neighborhoods through which the bus passed, which had no formal names and which, one after the other appeared and then fell away like the earth opening up and closing again... Almost immediately the sun had set and he was thrown into the gathering indifferent darkness of the street. People on the sidewalks were hard to see in the dingy air, the details of their lives also obscured as if they were whole and new.

Getting on and off the bus in loud, tedious traffic felt as if he was dipping into and out of sight, flaming in and out of Here-and-Now...

His neighborhood quickly disappeared: a *barrio*: neither rich nor particularly poor, an older part of the vast spider web extending through many *barrios* and *colonias* which, mostly, otherwise, were just broken streets and crude shack houses. Each seemed to die many times before and came back to a life.

Quickly the ride fashioned itself into a tube as he looked ahead to the front of the bus and the dashboard objects and decals plastered inside the windshield. The guiding gods of the road gave bits of confused meaning to the darkness. Playboy silhouette, flag of the Republic, skull-and-crossbones, and, arms outspread, downcast face framed by curly dark hair, features barely discernible, their coeval, Jesus. This Jesus was particularly elaborate: from a pulsing neon purple heart in the ribcage, chains of little deep red lights signifying His blood flashed on and off in rays out and down to the bottom of the tableau. Mostly these benefactors belonged, also, to the little concrete or windowless wood shack homes they passed with cement floors and families eating now, doors closed. The passage of the bus had its own meaning, shaped with a length indicated as two finites, point A and point B.

He saw, in an instant, as the driver turned his head, a big black beard and eyes wide awake with fatigue.

He anticipated, in forty minutes or so, getting off at the university into a different stretch and kind of anonymity. There, he became both less anonymous: on campus, part of a singular community; but one of thousands of students. Like any ape, he had an opposable thumb, but he was part of the two percent of the population who went to university. Somewhere there was a joke for his friends, for Mariaelena.

Why he wondered now if he would see them tonight had no particular rationale: why wouldn't he? Their connections to each other seemed molecular, spokes between them like an illustration in a textbook.

The better neighborhoods – Proceres, Reforma, Liberación, Las Americas: with a hoarse voice the boy called these out in practiced, sardonic cadence. And finally they were passing a rich, very old estate house behind walls topped with razor wire islanded at the demographic boundary, still within a big, dangerous precinct otherwise like campgrounds for street people.

A few moments followed of complete darkness, the red taillights from finer cars, and the grated entrances of cheap office buildings: the beginning of Zone Nine. Then another stop and many other people were getting on, stamping their feet – always the tired anxious faces, crumpled like they had been kicked in – settling into seats.

Spotlit mentally for a moment – resenting her but sympathizing: an Indian woman unfolded herself slowly from worn, but still vividly colored, *traje* in the seat opposite him. Her baby, black hair on the little head stuck up as if in perpetual sleepy astonishment, stared at him as the mother moved it in the shoulder pouch where it was cocooned into a more comfortable position. Slowly the woman turned her head to look back at him with a giant defiant rebuke. He looked away, then glanced back. Her eyes were a shadow of blankness, hollow, not seeing him or anyone as she pulled down one side of her jersey to release a big pale brown breast. The stiff dark protuberant nipple stuck out – a caricature of over-fecundity and plenitude... After rubbing it up and down against the baby's lips, she put the nipple between its lips, which immediately started opening and closing. The woman bent her head down to the side to look as the nipple slipped out of the now slack little mouth, the infant nodding off, milk sprinkling onto the dirty purple-and-red straps of the satchel and dotting her jersey. She glanced up, catching him looking at her again; she stared him down as if challenging him to confirm something.

Nobody belongs in this world, he found himself thinking...

He began to remember himself as he settled into the ride. Still the ride was more of a physical fact than he was. It was the same brown-black night, the same wrenching ride through warm black air... black the color of hair, black molecules, since everything was made of molecules...

A void of directional time shaped like a tube, otherworldly but familiar, but still able to shock – from sudden stabbings or carvings of light, white, yellow or red, from signs – but producing in his mind a filament, a dream, no, a brown forearm ahead hanging out the window the sight as if in an x-ray revealing the incredibly vulnerable bone structure... A glimpse of a splash of spilled tortilla mush, a banana peel, a pile of garbage: another periodic gulf of dirt and poverty like a basin collecting the haphazard detritus of the great slum that was the capital city of the country. Blood and other juices, orange dayglo Fanta sign reflected in a pool of water, flimsy plastic bags in shreds, a few spilled sticks from a broken bundle of firewood... They passed a guard in the orange light from a *mercadito* stuck in the side of an old mall, shotgun held between upper arm and the side of his chest.

But as if it were a normal city the stop was in front of a new car dealership with fancy cars, impossibly expensive, shining inside plate glass.

Relief beat through him when a tattoo like an alarm, on a possible *mara*, turned out false...

Immediately then were more piles of dirt and a construction site...

Then the bus went down a battered cavern beneath a gigantic Pepsi sign hanging above the overpass, producing a flutter, like confetti, of lime-green and papaya-red light wheeling spider-like through the bus.

In the poor light, the night was silky smooth. A dead chicken bus – named CECILIA in the scroll above the windshield – stricken by some engine trouble, was parked under some trees on an island in the avenue, just visible bottles and cans of oil and other fluids lined up on the bare earth.

Against the complete hopelessness and uselessness of the city, a little elation again: Mariaelena. But he was irritated with her.

After class, they could go to a restaurant to eat the first meal of the day. Then he would take her to his aunt's house, which he was looking after while she was in Mexico for cancer treatment. He would push her down on his aunt's big bed and soon his nose would be pressed into the bush between her thighs and she would moan...

Ahead was the tube in the darkness and slogans, some of which were written backwards: decals pasted to face front through the windshield...

Cartoon flowers...happy faces.

Militantly in contrast with downward or degrading sections of the city, which were like ejaculations sharp as a bayonet, was Luís and his crammed-but-ordered life – lived for part of the time in his mother's house extending back from the street in a better *barrio*. The dun-painted metal door with several locks was Luís' garage, where he parked his nice, toylike little car. Inside the door was a small front room, a corridor, really, with a mirror on one wall and

Jesus clinging to the other. Then a bigger room in front of a kitchen which itself was in front of a second story, the wall of sliding glass windows, evidence of how old the house was containing such strange niceties...including a hot-water shower in Luís' bathroom. And around the kitchen to the right another hallway leading back to the mother's bedroom and Luís' bedroom and office, with books and magazines, the scene of many meetings and discussions...where he and a few others had met just last night...leaving several empty wine bottles...

To mute the roar of the levered engine, and after checking for *maras*, he pulled out his walkman, put the little plug into his ear, and depressed the play button. Tinny guitar, drums, high nasal voices – like the *asistente*'s – filled his head, and made a space now around his isolation.

He was getting sick. A tickle in his throat... *La gripe?* He hoped it wasn't going to be bad because he would miss class...and the next meeting at Luís' house...

He wiped his runny nose with the back of his hand, then moved his satchel with his biology textbook in it between his feet.

Normally it was difficult to tell if it was an actual virus or was just the constant degrading wear and tear and which was cured only by *mota* or a music club or sex with Mariaelena... Hopefully, he was just worn out. The violent racket exploded passages of calm: mufflerless acceleration, drum rolls of engines knocking, vehicles driven long beyond their intended lifetimes by doglike men who subsisted at the limits either of great responsibility trying to feed their families with some sort of employment or of complete irresponsibility driving vehicles that were going to skid out of control and kill people.

A reflective, businesslike manner was required in order to pick one's way through any given day, going about errands usually of so small a purpose their routine required little mental energy even though all the little actions, together, gave the force behind the question: can one survive? This thought, also, produced a little elation: realistically, he wanted to be alive, to remain a living person, to continue to see what the country could offer him once he got his *licenciatura*.

What Luís did to manage his life: his errands were larger, part of a bigger scheme – despite risks, which he, Luís, smiled about, reassuring the little group that he had taken all precautions: no one wanted him dead, no one knew about him and what he was doing...

Hemming him in, a thought, then, as the walkman music kicked into nice rock and roll from Mexico: as if it were a gradient pitched steeper and steeper year after year, one learned from childhood to construct within oneself an overriding preoccupation with *The Small.*

He got up, clinging to the pole, stooping down to peer out the windows: long past *zona uno.* He really needed to be aware of where he was...

Because he was, to be sure, guilty of something, and the cops, if they saw him, would stop him – guilty, though, of what particular crime it was he didn't waste his time trying to figure out...but guilty he was – of conspiring, with Luís, anonymously, wordlessly, against the all-seeing powers that ran the country who gave no more thought to murder than stubbing out a cigarette or drinking a beer, who hundreds of times had foreseen the corpses of those they killed found by the *bomberos* in *barrancas* and which one saw pictures of every day in the papers, one of which, once, he, himself had seen, in the flesh, a crude blanket thrown over it, shoeless feet sticking out.

The *indio* woman had covered up her teat. For a few moments he felt powerful – he felt he could slide into the shadows of the dark streets, the innocent trees overhead planted as part of the Capital's token efforts to cultivate a civilized look. He could hear violins playing in his head, a superb, passionate elegy, playing for whom? For him? Always for someone, like in a photo, this one fading, yellowing with age in a few minutes, then that one...

All he was doing was heading for a night class at the university! No need for violins.

Stars fall to earth, imprinting a fabric, stenciled shapes like the pattern on one of Mariaelena's dresses.

As the bus got closer to the university campus there was very little to see – now and then a little trash fire burning, a single incandescent bulb, the chill pale bar of a fluorescent light inside a *mercado* casting a bluish sheen.

Little lights a bit farther back from the road, a *tienda* with its dim little light. A *cantina* thrown into view, red and orange light, the round *Gallo* logos and the Fanta banners, the drinkers seated at card tables or wooden picnic tables.

Nothing familiar had appeared yet and, because he was so tired, and a little dizzy from the cold or flu, he was worried he would miss his stop, and he hoisted himself up now to peer again into the darkness.

Then, seeing a familiar *tienda* where he bought cigarettes one at a time – he reached up and yanked on the bell cord and, after a second or two, the driver shoved the bus into lower gear and braked, suddenly and hard, at the old dark zoolike grounds of San Carlos, with its tall pines and bare earth.

He hoped he wouldn't be late... The class was taught by one of his teacher-advisors.

A step down the stairs and he pushed open the old, battered side door and got off. Throughout the ride and now striding through the darkness of the campus he had been and now was still thinking: at least as bad as the generals is the Church, *que puta!* the Church his mother and grandmother *que puteria!!* still believed in! He heard himself shouting without making a sound – what does the Church do, what does the priest do, what do the nuns do, what does the fucking pope do except make sure people do nothing!

Luís was studying law and had already published something on the Constitution in a Mexican law journal. He was studying the history of land tenure even though he, Luís, knew this was the single most dangerous topic for a future lawyer to focus on. It had become a matter of head-shaking among Luís' friends, meaning: don't ask me anything about it, we have warned him, he knows what he's getting into, just be happy he's still around. And Luís *was* still around, to their disbelief. Each time they saw him, were met by Luís' smile, they almost believed Luís had passed some kind of time limit for something to happen and now he was safe...

Mariaelena inevitably shouted at him to stop being Luís' friend – it was going to get him killed! – and started sobbing: this hysteria was turning him off, he told her, though he knew she had reason for it. Apart from the risks Luís might be taking, even merely because he, himself was a student, he knew people for some reason looked at him with suspicion. He had tried to guess the reason for this but could only think it had to do with the fact that most people around him, except when he was at the university or was out drinking or smoking *mota* with other students, most people suspected him of something because they thought he had something they didn't and couldn't have. University students were suspicious characters!

Justice and the *la mano dura*, was the campaign slogan of one of the retired generals of the army who was now running for president. Supposedly *la mano dura* was going to be used against the *maras*, the gangs that had started in another country bordering the Republic and had spread everywhere, to the most dangerous *barrios* in the worst, poorest precincts of cities throughout the region. But ordinary people, too, were being shot in the streets or were taken, and no one heard of them afterwards. Anyone could be a target! Luís had an old pistol, but he had only fired it once, accidentally, in his mother's house, putting a hole through an old Fritz the Cat clock, scaring Luís' mother so much she fainted.

Adjusting his eyes to the darkness of the strange, *generative* grounds of the national university as if simply by being on campus ideas popped up, abstractly thought and held in mind for pure speculation, ideas he wanted to use in conversation, show off to this fancy *gringo* expert who liked to laugh about how a *Chapín* could put a car engine back together with twigs, string, chewing gum, sweat, spit, blood, a bandaid, a bandanna, and a blow of *mota* smoke to make the spark plugs fire. Well, the *gringo puta* was right.

The campus was dark but he could still see the low buildings – a combination of modern and somewhat decrepit old architecture: big bay windows without glass, dirty roped curtains. Now he walked between the tightly packed, illegally parked cars, the piles of bikes stacked against the walls, manifesting a *focus*, careworn, but an intentionality attributable, visible, in the beat-up cars and piled bikes belonging to students who cared enough about their own lives and were cared about enough to permit them to go to university. The thought came, though, that no one outside of his friends and his mother and sister cared about him. Everybody needs to look after himself or herself – no one else is going to do this... And the individual should not live if he can't look after himself. The world and life say so. But nobody sends congratulations to the survivor. The secret machine of the state, the army, police, politicians, owners of the big monopolies, the *finque os*... the Church, too. None of them cares. Therefore, nothing, no one helps. Or can help. When there's trouble wherever one finds oneself there is never any help.

But, he thought, only a university student would be likely to know the reasons for the problems everywhere so long in the making... *Sensitive*, he was, then – trained to know the true roads of reality – where the facts took one, by necessity, unable to draw any other conclusions, therefore, roads leading to the end somewhere, sometime.

He walked past students squatting down on a curb eating – a little flat round tortilla with salsa, crumbled egg and cheese

sustenance as natural and normal as was the always profusely proliferating plant life that made the country a banana republic. *But we are not monkeys*. Killers, we have: look out, *gringo!*. The *world was wrong*. It was heading in the *wrong way*. For one thing, students shouldn't be so hungry, all the time, taking cigarettes from a friend's pack.

Striding in the interior, its lights at night yellow, making gray shadows, smelling of gasoline and diesel fumes, a sense of great age creasing the cracked and broken linoleum tiles, faces lit-up with excitement or boredom or anxiety, all as artificial as if everyone was on a theater stage because every student knew that having a university degree did not mean deliverance…

Then he was in Mariaelena's arms and she was kissing him. She tasted of jujy-fruit gum, smelled of coconut shampoo, and familiarly, of dust and smoke…

They climbed up the long stairs to the third floor in the yellowish lights inside that only lit up the tiled corridors and lino-leum stairs enough to blur things into shadowy dimness so that everything looked dirty.

A few girls passed heading down, laughing, not looking at them. On the third floor a group of four students was standing by the railing overlooking the open space. Ordinarily there were big razzing greetings, *abrazos*; but tonight, they didn't look at them. They were talking intensely.

One of them, Rafaela, saw him. At first he thought she was smiling but then he saw she was crying. He went over to her, Mariaelena clinging to him but standing behind him, as if she didn't want to ask or know what might be the matter. He asked, "What's wrong? What happened?" They looked at him – all of them young-looking, their faces grim but scared – very scared – and, he realized, almost lighthearted with shock. Rafaela alone was still crying, rubbing the side of her face with the back of her hand again and again.

"What's happened?" he asked again.

One of the young men, looking at him with a strained, astonished expression, said only, "Luís..." and then shook his head a little. And he knew immediately what had happened and why Rafaela was crying and the rest were looking the way they did. He knew particularly because of just last night.

There was nothing, and everything, to say. Marialena was backing away from them and he had to hold onto her. Things blurring around him, he looked down in the dim yellow light of the hallway. He put his hand on Rafaela's arm for a second. Already he understood what all of them were aware of... The circle they made was within another circle, a fast-sliding darkness. Things had moved very swiftly. Two of them murmured, *cuidate!*... and moved off into the dim light toward a classroom. He wanted to ask them, are you still going to class?

Mariaelena was clinging to him, then she was behind him, then she ran off, her arms raised in the air as if to say, I told you so!

He was left alone with Rafaela, who said, "What does God have to do with it?" and started sobbing.

"Come on," he said to Rafaela and, without asking where or why, Rafaela allowed herself to be guided back down the wide stairs...and in his head for some reason was a huge field of stalks of corn, cut down, and the cut down corn was like the students, so many of whom, like others in the country, were cut down to ugly stubble.

They came out from the building into the sodium light with its orange illumination encroaching only so far. In the shadows, outside of its reach, they became invisible. The almost black grayness danced, skipped, from a little wind toward the top of a great highlands pine.

Shapes of structures around them – buildings, a sculpture, its metal strips shaped like a running bull – evidenced some kind of effort made in the past to encourage people, to build things up, make things better, pretend there was no ugliness, no danger... Though, now, in the darkness, which was contrasted with the blinding headlights of cars coming and going, it was almost impossible to see, they knew their way across the bare grounds, to the curb and out into the bay of the broken, rutted street.

Waiting for the beater cars, wheezing, going round and round, the drivers looking for a place to park, he led her to the other side of the street. With her arms crossed as if holding in her stomach, she was reluctant, but the reluctance was a kind of skillful, or stylish, extravagance in feeling, and showing, grief and panic. *I am giving up,* she seemed to be saying silently. He maneuvered through the cars to the other side of the loop where they went into one of the little restaurants the group often liked to go to.

The fear is a lividity. But one gets used to it. It is no more than the air you breathe, the pulse of the heart. The fear is the cord of an exposed intestine. The cells may live for a while in organs ripped from a body.

Where was Luís supposed to be when it happened? Tecun Uman, she said.

He remembered an old woman in some village he had been in once – with other students studying the architecture of the old colonial churches – who sighed and said, God has forgotten us...

Normally, such thoughts he was able to keep deep down inside. But now... He took her back to the little concrete square room she shared with two other students, hugged her, told her he would come back tomorrow to check on her... She closed the door and he was walking out in the streets once again, looking instantly for a white van waiting...

His mind drifted further, filling up helplessly, though he didn't feel the need to react with alarm, no, that would not be right, competing though were these thoughts with noises from the streets, and the enormous arresting billboard overhead filling up the night sky with half-malfunctioning brilliant light buzzing, showing happy *Castellanas* with all signs of great good health, lifting a glass of the advertised beer with others, clinking their glasses together, smiles and laughter after work, now time for fun and relaxation with friends and this particular brand of beer...

Competing with the black thing that had happened – Rafaela, Luís' girlfriend, and Luís who had been taken even though they had warned him and he had scoffed, laughed it off, he, a serious-minded hard-working man. And, as the thoughts were competing to be thought, the first thing was that they couldn't even talk about these things! The white van, for example, that so often was spotted near where the disappeared was last seen. They had the strength to silence entire villages. Powerful men who ran things who moved in circles absolutely impenetrable to sight or accountability or specific understanding – except when their children were photographed for the society insert of the newspapers, smiling earnestly or rhapsodically, obnoxiously – only the basic understanding that these men held onto their wealth and their possessions, their trophy *finca* , their estates, their monopoly enterprises, their coffee farms, palm oil groves, sugar plantations, and that these men pulled strings that fed down into the special forces, the *kaibiles*, into the police, into the state and city and town and village politicians as they did in the *Congreso* and with the judges, even the judges of the Supreme Court, as they did, as well, in some yet more obscure way, with the newer powers in the country, the drug traffickers from Mexico and Colombia and Panama and elsewhere, although when the connections reached the drug traffickers, the lords of the cartels, you didn't really know so clearly any longer who was the string puller and who the puppet.

All of this they knew but never really spoke about in the way one knew but never spoke about one's own death. To do so was to jinx things.

The country was a shifting continent, with great portions, sides of volcano chains given over to growing poppies and marijuana, sugar farms where drugs were stored during transit... hot coastal slum cities or eastern slum ports or great tracts of rain forest where the killings took place. They knew all this and it was part of their waking consciousness, part of their day and their night and it lived among them, intruded into conversations and jokes, made backslaps into lies. There was only relief like a grayness that let them deny there was black certainty – a gray of possibility that it wasn't your turn yet, that nothing was certain, even if many things were likely.

Like petrol burned up. Luís. A fallen star or flower. Fallen to the pavements of the orange afternoons when the winds had sifted and rattled the palms, and the rains had finished and, once again, there was *nothing* in the gray rosy air but the acrid stink of diesel.

He rolled away from her naked body. She had come back to his little place and they'd had sex, which he knew she wanted, asking him for it, asking, *stay with me?* as a kind of consolation or reassurance. He might or might not tell Mariaelena about it.

Afterwards, they stood outside the metal door to the bare-dirt floored compound where he lived. It was raining. The rain was extreme, monotonous, enormous, encompassing, everywhere. The wind accompanying it was flinging the warm drops like mild whips everywhere, the drops seeking a body on which to heal with their wetness... Darkness, in comforting caches, womblike, or nets, on the wet, cracked asphalt, the asphalt with repaired sections of concrete jutting up that occasioned a big bump for the vehicles passing on the city road.

In memory, Luís. Medium height, with curly black hair, a thin, rather severe mouth, kindly raisin-black eyes, and thin arms covered with curly black hair. Luís leaning back, smiling, showing his little potbelly, saying something – what was it? – *we should give serious consideration to*…such and such. Whatever it was. Luís peeling his banana, taking a small bite. He was generally – almost always – serious and correct, and had a somewhat didactic manner with the rest of them in part because he was a little older and was further along in his education than they were, almost a lawyer, lacking only the final examinations to receive his *licenciatura* and already with a part-time job at a realtor's advisory service that catered, as far as he, Luís, could tell, mainly to *gringos* wanting to buy land on the lake. He, himself was standoffish with *gringos*, not to be cruel or dismissive on purpose but because he simply didn't see any overlap of his life with theirs. For a while some of the other students wondered if he was gay, a *hueco*, until his girlfriend Mónica made it very clear to them that he was not, he was straight and she got everything she wanted and needed from her man.

A few nights later Rafaela moved her head down from his chin to his chest. She sniffed, reminding him she was still upset enough to cry. He reached around to put the side of his hand under her chin, to tilt her face to him, but she shook her head and remained clinging to him, face pressed against his chest. She didn't ask about Luís because there was no point. They would almost certainly never know what had happened, who specifically had taken him, though they did know without a doubt what had happened to him by now.

To be killed was something he thought about often, but he knew his friends had the same general thoughts – so the regularities of the *campo*, of rain, sun, rain again, making the black volcanic soil sodden, clumping beside where it pooled, all of these regularities went on on top of getting killed. Torn fragments of clothing, a shirt, a shoe. A naked body curled up, foetus-like. But if this image was part of the necessary concatenation of images associated with being taken: *it may be*, he thought, because the imagination did not permit any image of the mangled body, but only the body reconstructed and whole, that he pictured Luís curled up as if in the womb, awaiting rebirth...

The rain broke open the lowering sky every day, like clockwork almost exactly in the mid afternoon – bringing overwhelming rhythmic sheets of wetness, cooling, quenching everything, as beautiful as if the city was in the jungle. It reminded him and everyone, probably, he thought, that they lived in the Republic, *this place*: the jungled heart of the so easily dismissed and overlooked Central America. Even he, though so used to the rain, could still attribute a magnificence to it, a reminder, so rarely, when the monsoons came, of natural things untouched by *invidia*, by corruption, by murder...

He had a dream after that, vivid with the green of corn and avocado flesh, the red of papaya, the green and red of mango, the silver of rain, the red-brown or black of mud. In the dream violins were playing, the strains floating sweetly through the air. And in the dream the rain was saying: *I am good. I feed the crops. I wash the piss from the pavements, the blood from the streets. I go with the people wherever they go.* And in the dream he saw people walking, hurriedly, huddling together under umbrellas or black plastic bags held, tent-like, over their heads. Grandmothers with mothers were pulling little children by the hand. Skinny store clerks, lacking head cover and completely soaked, were just walking as if nothing mattered. Workmen, grinning at the ferocity of the downpour, were dodging into doorways... Crowds, hordes and hordes of people, were breaking apart into this or that *colonia* in this or that *barrio*, like leaves falling from one branch of a tree and then from the next. And in the dream the desolation grew as the streets, increasingly broken and caving in as the water pooled and overflowed potholes and gutters, led into more isolated neighborhoods, cut off because the mounting primitiveness of the back parts of the city meant some kind of betrayal fostered onto the crowds who, now, had turned into *maras*, street gangsters, shaven-headed teenagers with tattoos showing through ripped tee-shirts... *I am hope*, said the rain. *I am renewal. I am new life, life reborn, sprouting from the mud, raised from the earth. With my surcease, and cease, comes a new day, that day when when the sky opens to brightness and you will see again your loved ones, your lost.* And in the dream he saw those faces that appeared in photos hanging on the cracked plaster of every wall, daughters in school uniform, *abuelitas* with mantillas, sons in black suits at church or *colegio*, all sources of such pride that when they disappeared it seemed there would be no more tomorrows – ever again… *Just as I fell on Jesus when he was on the Cross, through the nights until, on the third day, He rose again…* And in the dream he saw his own Jesus as He hung from a nail, behind cracked glass, on the smeared, cracked walls, with lightning behind him, on Golgotha. And he felt, then, that he was awake, though he knew he was not, and, as his head pounded with pain, he heard his own voice saying, *Ah Luís! – estupido! Ah, Luís!*

THE BLIND IMPOSTOR

It was marvelous. In a frenzy to get it down I concentrated on the details, but also the thick *sense* of it, so soon after it was over and I was back in the old colonial town. I had to record it, as much as I could remember before it disappeared, because I would have no time tomorrow – given to the hike up the volcano the boy and I would make.

I was, now, back at my wobbly card table, spiral notebooks in front of me. The boy was playing out in the mint-bright sunny air – rarified at five thousand feet – in the weedy courtyard of the house I had rented. The house was behind several-meter high stone walls, crumbling and with whitewashed plaster, painted and repainted, cratered with disrepair. The wind-gusty little place, stuck between other propped-up, centuries-old buildings, consisted of little more than a high-walled open space with two doorless rooms off to the side. At the back end was a tiny kitchen with a propane stove. This, then, was the temporary refuge to which I had brought my son, my private recourse where I lived while writing up my doctoral research.

The dry light outside the walls showed every detail – slow, somnolently waving bougainvillea loading the buoyant air with color, backdrop to the slow pace of the Indian women in *traje* colored as vividly in scarlet, purple, crimson, and orange, the women's movements somehow a chaste embedding of the slow imagined rhythms of country life – both charmed as "nature" and tinctured with the Real: poverty of the most extreme kind but which the tourist town hid. Like entering a maze, but ordered, like a topiary, this was mixed with the stinging of the different – the anthropological Other. It arrived to mind – the inaccessible, as if I could access it, could know, through some signage of wordless translation, a false nostalgia for a life *gringos* in fact could know only from the outside – the lie of the surface told by money: smiling tourist faces and which, in point of fact, hid the darkness of centuries turned upside down – or inside out? – by atrocities one could not talk about also seemingly *accommodated* accordingly in the mocking slow pace and smiles of the victimage.

I found I had written, with questions for myself inserted:

...The *xamanes*, like the *pastores evangelicos*, operate for profit, and the clients of the former, like the members of the *pastores'* flocks, say little, words insultingly indelicate. Their fervency makes the supplicant easy prey for the whispered solicitations, the pious insinuations, for donations. If the ceremonies are held outdoors, the god sits in the center of a courtyard carefully swept clean beforehand of garbage and litter. A big-brimmed cowboy hat is placed on his head – (*black for the bad guy?*) – and a blanket is stretched across his lap and legs. The *xaman* then measures out lines of sugar, salt, and maize kernels, and stacks up little bricks of sweet-smelling *pom* incense, adding many white candles at the end of the lines, ritual emphasis for the four directions.

The customary gift for the black wood effigy is a bottle of Johnny Walker Red or Botrán rum, or, less well-received, cheaper aguardiente, which the god "drinks," the *xaman* tilting back the statue seated on his throne-like wood great-chair and lifting the bottle to the carved red-painted wooden lips – carefully then wiping off the dribbled liquor. A cigarette is stuck in the effigy's mouth and lit, the fag, of course, burning down as if the god is inhaling. If they're aware that cigarettes burn untended, they don't care. *(Ah, but* no importa – *it's the belief that animates!)*

I glanced outside. My son was out of sight, but I could hear him smacking his machete on a big wood stump in the courtyard – the machete two-thirds as long as he was. (I had made sure the blade was dull; the continuing thrill was that he was here, as if I needed to be reminded...)

...In the middle of all this show the gullible client, particular focus of the *xaman*'s ministrations, is placed in front of the effigy; other subordinates, audients and spectators, sit on little stilted chairs or on the ground facing and within the charged space around the god. If further efforts are required, or the magic needs to be concentrated, or a highly specific wish is brought, the piacular rituals may be conducted in private, in front of a glass-framed San Pasqualito, this latter deity manifesting in the form of the upper half of an actual skeleton (*whose, I wonder?*) – skull, clavicle, some ribs, arms and hands, skeletal fingers beringed and a paste-jeweled pectoral hung around neck bone. Pasqualito, in general, represents "white magic," Maximón, at best, mixed black and white but, more often, black. More powerful than the "good" skeletal god, Maximón represents forces controlled only by his unpredictable personality, and his particular power, then, is far greater than Pasqualito's because there is no shared power. Nor is there a visible *quid pro quo* – the liquor is gift without a promise. The god's whim decides the issue. There is nothing one can do to coerce or do the trick, as it were, and one must conclude that the *xaman* is calling upon the very greatest powers of persuasion with so much at stake, or possible, with Maximón's intervention. The efforts then might seem almost like that of a lawyer arguing a client's case, conversing with the deity in a respectful give-and-take; for his part, the mascared eyes are wide open, the frozen carved red lips smile, the stiff body is tilted back regally –

As I wrote I thought of what had brought him to me. As with any story one tells oneself, this story begins in the middle. Things have already happened, I reminded myself, and I could not change the past. *Accentuate the positive, appreciate what you have!* I said to myself then. I found myself, also, the breezes tapping at me, cupped within a jubilation. Searching for the right words to describe the ceremony I had just witnessed seemed nonsense, trying this phrase out or that one, as if the careful precision mattered, when what mattered was I was divorced and the little boy so miraculously was here with me now – and if I had any particular claim to being a "good man" it was that I loved my little son, truly.

Ghosts follow me. The question since the divorce: *was* I a good man? In most ways I was a walking wounded, a typical middle-class white fellow suffering from typical pains and complaints, divorce included, preoccupied uselessly with wondering if he *was* a good man – although, if my ex-wife could be believed, I was criminal, not just selfish and hypocritical... If I really was interested in being a good father, how could I expose him to the risks down here? But the recriminations only came after the divorce.

Or I chase the ghosts... I had flown half around the world to see my eight-year old son, the flight in my mind consuming several dusks. The world beneath my feet by thirty seven thousand feet I was still quite deranged by the breakup. In an odd moment because I was flying closer to *her* I found myself thinking I was heading "home," simply because Auckland was where she was, while the reality was, all of that was dead. His mother, my ex-wife, with whom he now lived, I considered now, bitterly but with an ache, to be a bitch, of course, who I still loved but who had caused me such trouble – heartsickness over the failure of the marriage, guilt about the boy. But still, beneath my hatred – still! – I loved and missed her: a five-foot-two, career-addicted blonde New Zealander with a musical voice, a briskness and, somehow, an inchoate poignancy, behind which was a wonderful black sense of humor. For the first three years of the marriage we never slept apart, and the intimacy was so skin-to-skin, breath-to-breath close that when, infuriated and cold, she suddenly decided on divorce, I was both desperate and stunned, numb with shock and disbelief.

My thoughts cycled back, as they often did, to the botched marriage. Effectively it was over after a couple of years, after the boy was born – I had turned out to be quite less than perfect, ranting and raving, ever-dissatisfied. Because she never explained it – too proud to ever point-blank ask – still in pain and uneasiness by the time of my son's visit I had to try, had tried, to guess why she did divorce me. But she never explained; one of her favorite sayings was, if you can't find something good to say about someone, say nothing – but what then had changed so sharply in her feelings about me? For lack of any explanation to fill in the huge hole she had left, I had only ever been able to conclude it had to do with both my *ambition* to find things out – to be able to explain to myself the vast mirror of reality – and to become someone I was not, or was not, yet, and which seemed to require, in my case, going more and more to exotic and difficult places...reasons that set me searching into scholarship and brought me to this Third World place, and then had made me despise being a *gringo*. Admittedly, I was tortured perhaps a bit more – only a bit – than the customary *gringo* with just enough idiosyncrasies, smarts and talent to be convinced I had to be extraordinary. Tortured by the worm of dissatisfaction – how quite sickly agonizing – a burning but hazy ambition led to "life mistakes" culminating in that decision so poisonous to marriages within our stratum, to change careers, in this case to pursue expertise in a quite exotic discipline, although at the time I had no idea I would live for so long in such a place as this – nor anticipate such a circumstance in which my child and I were embarked on a volcano climb! Foremost, as usual, was pity, or sorrow, for my ex-wife, who had, in her own way, trusted me, given herself wholly, yet whom I had so bitterly disappointed, so badly, indeed, that she could never tell me why, ultimately, she ended the marriage to return to New Zealand – as if, if not for the boy, the marriage had never happened.

For myself, I felt I was a lightweight, *and* guilty of the particular sin of inflation of my own importance. In confirmation of this were the beautiful surroundings, making any complaints I had precious self-indulgence, the busman's holiday political commentary I was now and then trying to write just what I called WASP-in-the-bottle rants. What I should have been doing was devoting my energies only to the scholarly task at hand, writing the dissertation

my own personal peak to climb...

Undoubtedly conveniently, I. did find myself angry at my ex-wife also for being so ignorant, like all the rest in *gringo*-land. But could I honestly blame her for not knowing about all this, these awesomely deeper realities? – how the citizens of the Republic, for example, had suffered and were suffering from the most monstrous, ugly, and tragic of histories. *They* had a solidity, a universally justifiable *raison d'être* – managing their daily survival, with their own fevered, spent *bricolage* in a world which they had done and did now nothing to create but, nevertheless, had to suffer and struggle within in order to survive in the meanest fashion.

I was a gaudy dragonfly by comparison.

At least he's here with me now, I told myself, again, remembering how she and I, when I had returned home for a visit, missing the child so terribly, and then, having to return to continue my work, together we had placed the boy in the impossible position of choosing whether to stay with his mother or accompany his father half around the world again, back down to this extreme and frightening place... Well, the child had quickly and freely picked the latter, so there was no excuse for the terrible scene she made the next day when

I and the boy were driving off in the taxi for the Auckland airport, and, uncharacteristically, she had come completely undone and had started walking, then running, beside the cab, sobbing hysterically, tears all over her stunned, strained face, usually so grimly controlled. Anguished for how this must have been affecting him, I glanced at the boy but saw his face was completely serene and I felt, ashamedly, a satisfaction at the knife his decision had turned in her heart...this woman I had known so well but who had become such a stranger.

Cumulatively then I felt a bit dark as a person – somehow "third person." But maybe there was light there, too, inside...as if I were to angle my body and different scales of light and dark could be registered – occluded at one angle but, like a marble, clearer at another.

Often it felt simply that I was merely side-tracked by the butterfly-vivid life all around, with fresh attempts to catch more than a mere glimpse, to see through the skin of things. As always, a customary blindness, the inability of that so very stupid animal, the *gringo*, to find some foundation incorporated in the grist, the *matter*...that every life ends in disaster.

It wasn't that I was necessarily bored by the minutiae of scholarship in which I was supposed to be immersing myself, but I was afraid that the necessary intensity, the scholarly fever, might be flagging bit by bit, the longer I remained in the cushioned amenities of the town. I needed to get serious: which was even harder because of what was at hand: two facts – my son, for whom I was responsible, and then that otherness, the sense of which was deepening into much more than I could ever hope to figure out

because there *was* just too much, it *was* too dense with meaning for me ever to scratch the surface. Again, and too often, I felt like an impostor, or a blind man, or both, who was supposed to be the expert, in front of the elephant! Fundamentally the question was: What the hell was I doing, presuming to understand any of this?

As always the palliatives of my whereabouts – what had to be "good" in some way for my son – the colonial town with its several centuries-old cobble streets and whitewashed buildings, made my doubts seem self-indulgent. It was now getting dark, and the rose-colored air was peppery with the sweet scent of firewood; I could smell, also, the warm odor of corn tortillas baking on the griddles inside the locals' houses. Soon the twilight would turn to a quite magical dark, cool and velvety, when, before I brought my son to stay, I was in the habit of strolling, solitary, through the streets – an experience which always seemed accompanied by imaginary cello music – as if I were in the middle of a dream, sleep-walking in the silence, light and color suddenly opening from one of the makeshift restaurants or crude cafés catering to the foreigners increasingly arriving in the town, drawn by adventure and novelty, these clutched tightly to their senses of self as if they were the recipients of a highly exclusive prize. At night, apart from the crowds of students and expatriates mingling with the locals, my solitude was steeped in a hole full of stillness – the town that had somehow made its way into an agreeable, sighingly tranquil tourist destination, the distillation of an undisturbed past like a blemish in the chaos of the world-forgotten Republic outside. In this venerable old place, I was able to do my research a few minutes' walk from the ethnohistory library – a walk past a four-hundred year old earthquake-tumbled church. The great tent-flapping fly-buzzing *indio* market was down the street. The sun each day shone right overhead like a brilliant bulb. Otherwise hot, the altitude cooled the swells of breeze in the thin air, the sun as solvent as gold, itself – like opening the door out of a photographic darkroom sometimes such was the shadow cutting through drowsy shaded squares and lanes to come out to the central *parque*.

But *what* research! Again, how pathetic in the face of Mystery – mysteries of the resolutely hidden, the completely inaccessible... But I read and studied and wrote against the backdrop of the great volcano looming to the south where it filled a full third of the sky over the postcard-pretty streets, the thick walls of lodges, the Italianate villas covered with brilliant bougainvillea, scarlet, orange, pink or purple. Sometimes, the lacy clouds hid the summit like the skimpiest, most diaphanous lingerie. The "water volcano," it was called, because an eruption sent not lava but a giant mud-slide down one side of the volcano that had wiped out the entire seventeenth-century colony of Spaniards.

The town, mindful of the recreations it provided its own, offered charmed walks in the sun for the tourist as well as lures for students from Europe and America, ostensibly to study Spanish. Many language schools had sprung up even before the signing of a peace treaty some years before that had ended the so-called civil war, and the first "alternative life-style" arrivals decided to stay; more and more came every year. The peace treaty signed between the army and the rebels was, like all the facts of history here, somehow both unreal and dramatic – it had put a coda on the otherwise overwhelming event of genocide: hundreds of thousands of *indígenas*, earth-weathered silent figures now, had been killed in the little villages in the highlands, unreachable for tourists but not for the death squads. In the back of one's mind always were imagined machetes hacking necks or the heads of infants dashed against a piss-smelling wall – great brutality and malevolence such that the serene sun and the murmur of *indígena* vendors – the little intaken gasp of daily greetings, the glottal clicks – was a fabrication, a weaving around the upturned throat of helpless innocence, trying to busy itself with necessity....

While ever-present *was* a sense of threat, in the town the violence was latent only. Nights seemed reserved for lovers' trysts, a fact, for me, poignant if not painful. Divorced and very lonely, I would walk past, so often, it seemed, *novia con novio* from the town, or young American or European women here studying Spanish: seemingly willing and available. But nothing gelled in my own little expatriate group of friends. I guessed this was because I was a bit older, and there must have been something betraying that I was here not for play but for work – intellectual work – and, therefore, I assumed they assumed, I was one of those obnoxious "experts" who would inevitably condescend... In the twilight, strings of firecrackers were going off beyond my walls, the ever-ephemeral frolic of children playing in the freedom they had at the end of the day, stark contrast with the cloistered houses and earthquake-toppled churches asleep in their deep past, the little kids ricocheting around like fireflies. They were the more visible *Antigüeños*, creating bubbles of chaos, slyly appearing then disappearing, graduating from the strings of newspaper-rolled *cohetes* to handheld rockets, little pockets of zigzagging energy, unleashed until almost dark when the commands from grandmothers recalled them inside barracks-like bungalows behind crude little yards and smoking piles of garbage in the bay of the street; these were higher up toward the back-end of town where the *gringos* did not venture unless, seeking quieter hidden charms, they got lost, disoriented by the town layout even though it was set on a grid, wandering away from the center where the language schools, restaurants, and money-changing banks were. One could easily pick out the recently arrived, looking both cowed and proud of their adventure in such a tamed setting! – with mass graves not far away; I had taken a walk with the little boy a few days previously along the sidewalk by the fountained *parque* when, passing a solitary guard in front of the old metal doors to the courtyard of the town jail, the man had motioned and, opening his palm, revealed some bullets... so bizarre it made sense only to me later: the fellow was absolutely desperate and had nothing else to offer to sell! I certainly had no gun (though in moments of crazy daydream I had contemplated getting one). With a startled *no, gracias*, I took the boy's hand and was walking away when the skinny little fellow caught up and, making himself as circumspect as possible, asked if I could get him a job in *los estados*: so much for the town's hidden charms and the protectors of the social order! Protectors of the flocks of *gringos*, anyway, who thought themselves so clever and adventurous to have found such a charmed, such an exotic, place.

I read, read more, made more notes. Stopping for a moment, concerned I was neglectful, I leaned a little forward in my chair and then half-got up to see the little boy's Australian wide-brimmed fedora, low over his face, his expression, as much as I could catch of it, intent industriously on his thwacking. I put aside and anchored the papers, fluttering in the breeze, with a paper-weight – a bamboo cup the *xaman* had given me full of an unexplained cold and bitter liquid I drank during a later ritual in which I was the supplicant but, for some reason, cannot recall in any clear detail; nor could I say why I kept it. If my son had asked me about it or any particular object or detail in my life – he didn't I would have been stuck for explanations. I had notes about it somewhere...

The boy's life wasn't filled with much, but he seemed not to mind, didn't seem bored. For a couple of weeks I'd scouted out alternate schooling – there were enough expatriates in the town for an English language school. But on a visit, its cloying bohemian slovenliness did not impress and the boy was simply not interested, anyway. So I arranged for a tutor to come every day to teach him Spanish, and, as much as my time and energy would allow, I planned to take the child around on trips, the idea being, obviously, to expose him to different types of people and their ways, believing that some of this would be of long-term benefit, history, geography, "social studies," whatever, in some generalized process of osmosis.

First on the list, unequivocally, was the volcano. Even if I was dismissive of other *gringos* thinking they were intrepid adventurers, the town *was* set at the feet of the immense perfect cone just to the south, so there was a ready-made adventure for the two of us, father and son.

Thinking of all this and for other reasons I was consoled that, that evening, we would pack our knapsacks for the climb the next day – an adventure so big, in fact, I wasn't sure we could manage it. The climb up the volcano was promised payback for his waiting for me all the time and reassurance that things would be different.

The day before had been "horrible," the boy had said, vehemently, voice quavering in admonitory admission, out on a walk with his dad, needing to go number two, with the only place for his business some bushes, and, unfortunately, the bushes were stinging *chichicaste*, the leaves with which, on his father's stupid urging, he had wiped himself. So I held the little boy's hand all the way back to the ramshackle house, tears squeezing down the little oval face, mouth trembling with resentful bewilderment. In my mind I could hear his mother screaming at me: *what kind of father are you! I should NEVER have agreed to let him go with you!* And there had been another incident two weeks before. After many inquiries to see if I could buy whole cow's milk safe to drink to make sure of proper nutrition for him, I had found a vendor near the big crowded market – a confident, quick-talking, reassuring young guy who declared his milk was absolutely safe, *pasteurizada*, perfectly fine for little *gringo* stomachs! Duplicitously, it came in a carton that looked almost, but not quite, like a carton of milk I might buy anywhere. And so, feeling very pleased with myself and glad I was meeting my parental responsibility, I, the erstwhile dad, bought a half-gallon and, that morning, poured a generous amount of the milk into his cornflakes. A short while later we caught the chicken bus to the Capital – to visit a colleague doing his research in the bumpy squalor of a rundown "middle class" *barrio* near the airport and while we were riding the bus, bouncing over the potholes heading into the outskirts of the great crazed city, the boy leaned over as if to pick up something he had dropped, got up suddenly out of the lurching seat, and threw up every single half-digested bit of cereal, and every drop of the goddamned milk. The spout erupted from his mouth and the mess landed next to the black draped skirts of two nuns, who glared angrily and disgustedly at my son and snatched back their robes to avoid the lacings of saliva and puke – their response managing to incense me totally. The only way I could make the situation better, later, at my colleague's run-down box of a house, after spooning some mild tea into the boy to settle his stomach, was to make profane jokes about the nuns' un-Christian reaction to a child's distress – to which the boy, still shaky and face tear-streaked, laughed, thank god – loud and defiant.

But the misfortune of the stinging nettle was yesterday – the bus incident a few weeks before that – and each had been resolved or weathered, successfully: no lasting harm. Thinking then that these were tiny crises resolved in the bigger perspective, I got up next morning in the chilly dark, well before dawn – for this, the big adventure, I had calculated the climb would take six hours to reach the top and six to get back down. Tapping gently on his shoulder, I saw in the darkness how, vulnerable and toy-soldierly, the boy tugged on his hiking boots and pushed into his little green jacket – the miniature movements somehow charged with his own drama, as if with destiny – and struggled to attach the cumbersome machete to his belt.

Still half-asleep, the lurching bus particularly violent, I helped him down the steps after the short ride to the little village nestling on the first slopes. The darkness was just lightening to pre-dawn gray visibility. The lacings of sun, rising behind us, fool's gold-colored, revealed to the west and in front of us more and more of the green, feathery-leather texture of the massive volcano, a little broader for the first third of its ascent, steepening thereafter, and already the top hidden behind a demure cloud – as if the volcano had decided at this hour on modesty.

The sun's rays, palest brass, flickering and weak, glanced off our heads as we walked in and out of little canyoned lanes, dipping level now and then back into dim dawn, passing corrals, a pig in one, in another a rooster pecking at the ground, the corrals turning into more slat-board walls of houses. I saw then the white-washed church wall with a graffito that read, *Mano Blanca*, next to a stenciled white hand in outline, and I was suddenly apprehensive, for this was the name and insignia of the most notorious of the death squads, which were supposed to have stopped their killings with the signing of the peace treaty a few years before. But in the dusky air now topped with sun, clouds of vapor from dew arose around us, and I was full once again with attention to the boy and to the smell of fresh earth and the sourness of pigs, and the sense of things as so clean and wild, the rusticity all around us so unpremeditated and innocent, the death squad logo, as jarring as it was, seemed little more than daubed paint.

The steep little lanes seemed interminable but, in surety of the size of the adventure, we began climbing at a more steeply pitched angle, negotiating the massive broad-angling, green-swathed heights. Little lines or points higher up from lighter-colored trees shone – some reflection of something. Above these shoulders of the volcano, clouds still completely obscured the top. Then we were hiking up a cobble-rutted, soft-loamy path laced with thick erupting tree roots that led to a kind of narrow road, though not navigable by a vehicle, the deep ruts prohibiting passage by anything but foot.

Great trees with long dangling parasitical vines gave through increasingly as we climbed to views of vintage countryside long and far away, and it felt we were more and more remote from everything. The boy was doing well, though I could see already he was getting tired – prancing ahead, talking to himself, which he often did, making up imaginary fights, swinging his machete. I was struck by how little affected he seemed by such a fantastical adventure for an eight-year old – and was surprised, as always, by his trust in me, as if he felt he was home no matter where he was, as long as I was there with him..

Idly, I found myself thinking of places I had wound up in for no sensible reason. Some months ago, with every mild and generalized intention to explore the country better, I found myself heading north and west for hours, northwest where the highest mountains and the most Indians still lived – on a potholed but manageable narrow gray macadam – but then I was halted, brought to a complete and incomprehensible stop, by a pile of rock and dirt blocking the mountain road: the road just stopped. On one side of the pile, mountain jutted, banana trees and tall volador – that lonely tree famed for the suicidal high-wire acts unwinding in a swan dive to near death like the unspinning of a shroud – sticking out at odd angles heading up, on the other, no more than a few feet away, the cliff falling off down a quarter- or half-mile to fields cultivated with maize or some other crop.

I had set out to visit a highlands town, high up in the western mountains, renowned for its syncretistic Indian ways – worshipping Jesus as new corn. I had to turn around and, as it was getting late, made it back down a bit to the department capital, just as inscrutable as it, too, was crazed, where I bought a beer in an impossibly primitive restaurant with plastic tables and worked my way through the ink-bled regional newspaper. The weekend drive, precipitated by what, later, I would have to admit was nothing more than "sight-seeing," as if such an innocent adventure here was possible, resulted in drinking my beer while making my way through an article describing the finding, in the Capital, in a forgotten warehouse somewhere, of a trove of files of the Disappeared, the faceless lost of the civil war.

As I sat there in the sunlight, flicking away flies, these events had seemed very far away, and the article concluded on an uncertain note about what might happen next: one assumed there would be repercussions, journalists kidnapped, witnesses murdered, denials by authorities. But the discovery seemed like a familiar shadow and inconsequential, to me, at least, despite its confirmation of what still was but a garbled fable of horrors peculiar to the Republic; the good and the bad alternated like in a *patolli* game or on a checkerboard:

iniquities of darkness, then squares of light, the consciousness or memory of which instantly burned off in the raging hot disorder of the streets...sort of the things I was not supposed to see, for the same reason one is not supposed to wonder if there can be redemption without illusion.

This was when, in another curious episode if asked about I could not possibly explain, tired and looking for a place for the night, I had stopped at sundown in one of those impossible-to-foresee *nowheres,* capacious for their presuming to exist in the real universe, that present themselves, often on the outskirts of some regional city. The only option, appearing at an intersection not locatable on any map, was a series of pillbox rooms, advertised as a "motel" – the sign on sticks – as if they were built and offered, ludicrously, as some kind of resort. The proprietress – owner? manager? – a curiously emphatic but obstinately vague woman, led me down to an appalling subterranean hole. For some reason, she seemed to think the deal made for the room even though, feeling waylaid, when I looked inside the door of the "unit" she was offering, I saw, in darkness without electricity, painted all in the darkest green or black, nothing but a mat on the floor. In a daze I found myself following the wave of the woman's hand into her pillbox home to pay for the room. It was only when I "came to," as if realizing I had left my bag in the rental car that, while amazed by the prospect of actually putting myself to sleep in such a place, what caught my attention otherwise was, in a makeshift unkempt cage on a partly tree-shaded roof, sprawled by slop-bucket and rinds of rotting fruit, a captive ocelot, superb, very end of long, thick beautiful, ringed and spotted tail twitching, eyeing me lazily, aware of its own superiority. Instead of replying to the woman about whether the room was acceptable! I found myself instead thinking that this beautiful creature, insufficiently camouflaged for being *too* beautiful, undoubtedly had not long to live.

The ocelot I remembered in odd moments continually for years, long after it had to have died, probably not too long after it had taken note of me and then looked away, as if magnificently bored, indifferently ready, or not, to join the ghosts that would revisit me later.

Paying the animal no attention until she saw my startled interest in it, the woman looked more sharply at me, sensing a vulnerability. And then she was walking sturdily up to me, exclaiming and gesticulating excitedly, as if – I could only guess – I had promised her that I would rent her little room of certain insanity out there in nowhere, that I had somehow misled her!... as if, I could only guess, she had turned down another person's offer on my promise to take it – which was as weird as the guard in the *parque* offering to sell me his three bullets... I stopped, shook my head, and turned back to go to the car. As I drove away, bouncing in the potholes, the woman's face, as I looked back, was full of some final judgment – full of anger, disgust, or disappointment. The ocelot, I saw, was watching when she started yelling, then turned away again as if it knew I could not save it and there never could have been any other outcome from this meeting at a time of terrible misfortune.

I managed to stuff this bewildering, ugly craziness away somewhere in my mind, and from the chill of this memory I was so glad again my son was with me. Thank god, he had no idea what ghosts I had been remembering! It was, however, one of the first of other inexplicable encounters and errant events that seemed like – and I could characterize them as such – punctures in my expectations of a seamless reality.

And, normal for such a great adventure, then, periodically we were hiking up in the broad, open sun.

With relief we found ourselves, briefly, on a more level stretch, by a whitewashed little shack, apparently unused, the shade by the shack a bit of relief, and we stopped and shared the water bottle. As we started up two figures emerged, walking across a steep maize field pitched immediately higher above the path.

The two were a thick-trunked, powerful little *indio*, the other, undoubtedly, *his* son, both bent nearly double with enormous bundles strapped to their backs – scavenged firewood, probably poached – and from his exertions the man was sweating and breathing hard, but he stopped a few feet from us and smiled an open-mouthed wide broken-toothed greeting as he looked at the two *gringos*, big and little. Even as my immediate thought was that the man was trying to reassure us he meant no harm, as if he might have, the encounter provoked a pleasant amazement: I was aware how we, the big *gringo* and the little one, came from and returned to a world of privilege as remote from the other two as was the moon. I looked at my son and then offered the man the water bottle; short, even shorter when he was stooped over double with the enormous bundle, he tipped the wood off his back to accept the flask, then returned it after slow careful wiping. I caught the strong sour smell of corn all over him. I, myself, was conscious of a singular fact, face to face with these two, the only bond was that we were all the same human animal – nothing else. The little man may have been thinking the same thing. Showing gap teeth with a completely unaffected, guileless smile, everything about him be-spoke the simplest barefoot *campesino*, the human as ape, indeed, trussed up like a pack animal, a *traje*-vivid sweat band tied around his forehead as tumpline. The man's son, who had hefted off his back an only slightly smaller bundle of wood, looked down at the ground – as the *campesino*'s offspring, subordinate to a subordinate? My son, little child of the West, by comparison was impatient, accustomed by now, of course, to his father's insistence on treating these *indios* in such a way as if to reverse the subordination history had yoked them to, for were we not all children of the Sun? The boy took as natural what his father did as he listened a bit to the few exchanged words, then lost interest. Nonchalantly showing off his machete prowess, he set to slashing at a flower stalk, then squatted down with his Swiss Army knife and began throwing it at a little piece of wood.

In a high, drawn out, coddling voice, the *indígena* nodded at the little boy and, taking note of the machete, with an egalitarian smile of appreciation and, to compliment the father – the little boy is a little *man* already! – crooned "*Campesiiiino... campesiiiino...*" because the machete was the ubiquitous and standard tool in the *campo*. The little boy thwacked at a root. In an ensuing silence, it may have been that the man and I were thinking the same thing, of the gulf between people, in this case, *campesino* and *gringo*, and that he may have been trying to reassure me not to feel guilty about the past. I had the sense that he knew about me, simply from the situation – a father and son, no wife/mother present – that he was aware somehow of my loss, but only from within *his* reality.

The other two picked up their great bundles and proceeded tramping down the slope of the road, balancing and readjusting the loads to avoid tottering to the side, still managing deftly to avoid tree roots and cobbles. Then they were gone off on a tributary path. I turned to my son. He looked away and took another slash at a stalk. Then we started up again.

These were the only others we met on the climb, except for, another hour further up, a dispirited group of three who had turned around in defeat and were on their way down.

Then for a long time we walked and the slope got much steeper.

Once, the boy just stopped. He squatted down and I had to turn around and encourage him. "It's not much further! Come on!" He got back up and followed me. This happened again, several more times, the boy beginning to resist the climb, once telling me he did not want to go any farther, he wanted to turn around and go back, which alarmed me – and I was aware of an anxiety to accomplish the feat, so that, as I told the boy, he and I would be able to tell ourselves, we had done it, we climbed the volcano!

But it did not get easier the higher we climbed, only much harder, and I kept looking up, always disappointed the summit was still far away, apparently even though, clearly, we were very high up now and had advanced very far, because the mantle of cloud was below us, a fluffy white seen through the trees – their deeper, greater magnificence somehow a stinging reminder this was the wild. We surprised a swarm of brilliant butterflies, white and purple, and for a few seconds they exploded all around us – silent, imagined thunder, innocent busybodies, and remembered thinking that the longer one lives the more ghosts one makes from shuffled-off lives, seemingly more effortlessly at hand, not dead, flittering, everywhere.

The symbolism of our immediate situation was so obvious it was as if it was spelled out in capital letters on some billboard: the boy, starting out in life, myself, already having botched things up, in some ways, at least – the divorce, its impact on him perhaps unforgivably, but, more than merely gamely going about the effort, in degree as arduous, presumably, as would be the gain of the accomplishment. So, at this particular juncture, and despite my proven failures and mishaps, *presuming* – necessarily! for I *was* his father – to serve in the role of guide or shepherd, heart more than half-full, hoping to scrounge something up, I was hopeful, perhaps, of doing something magnificent despite my messes in life. Then, the countering retort: getting to the top, though for what? Beyond the physical achievement, beyond the goal set, a difficult one, yes, to be sure, for the two of us, beyond all that more or less prosaic or even trivial good-luck attitude of a climb up a volcano, beyond was...the *simulacrum*: the "As-if " – the automatic, fabulously interlacing intricacies of the simultaneously acted and re-enacted, postscripted-prescripted world we occupy, always a step behind so as to be a step ahead, the world seen, constructed, and reflected back to us, a hall of mirrors. This, I realized, was how I could characterize my search to understand and explain things.

For what were we going to do when we got to the top if we did get there? We would look out, *see*, far away, but to what I knew could be nothing but the real-life trashed countryside of Guatemala, its *llanterias* and *pinchazos* and *tiendas*...from up high, miniaturized and neatly ordered, the perspective, thus, both a lie and the truth: the vision we made and were given to see out of the ordinary flow of things, out of the biology, the *matter*, of the human creature – the liquids and ligaments and gravity-prone flesh seeking the sedentary – nevertheless, given the capacity to *see*, not necessarily because we are these marvelous beings and not just animals, but, really, simply because we are alive. And why do we strive to *see*? – because, for whatever mysterious reason, we exist, and it is not just any existence we're thrust into, but *this existence* – and we hold on to it.

In circles, then, I kept coming back to the obvious symbolism and how ultimately useless it was beyond itself... The little legs climbing, the boy at the start of his trip through life, mine already metaphorically tripped up in missteps and perhaps sidetracked into foulnesses, turned back on itself, having strayed from the path, proverbially, whatever – but alive, for a life – a while.

Of course I hoped he would never have such thoughts.

More than once again I had to coax the boy not to give up, and by now he was crying a little, angrily, and I was worried I was forcing the boy on for me, instead of the boy doing it for himself and that, now, even if we did make it to the top, I was robbing him of the pride of having done it on his own. Again, I could hear my ex-wife asking me, shocked with anger, *how could you?*

Now, as we continued on, for some reason guilt arose for a host of other failings, secret sins, little darknesses in my past – cruelties, indifference to others, insistence on gratifying just myself, small, venal things I had done... going with colleagues once to a grimy sex club in the Capital, staring at the naked girls, knowing they were prisoners in a country with no laws, and they were helpless, sold for sex... thinking, given all this, how my ex-wife must have been right to divorce me, and how I was, frustratingly, sadly, as much a creature of darkness as of light.

The climb then became much steeper – impossibly difficult.

Though we were more or less out of tree cover now and so high up it felt we had entered a stretch of much lower altitude grasslands and rock, the boy again started crying, and I made an even greater effort to plead and cajole. But then he stopped crying, I think because he saw his father – a marble more occluded than light – would not heed him, and so he continued on, having gained, surprising both of us, it seemed a second, or third, or fourth wind, even when it became so steep we were climbing hand-over-foot and feeling a vertigo as we looked to the side, through the trees, where we saw only space of sky, deceptively benign, and clouds well below the space. But still the summit did not appear. I could see above us the edge of the trees and the slope upward, as if it ended, and, believing we were near the top, was very disappointed when it turned out it was not, but I had to keep this to myself, so we kept doggedly going.

And I became exhausted, so much so that *I* began to think of giving up... But something – maybe mere momentum or, something else, a little fear that I was crazy, and always had been, and to stop would be to acknowledge this, that the climb all along was absurdly unrealistic – kept me going and the boy continued climbing, surprising me when he was now and then in front of me. But then, as if in a little dreamed second of withdrawal from pain, of release, of "how easy it is, after all!" completely unexpectedly I saw a clearer patch above us of unencumbered skyline. The boy was right beside me now, a tiny figure tucked into my shadow, and I stretched my legs double and reached for hand holds, and he scrambled up beside me, on a steep rock slide, my hand holding his arm as he slipped and slid a little.

There, as if in the clearing of everything halted by a vision, all of a sudden we were on a jagged rim, the unmistakable proof that we had made it to the top leaping below us: what seemed a preposterously tiny crater, looking exactly as one would expect at the top of a volcano, and under the sky so deep blue from the thinness of the altitude it was cold and dark: the crater's roundness seemed too perfect to be real. At the bottom was the small unused church constructed entirely of cobbles we had been told about, white cross sticking out from a brown slate roof. Then, with the headiness of the weird improvised top of the world – or at least the top of the beat-up Republic, unreal as it seemed – the moment of triumph was already passing, the capacity to fully experience it beyond reach.

But in the echoing silence, the silence of an anticlimax – for it seemed unreal that we had *done* it – I gave a *whoop* and the boy followed suit and I whooped again remembered the surprise I had for him, and pulled from my knapsack a string of *cohetes* brought precisely in anticipation of this moment, and the boy shouted, yeah! Together we lit the fuse and tossed the whole string of firecrackers over the rim where it dropped several meters inside the crater wall and then, just as a warm patch of sunlight appeared on it, it started exploding *rat-tat-tat* right in our ears in the somber air like a muffled gun, the blue smoke dissipating in the darkness of the cold unnaturally dark blue sky above. And *then!* A miraculous little bonus gift tossed to us by the volcano, there was a rainbow in the crater, the spectrum trembling and iridescent.

I turned to him, offered my hand, and, I couldn't help it – I gathered him up in a big hug. Resisting, he said, "uff!" as if I knocked the air out of him. But he was smiling, though he looked a little dazed. Although what his *real* thoughts were I had no idea, except, at times I did realize how much my presence occupied his consciousness – the instant thought again was if I was already looking back on how we would think about the feat, the experience carefully constructed by the two of us together, and I felt we were turning or had already turned to the other side of it, of that moment.

I felt the child shiver involuntarily and I, too, felt the chill of twelve thousand feet.

Glancing at my watch I was instantly alarmed – already it was three in the afternoon.

How to document the triumph…with, too its whollity of sadness for how this all inevitably would be diminished in the future until it was vague at best? For, already, we *had* turned to the other side of the moment – though couched in my mind were somewhat consoling images of being safely back down in the town, and I thought for some reason of the dark vivid green of the trees and the flowering bushes and the boxes of impatiens and iris in the *parque*, picturing the two of us – wishful thinking as if we already had made it back – at one of the cozy ancient-walled restaurants, having a celebratory meal. But without letting the boy see my apprehension about finding our way down in the dark, I said, "We have to leave." And he turned away from looking down into the crater and we started sliding back down the rocks to begin the long hike back.

The ghosts started assembling, of memories I would be visited by in the future, although – another painful minor chord! – the significance of the climb, father and son, I knew would continue to pale also because of the enormously heavy charge of sense and never-clear insight delivered in this terrible place, how, for example, the ghosts in the pasts of the citizens here, were everywhere and constant, fulminating against bad deaths, or the grills or grates or trellises of wrought iron on buildings in the Capital in what represented hopes of the *gente* of the *barrios*, ornaments of a hopelessly lost gentility.

Hour after hour we came down, shadows of ourselves to the experience, backs descending away from the sun.

There was still light, but it was cool, late light, by the time we reached the bottom of the overgrown road where we recognized the turn-off onto the path that would take us down to the village. But quickly after that it became very dark, and I remembered how long it had taken climbing up the first path that morning. The only light came from a lacy Spanish moon, so we continued tripping down the broken path, trees and bushes leaning close on either side and arching overhead in blackness. Hiding my anxiety, I had no choice but to plunge confidently onto what I guessed were other paths heading down, and we still walked on and on for hours.

I only realized, with enormous relief, that we were going to be all right when the tilt of the descent lessened and we found ourselves in warm night air out in the open by a maize field and under stars so brilliant I could read the map by their light, only slightly outshone by a milky moon so close it seemed opacified but grimed with little lines and erasures like markings on tracing paper.

Cutting through the field we wound up to the east of the *aldea*. But we walked on a dusty road and found a taxi, a huge-finned old Chevrolet – parked next to the *pila*. The laziness of the scene – the little trash-littered *parque*, some closed *tiendas*, the smell of grease – tempered the great relief, because it brought back to me, starkly, the sullen reality one encountered everywhere outside of the charmed space of the colonial town. For some reason, perhaps because the night was hot and we were so tired, I was angry at this impoverished nation that lacked the barest amenities, that was always and everywhere full of threats – of sickness and violence and intimidation. This was made worse when I could not talk the driver down from his extortionate fare to take us back to the old colonial town; fat, mustachioed, sloppy, wearing a big hat, as if good-naturedly he refused to bargain, not retreating from his exorbitant demand because the buses had stopped running some time ago and, plainly, we two *gringos*, man and child, had no choice. After thinking about, then rejecting, the idea because of the late hour, because we were hungry and tired, that we could just walk the several kilometers back – enraged by the driver's calm refusal to budge, to see reason! and by my own impotence, I gave up, and the two of us got in the battered old vehicle. Seething, unable to stop myself, I motioned silently to the boy beside me on a back seat that from its polish seemed carefully maintained and pulled out the Swiss Army knife I remembered now that I had brought and made a long slit in the seat, aware I was setting a bad example. I told myself I did want to teach the boy not to be taken advantage of, for we had been swindled and there was nothing else that I could do about it. The boy's reaction – wide eyes, a little nod, but no judgment.

When we got back and had washed up and had a meal, from the stable-like public telephone building packed with crying children and tired mothers, where one had to wait for an individual stall, I made the call to the boy's mother; I had told her about the planned climb – typically she said almost nothing to me but was stiff and tense.

The boy listened to her, responding in monosyllables – I could then overhear her telling him how much she loved and missed him, but that she was doing fine. I could tell she was crying. I took the phone, intending to reassure her but, bad luck! perhaps because I was hearing again her New Zealander accented voice, which I had so loved, and forgot we were divorced and could no longer tell her anything, let slip about the near mishap of getting lost on the climb down; at this, thousands of miles away, I sensed her freeze. Then, hearing her pause, from out of nowhere a picture of us making love sprang to mind. A little shocked, I realized again how she must hate me, even more than I hated her for the divorce and for the bifurcation that left me a single parent and alone in life; I also hated her even more for not being able to appreciate all the things I was coming to understand down here, hard but absolutely certain truths, how this benighted country had opened my eyes to how, for example, the mass of the past – all the ghosts of the maligned and anonymous dead – *was* The Real. And yet, as I kept talking, trying to reassure her the boy was fine, and promising there would be no more risky adventures, I was aware of a second voice in my head, how great the divide also was between me and the disaster of the life around the boy and me, *now*, how incredibly messed up everything was that would permit such a country as this to exist, and again, then, how what a sad mistake it seemed to be so far away from this woman with whom once I had been so close.

Simultaneously I was aware of a solitary drama looming ahead – the futility of the insights multiplying within from this piece of gristle and *badness*, this place, the issue at hand, now and always, how pathetic my attempt to grasp it all, the mass of actual people, perishing so quickly everyday on a burning surface, who lived in a place that was nowhere, a land mostly of nullities, nowheres, but nowheres that were inverted inside their nullity, because people *did* live in them, to try to be somewhere: thoughts here in this land: circles within circles, for me, at any rate.

There was an epigone. A few weeks before I had to return the boy to his mother I took him to one of the parks where an enormous ruined city, a thousand years dead, built of limestone filled with the most curious but now speechless iconography, lay almost completely covered in jungle. We climbed to the top of temples and I tried to explain to him what we scholars thought they meant.

Then we went to the Pacific for one last adventure. Coming into muggy Reu, a Wild West version of all slum cities elsewhere, we found, on the outskirts, what the sign said was a hotel. I wondered who the patrons of such a place could be. A tremendously powerful wind was fanning and then lashing and bending over almost double the palms. The dank little room had no hot water and the lamp did not go on. So we went almost immediately to the "restaurant." It was getting on to six o'clock, anyway, but we noticed no lights on on the big terrace. As we sat down at a picnic table, a waiter came over and told us – hard to hear him in the wind – that a big hurricane was approaching that had cut off the power. The generator for the refrigerators was not working; but *no se preocupen!* the man said briskly – the bulletins advised that the *huracán* was veering away and would not hit. Because of this we could order anything on the menu for almost nothing – the meat and fish were going to spoil, anyway. We could even have second or third helpings at no charge.

The sky was brilliantly dark, more darkness loomed swiftly, the strange warm winds were now lashing, beating the palms, there was a curious fish smell, and the waiter gave up trying to relight the instantly blown-out candles. Occasionally, a big warm rain drop fell on us. The boy and I ate our meal – choosing the most elaborate platters of giant shrimp, he, of course, only able to eat a tiny amount – and we couldn't see our plates were it not for oversized fireflies bashing softly into our faces, landing in the food, then fluttering away. Some skulking invisible animal rustled and pushed against our legs; must be a dog hunting for scraps, said the boy, for some reason delighted. I took a picture of him with my flash – he in his Australian broad-brimmed hat, looking directly into the camera but squinting a little, heel of one hand resting on the handle of one of his machetes. Fixed in the image forever, he was smiling, proud and confident.

A few days after we got back to the town, I came down with malaria. For several days I couldn't move from bed – marveling at the clockwork predictability of the cycles, an hour each: the teeth-chattering chills, so extreme all the blankets and coverings available piled on me were not enough to stop the violent shivering; this alternating with the sweats so bad if I had any strength to do so I could wring out the sheets. I had to ask him to look after me – bring me tea and powdered soup which he did, spilling things a few times. I remembered that, as a baby, what was guaranteed to make him laugh was when things "fell down." But he took the nurse role seriously, with tablets and blue bottles of stuff I managed to buy for myself at a *farmacia*. Still, throughout those days even during fever I was aware – as I was, of course, throughout all those months – how precious the time was with him, with changes in both of us happening so quickly, how this time with my son post-divorce would end soon and then be gone. I thought of it, I remember, as like the end of the fertile rainy season.

I recovered. Still weak, I took him in a taxi to the old airport in the Capital, where I turned him over to the nanny the boy's mother had sent to bring him back to the other side of the world. A post-malarial mental fog rendered my goodbye perfunctory and anticlimactic. But as I watched from the old balcony above as he was led away in the well of the beat-up old airport, he made a slash with his arm as if he was holding his machete, like a little reminder to himself. Then he stopped, despite a tug by the nanny, and turned around and gave me a little wave. Exactly as he was in the shadow of the lights – the closeness of memory, the intimacy of the moments one remembers – I recalled, very clear and vivid, leading him down in darkness on the side of the volcano.

Driving back to the town, then, I cursed myself for exposing the boy to the garbage and pollution, the shitty water and the cholera and the malaria, all of this everywhere as part of a huge chaotic violently devolving social crack-up – a giant chicken bus nose-dive crash of History so bad even Christ would not bother. Returned to the empty lonely house a day later I got horribly, demoralizingly sick, once again, this time with amoebas.

But I was then still so fresh to being a father and to my work. At the time I *could* see how these sicknesses happened only after the marvel of the volcano climb when I felt renewed joy and optimism with my trusting son. For years afterward I was apt to remember, and still do, today, with a shock of longing for what was unlikely to happen, how, the night after we had returned, utterly familiar with each other despite, or because of, the jerryrigged life we had together post-divorce, I ate a quiet dinner with him, little boy across the table, and I was full of future nostalgia, and proposed a vow – large hand enclosing small – of a repeat climb up the volcano someday.

For years, then, I was apt to remember that this time had been a beginning, again, with hopes for a whole new life, uninjured.

The post-visit days passed. Then weeks, and then months filled up somehow. I had a fling with an American Spanish language student. When we had sex and I was behind her, I could faintly smell the shit – casualty of Third World circumstance: so often, no toilet paper. But she turned out to have little interesting to say, at least not given my past and current preoccupations, and, even if she had wanted the thing to continue, it would not have lasted much longer, anyway, because I spent so much of our time together obsessed, for some reason, still with my ex-wife, brooding, for example, on the many frozen hysterical phone calls when our son had been with me. She had asked almost never about the country we were in nor the adventures: she simply could not, would never, understand what I now knew to be crucially important: grasping whatever piece I could of the gristle in front of me.

But such thinking, of course, was useless. I felt somehow wooden, not-me, empty in the face of futility and the meanness only of survival, this *the reality*. It was all so complicated, so very, very complicated! and how pathetic was any attempt to grasp it, because masses of actual individual souls were perishing quickly and constantly, stumbling into the fires of transience, disappearing into the fires of any particular day, as unextraordinarily as if into the stalls of a *mercado* in the crazed, bottom-up cities I wound up in – they're alive, talking away to each other, all of them, then they're gone.

My research stalled. At the same time – the somewhat terrible truth of the matter – for reasons I could not clarify with him nor understand, my son seemed angry with me, though he never offered an explanation and even denied he was angry. He moved with his mother from place to place and, though of course I wrote and called, I saw him not more than once or twice over a period of several years.

During this period – faltering in the profession – I was apt to remember, with an odd stab of shame, still reverberating after years – parts of our climb up the volcano and how, all the while I was aching with bitterness at my ex-wife – this had really consumed me during the climb – how stumbling beside me had been that little figure as we were making our way up through the groves of high trees and vine underbrush. This led to a panic that he was almost like an afterthought, no more, and this, in turn, to an even colder panic, for myself, and then especially for the child ejected into the inexplicable randomness of things – "what happens." And these feelings had grown as we'd climbed, as if on a healthy adventure in a wild place. But then, simultaneously, I was able also to feel a real joy in the volcanoes and jungles, my wonderful immersion in the land of the Other, and how that was when – those first years in-country – there was a great loosening of my spirits and the novel belief that internally, as if I was a tree, I was putting down new roots, and growing new branches out in the magnificent void of the Wild, the void a lucidity, I was sure, if only I could understand it!

After some years again I tried to see him as often as possible, arranging to bring him to me a few weeks each year on those incredibly long flights. An anxious year passed when he was obsessed with guns – because of the divorce? (he denied it, when I could get him to answer my questions, saying only he was being picked on in school), the boy grew into a tall, wiry, stiffly proper young man, reserved, but, every now and then, unpredictably, exploding at me, to the point of sobbing which, then, instantly, very awkwardly he stifled. It was as if now and then an alarm went off, revealing how close to being pushed over a line he had been, or maybe he had been pushed over it, a line I surmised he had set for himself sometime far back in childhood that led into a maze that led finally up to a wall, on the other side of which was his innocence.

But then I would remember how when we climbed the volcano I may have stood tall for him and cut a great and noble profile, although what I realized in those later years, was, Jesus! to the contrary! how small I stood! - certainly against the greater history of things which was like a massive wall, elaborately shadowed with the jungle of events, great and small: the "scholar" in front of all this chaos, this thoroughly and completely fucked-up hell permitted by the world to exist, god-forgotten millions, forgotten but never-known, this *the reality* – which later was reduced to little more than an odd pain, because there was, there is, as always, an end. And yet, and yet! Neglect: it was as if back in some lost world someone had left the light bulb on.

Hazy, though, among other memories like little shallow antique shelves, opening and closing, aromatic of pepper, one, in particular, I had forgotten, or deliberately pushed away: in the taxi with the boy back from the climb, and I was asking the *chofer* about what he remembered from the civil war, and the man, after a moment, laughed and said something about how there were a lot of former *guerrilleros* walking around without their dicks – they'd been chopped off with machetes... *You* know? the man asked, as if happy about this.

Looking back, different problems for me began after I left. The self-castigation continued along with recurrences of malaria. I found refuge for several months with a Salvadoran colleague – his family welcoming and affectionate. But, drawn back to my real home, as I felt it to be, I came back, again and again, to what I considered the bottom of the world. I tried to continue my research, and resumed the round trips on the chicken bus into the Capital and then, hopelessly, wondering at my persistence with the old manuscripts, heading back to the colonial town... It was then, really, I felt my life was not just degenerating; it was crumbling, or being ground away, putting me more and more into the darkness of the self.

I still went to the annual conferences and exhibition openings, where I met colleagues – friends and enemies – once, several years later, one fellow who had some big grants but whose project had run into troubles; he told a wild tale about asking the Interior Minister to "disappear" a local fellow who was running a scam about compensation for service in the *Guardia Civil* during the civil war and the epoch of the death squads. I thought the guy was making it up – he was kind of a type for whom a certain pirate pride in the outrageous was normal. I made up my mind not to check his story... I didn't keep up with him and never saw him again. Those coming to the conferences seemed to change every year...

Little things began to provoke a silent rage. So many times I found myself running, horribly depressed, across the tarmac of the broken streets and the rubble of the great slum capital city, in a sunset blood-red from pollution, frantic to catch the last bus into the volcanic mountain passes back to the town. At those times I felt more like a ghost than a "scholar," less sure than ever what the word meant. If it did mean anything at all, what value did it have? I felt I was dematerializing, tailing away in the fumes and vapors of twilight dimness boiling everywhere.

Strange memories became imprinted: climbing onto the chicken bus and finding there was no space, four or even five little *ladinos* crushed onto one seat at the very back, others standing over them, the proximity so close as to be skin to skin, yet all of them oblivious or indifferently hostile. If I found a seat my large *gringo* frame squeezed, pressed into somebody else's body rank with sweat, squashed hard between little doggedly unyielding brown people, resiliently pushing to protect their space on the seat, with every violent lurch of the bus immediately taking advantage of a gap that opened to aggrandize a bit more space, and, if I resisted, pushing antagonistically back, all the while not looking at me or acknowledging the strange existential combat which is all the fiercer and uncompromising the poorer you are, the more towards the bottom of life you are. Gibing with this inexpressibly tiny combat, little became littler: having to stand, gripping the metal stanchion, wrenched this way and that as the bus, swaying, blustered through rattling gear shifts and careened wildly around curves, back hatch-door banging open and shut... And when I regained my balance, looking down at the part in the black hair of some young woman, thinking she just washed it but the effort was hopeless since the water was full of fecal matter...thinking even then she could have no interest in me no matter how pretty I thought she was... And then, as the lacework of thought scrolled out further, ashamed of myself to admit it, automatically she counted for less in my eyes, because of this — because she was dirty. Along with these scarce-worthy memories imprinting themselves in my brain I was ashamed, too, to think that *I* was somehow contaminated, also, because of a life spent too long now down in the cesspools of this country.

I found myself faulting the *place*: what kind of country can it be when you're packed four- , five- , or six-times too many into a battered old chicken bus named *Juanita* or *Esmeralda*, an old American Bluebird down here for a second, third, or fourth resurrection, the brakes and transmission leaking, unreliably negotiating wild, steeply descending curves, skeletons of past disasters rusting hundreds of meters down just over the side of the road? On these trips into the Capital and back out again I always remembered how, during my first year here, the entire folk ballet troupe of a neighboring country was killed one early morning when the brakes of the tour bus taking them to the old colonial town failed just as the bus barreled around a curve and plunged right over the side of the cliff. I could easily imagine the dancers jacked to the back as the bus fell through a rosy gold, each molecule of air hoarded as their last second, the moral: Life, how cheap a joke... And I asked myself: did the *xamanes*, those many years ago, know this? And were they just dancing around the void, unable to face life without some tricks? – Maximón, himself, whatever he is, a hopeless amalgam constructed in the emptiness of a ravaged culture?

Only much later, as the boy grew up, during the intermittent times we saw each other, I saw how changed he was and I realized I, too must have changed – become "leaner and meaner," "Third-Worldized," I might say, kind of absent-mindedly, to others when the subject arose – how I managed to live with so little amenities, the lack, truly, meaning little...

I am standing, half in sun, half in shadow.

I would say I am still on the journey...but still have little understanding of myself and this world.

When not stopping to write this down – to transcribe later stuff that I felt I *had* to get down, I am walking along the battered highway outside the Capital. Of course, the bus broke down and all the riders had to hike, though where to it wasn't clear. I have been away, for some time, and have returned. Around me, so familiar, the same country decomposes, in the air, always, the smoky smells of wood, tortilla, burning trash...perhaps for the *gringo*, somehow redolent of *distance*. The country evening. Bustling, or frantic, or sad, hopeless people, anonymous even to themselves, find paths off the road, going somewhere... I think: *I have been at the bottom of the world! looking up from inside it to a very clear, very dark blue reality, as if I have been in a bowl, a crater!*

Even so I find myself again in the complete opacities of the present, this moment...in an otherworld of rutted, battered corridors of so-called highways. Behind me is the infinitely jaundiced life of the Capital, lived out to its various ends in shacks and broken cinderblock *llanterias, pinchazos,* blanket-doored *cantinas...* The fabulous *indio* I have studied...his days that disappear inside a *maquila*'s razor-wired walls, inside huge, anonymous, domed buildings housing immemorial deracinated tedium. Always, at the beginning, of course, or for a short time, is a brief splendid radiance. It glows, envelops – that instant and absolute faith that life goes on. But how briefly does that radiance continue. Fitfully, even in the quiet shadows that obscure the hardship, all is mysterious. And *this* then is gone, forever, little gains overthrown by events, again and again. Even the little lost people here, as children, feel this, for a while... No matter on what thin pallet, in what cell-like room, in what shack home in which you wake up, no matter how dispossessed you feel with the constant reminders of your plight, you will wake up on the same dirt floor shack you came back to last night, you will leave to wait for the chicken bus as the dirty breeze blows dirtier air, and the trash flaps in the highway winds, or it burns... You will walk, after some time, kicking off your plastic sandals because they are worn out... (I have often noticed the most common physical artifact here for future archaeologists are shoe soles, worn completely out, because the main mode of transport is the foot, in endless, fruitless peregrinations.)

The withered brown faces of the *indio* women will gaze out stoically as they slice pineapple, papaya, coconuts, dunking dirty knives in gray water... then bag them in plastic to hang and sell from their carts' rail...as hopeless in their tiny commerce as other vendors with their shoulders to racks, giant with tiny wheels, pushing and pulling them into position, all up and down along narrow, packed *Sexta Avenida*, that great clogged street of pirated goods, to sell their cheap pants, or socks, or tee-shirts...

Even the uniformed children parading to school in the sun-stricken streets will pass by, as if they have futures...the *asistentes* on the buses will yell, and coax, and cajole, then smile...all this the *bricolage* of Maximón...the living and the dead.

(Reading over this there are several lines here but I cannot make them out.)

But I feel that I, anyway, can walk... And to walk is to be free in a way. I feel I can keep going forever... Here, underfoot – no sidewalk of course – on the tussocks and roots of hump-trunked pine and enormous tall eucalyptus. The trees interlaced over my head providing the close beddings of needle and twig, with wind-frayed shreds of plastic, the residue and product of the world's engine. Pale and paling to misery here.

But what they call a highway here *is* going somewhere...a journey, epic, to the clear sundown, then into the darkness that hides the trash and the smoke...and the failures of humans to do good things. There is the respite of the *bosque* with its marvelous birds and then the still highlands out there and which the volcano foretells as the first in the long rim of volcanoes stretching west – reachable, safely on foot, after a life-long hike! If not on a chicken bus that, perhaps, might crash through cliff 's edge vines into weed and trees at the deep bottom of an abyss...

On the corridors of highway the beater cars are racing past, chicken buses and great trucks roar here through Nowhere, blasting black diesel tornadoes into the air... *What am I doing here?* I continue to feel a trace of something I have carried with me for years now, something hard to describe or express, that there is, out there, some distance west, where the rosy sun sets, in this place so much destroyed, some kind of home to replace what I lost or gave up?... beginning with the divorce...the killing of some great part of my son's childhood...friends gained or lost, dead, or just gone somewhere... But perhaps if I walk far enough I'll find some *true* home waiting, a slat-board hut, a blackhaired woman in it kneading tortillas by a stone hearth – maybe I'll sell bullets! and have wandering off his chain in the garden, an ocelot... and where I will walk on stones, in dried creek beds that somehow I know so well, through the same bottom-up little crossroads towns, thinking of all the things and times...and maybe get lost again...

And I remember then how those many years ago my son and I had shaken hands – his eight-year old hand in mine – when we came down from the volcano, vowing to make the climb again – like some coda or bargain for something! against – what? – time and failure? I have often thought of this and how we would climb once again up to the top, to that little crater – but that he would have to coax me on up, this time around.

After I find another bus and am back I try to read and rewrite these notes but much I just cannot reconstitute. Now though as I type them up, despite how important they seemed, I remind myself, maybe it doesn't matter, because I go to the airport tomorrow to pick up my son. We haven't seen each now in several years. He is twenty-two and has, detectable on his recent calls, a pronounced New

Zealand accent. With all that he has sounded good; his tone warm. But I find myself asking if, hoping, he will forgive me – he stands out, particularly clearly, against what seem a bunch of ghosts – for things only that ghosts, even most beloved ones, can forgive…

That night I dreamed about that strange "motel" with the crazy woman and the ocelot. The dream was cold, a nightmare, with both the woman and the cat disappearing somewhere in the middle.

But in one of those nonsensical, quite masterful, dream transitions – quite jovial – my son, black-faced through the diesel fumes, then yelled, "Are you ready to climb the volcano?" In the dream, I told him, then that, first we had to go look for that big cat.

Author with son, Santa Maria de Jesús, Sacatepequez, 1992

ABOUT THE AUTHOR

Jonathan Reynolds (a *nom de plume*) was educated at Yale. For part of each year over the last decade he has lived in Samayac, Suchitepéquez, Guatemala – renowned as the home of more Maya *xamanes* than any other city in Central America and Mexico. Under another name, he has published in *The Antigonish Review*, *The Texas Review*, *The Birmingham Poetry Review*, and other literary magazines.